BUNNY
and the
STUFFED
ANIMAL SQUAD

BUNNY and the STUFFED ANIMAL SQUAD

MILES NOBLE

CONTENTS

Dedicated to all my stuffed animals. (Especially Bunny, who truly is part of the family.)

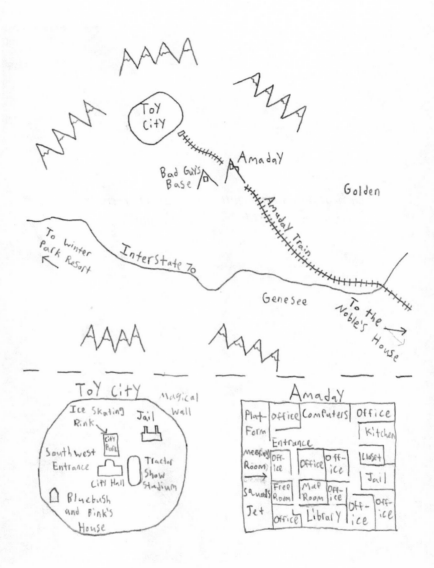

PART

ONE

THE RISE OF THE SQUAD

CHAPTER

ONE

HOW IT ALL STARTED

A long time ago, there was a Tortoise.

He was inside a tall mountain that loomed over Antarctica, rising so high that its peak was hidden in the clouds.

Yes, let me tell you again. A real Tortoise—an Angulate Tortoise, to be precise—in the middle of Antarctica.

He climbed some stairs to an arched doorway, took a deep breath, and walked through. This Tortoise's name was, well, Tortoise. But before that, his name was Mwana, which means son in the language of Swahili. But he abandoned that name when his father disappeared. You see, a mysterious mist had swept through his homeland in Africa, whisking away Tortoise's friends and family. However, his gut told him that they were still alive…somewhere.

Tortoise missed everyone, but most of all, he missed his son, Rudy, who was only seven years old when the mist swept through. Because he was the only one to escape the mist, Tortoise needed to find his family and get revenge on the mysterious curse! So, about a week and a half earlier, he had begun his journey to follow the mist and find his relatives. According to his knowledge, he knew the mist had traveled south. So, when he saw a wooden boat heading down a local river and towards the Southern Sea, Tortoise knew that it was his chance. He positioned himself on a rock in the river and gracefully jumped into the back of the boat.

Okay—let me rephrase. He jumped gracefully onto the boat in his imagination. In reality, he jumped onto the boat with an adjective opposite of gracefully.

First, Tortoise struggled onto the rutter of the small boat before losing his grip and barely clinging on, his behind skimming the water. Then, he managed to jump onto a wooden ledge (after sixteen tries) and carefully sat down behind a crate. Tortoise never saw who was on the boat, but most importantly, they didn't see him. Tortoise rode the boat for a few days, breathing in the dewy smell of the sea. He sat there looking bored, but his brain was busy. He wondered what the mist was and where it was headed. Far off in the distance, he could see its familiar brown fog, almost like a sandstorm.

Tortoise was deep in thought when the sleek and icy Antarctica came into view. *Finally!* He thought. But then the boat made a hard left turn, going straight toward Australia! Tortoise watched the mysterious mist continue south. He sighed. He knew what he had to do. *Hopefully, those cheap swim lessons will pay off.* He thought, trying to stay confident about swimming in the wavy ocean. (Hey, I didn't know Tortoises had swim lessons either.)

Tortoise had a little bit of practice swimming, but he hadn't mastered it. But still, he knew that he needed to follow the mist. There was just a feeling in his gut. So, without another thought, he jumped!

JUST A TORTOISE NAMED TORTOISE ON A CONTINENT WHERE most animals would freeze to death. Not your typical day. You see, something was allowing Tortoise to survive, something very mysterious...

He barely made it to the shore of Antarctica. His swimming wasn't pretty, but he made it unharmed and undrowned. (Is that a word?) After lying on the icy and cold shore for an hour, the first animal he was greeted by was a polar bear. The furry beast had pounced and tried to eat Tortoise before deciding that he was not exactly an A-rated snack.

Even after the bear left him alone, Tortoise fled into a hole in the ice to stay safe. Unfortunately, he crashed right into some seals taking a nap. They woke up and started barking at him. Tortoise wasn't in a good mood to begin with, and he couldn't stand the barking. So, he punched the two seals directly in the nose! The noise that the seals made as they ran out of their hole was funny. But the screeching noise they made when they saw the polar bear waiting outside for them was frightening.

After the polar bear finished her yummy seal dinner and walked away, Tortoise peaked out of the hole. He looked across the barren ice sheet and knew that the coast was clear. He slipped out of the seals' burrow and into the open. Tortoise started walking, having no clue where he was going, upset with losing the mist's trail.

He wandered Antarctica for a while and was about to die of frostbite when he ran into some penguins. There were five of them, sliding down an ice hill on their stomachs.

Even though he didn't want to get involved with other animals, Tortoise knew he needed some help, so he walked forward, and the penguins stopped sliding to examine him. *Squawk!* They said, eyeing the new creature. Tortoise took this as a welcome, and he stood broadly before them. The penguins got the message. They're intelligent creatures, I'll tell you. They signaled for Tortoise to follow them, and he did, surprised at how patient the penguins were with him.

Soon they arrived at the penguins' nest. One of them nudged Tortoise inside, and immediately he fell asleep, despite the cold ground. He dreamed about the mist, and where it and his relatives were. Then he started dreaming about dead fish… *Wait a minute!* Tortoise thought, as he opened his eyes. Sitting in front of him was a large, dead fish. It looked similar to the live fish back in Africa. But this fish was different. It was dead.

You see, Tortoise had always eaten plants. In his opinion, they were the best food in the world. But here, he knew that there were no plants—just dead fish. He sighed and took a bite, knowing that starving wasn't worth it. Tortoise slowly started chewing his dinner. But he regretted picking up the dead fish immediately.

Disgusting! Tortoise thought, unfortunately, right as the penguins waddled into the nest. In spite of himself, Tortoise spat it out right below their feet. "Sorry," he said, before remembering that he couldn't communicate with the penguins. Then he ran as fast as he could (0.4 MPH) to the nearest water source he saw, a puddle, and slurped it up.

After the taste of dead fish was finally gone, Tortoise spotted the mountain. He simply saw it out of the corner of his eye, far off into the distance. But right there and then, he realized that it was where the mist was. Somehow, he just knew it, similar to how he knew that his relatives were still alive.

Tortoise slept restlessly that night, thinking nonstop about the mist. Finally, early in the morning, he snuck out of the penguins' nest and headed out for the mountain. Tortoise abandoned them, after all of the trouble they had endured for him...but he was too distracted with finding his relatives.

After a long day of walking in the freezing cold, Tortoise finally reached the mountain's base. If he had a Fitbit, he would've set a personal record in steps. Tortoise rested for a while before noticing a mysterious cave. He figured that the mist was inside, so he got up and walked through the cave. Inside, he looked around in awe, very surprised. There was an elevator. Remember, this was well over a century ago, so elevators weren't invented yet. Besides, even if they were, it's not like tortoises could press the elevator buttons given their short stature.

Tortoise cautiously boarded the elevator, the gold doors closing behind him. The next thing he knew, the elevator started shooting up the tall mountain. *What's happening?* He thought frantically. Soon it shot into an open part of the mountain, and Tortoise gasped. There were critters of all sorts, just living their lives in the middle of the mountain. It was like a village. He kept riding, his stomach queasy from eating the dead fish. (Even though he had eaten it last night.) Finally, the elevator slowed to a stop. Tortoise stepped out and took a moment to breathe, trying his best to get enough air, as the altitude was much too high for a tortoise. Once he caught his breath, he looked around.

Now, this is the mountain of the future! Tortoise thought to himself as he admired the round room. It had decorative paintings, each of classical artwork. On top of that, the temperature wasn't as bad as outside because of some unearthly vents in the ice-covered wall. After Tortoise finished a circle of looking around in awe, he noticed a staircase, and quickly, his mind returned to his mission.

I need to find the mist, he reminded himself. Tortoise started walking down the narrow staircase. He arrived at an arched doorway, took a deep breath and then walked through. Inside was a small room, and right away, Tortoise smiled. Finally, he had found the mist! His gut told him it was right there, in a purple chest sitting in front of him. He was scared and excited at the same time. Tortoise took another breath, inched forward, and slowly opened the chest.

Nothing.

He gasped! He had been positive the mist was in that chest.

Is it back in the lower part of the mountain in that village full of strange creatures? Tortoise thought. But then he felt a bizarre feeling. *What's happening?*

His whole body started shaking, and the pain escalated quickly. Tortoise fell onto the floor and tried to stay calm. But he really couldn't. He felt as if he had been stung by fifteen wasps on the same spot. Tortoise groaned on the floor, going through the most physically painful moment of his life. Finally, after an hour of experiencing that misery at the top of the mountain, everything stopped. Tortoise slowly got up, shaken but relieved.

Soon he realized that he felt better.

I feel even better than before, he told himself.

Tortoise felt like he knew everything!

He felt magical!

He felt confident!

He felt powerful!

He felt…stuffed?

Yes, Tortoise felt stuffed. By this, I mean full of beans. (Yes, the first stuffed animals were not as high-quality as today.) Tortoise scratched his back, and sure enough, it was soft as a pillow! *I've lost one of my defenses!* But he was smarter now, and he understood that it was happening for his protection.

Tortoise realized what had happened. The mist had gone into him! Suddenly, he had mixed feelings about the mist. Maybe it wasn't so bad after all? But then Tortoise remembered Rudy and all of his relatives, quickly reversing this thought.

Suddenly, a booming voice said, "I am the ruler of this mountain."

Tortoise froze. "Who's there?" He carefully turned around, but he was alone.

"Go back to the elevator," the person hissed. "Stop halfway down the mountain and I will meet you."

Tortoise gulped. He did not want to listen to this mysterious voice, but he knew it was necessary. So, he turned around and walked back to the elevator.

TORTOISE APPROACHED THE PERSON, WHO WAS SITTING ON A golden throne the same color as the elevator. He was wearing large purple robes and a weird gold mask that covered his entire face, making it so that Tortoise couldn't be sure if he was human. He had seen people before, but never so close up. Tortoise had always been focused on their big sticks that made loud noises, causing larger animals to fall.

Anyway, he took a deep breath and straightened out.

"Welcome," the figure said.

"Who are you?" Tortoise asked. As of becoming a stuffed animal, he could talk just like humans.

"Oh," the person responded, "just the Wizard of Pines, creator and destroyer of stuffed animals."

"Uh..." Tortoise looked down at his newly stuffed body, "do you mean me?"

"Yes, you are the first of your kind." the Wizard said.

"So, you're the creator and destroyer?"

The Wizard chuckled. "No, I will not destroy you. At least I hope not. The species of stuffed animals will go extinct eventually, when the time is right."

Tortoise stood there pondering on this. He had trouble thinking this many years ahead. "But why are you going to destroy stuffed animals?"

"I am the creator of the mist. I have complete control over your species as long as I have control of you."

At the mention of the mist, Tortoise thought about his family. "If you have control over the mist, then can you give me my family back?" The Wizard tried to continue, but Tortoise interrupted and pleaded, "I want my friends and family back. I want my friends and family more than anything."

The Wizard of Pines stood up and stepped down from the throne, his purple robes touching the icy floor. Tortoise looked into his mask, dreading what was going to happen next.

"You are part of my plan in taking over the galaxy once and for all," the Wizard said.

"What?"

The Wizard looked Tortoise in the eye. "You will start a nation of stuffed animals and build their power, as you soon will have the ability to create more of your kind. And some day – some day – you will be glad that I am doing this to you."

Oh no, Tortoise thought.

Then the Wizard of Pines raised his hand. With a flick of the wrist and a flash of light, everything went black.

A FEW HOURS LATER, A TORTOISE EXITED THE WIZARD'S mountain. But he was no longer named Tortoise. He was now King Gewis, the first stuffed animal and the one destined to grow their population. He was a little shaken from his encounter with the Wizard of Pines but looked across the vast sheet of ice with a smile on his face. Gewis didn't need his old life anymore. He would not ponder on the past anymore, would not think back to his old self, a pointless Angulate Tortoise, but rather, focus on creating more stuffed animals with his new magic. Gewis thought and then said aloud, "Hooray for the stuffed animals!"

Since then, years and years have passed, but stuffed animals are now stronger than ever. Their population grew, and eventually, they became well known in the world as humans started snuggling them and playing with them.

"Stuffed animals have the best life of any living creature," Gewis once said. He left Antarctica using his new magic and kept his words of creating more stuffed animals. Gewis soon became the powerful leader of his kind.

Yes, although stuffed animals spend most of their time with their beloved human owners, they are forbidden to talk to them. This strict rule has worked for over a century, and no stuffed animal has ever talked to someone besides another of their kind.

Or so they thought.

CHAPTER

TWO

BUNNY AND THE NOBLES

"Ice cream! Ice cream! Ice cream!" Miles and Louisa chanted.

Many years after the creation of stuffed animals, the Nobles: Darren, (the dad), Leigh (the mom), Miles (kid one), and Louisa (kid two), were sitting at their dining table, and Darren had just pulled out their favorite dessert. This family was pretty normal. But one thing made them especially unusual. The rabbit. Bunny Bun-Bun is his name. He's a stuffed animal. The first one, in fact, to ever talk to humans.

A few months prior, Bunny was tired of being quiet. He couldn't be silent in front of the four people he had been with his entire life! *I'm going to talk to someone other than a stuffed animal,* he had told himself for quite a while. One day, that's what he did. Bunny went up to Darren and said, "Hi, Big Guy!" These were the first words a stuffed animal ever spoke to a human.

The Nobles and Bunny have formed a great relationship since then. Bunny quickly realized his mistake of talking to humans, but he did a decent job covering it up. He had told the Nobles that Joe down the street was cooking up potions to turn objects alive. Okay, never mind. Bunny did a terrible job covering it up. The Nobles didn't believe this story. (There was not a Joe down the street.)

When Bunny couldn't convince them, he simply lied, saying that he had no clue what had happened to allow him to speak. After a long conversation and many confirmations that the family wasn't in a strange dream, the Nobles accepted the fact that Bunny, their beloved stuffed animal, can talk.

Alright, back to the story.

"This is fabulous ice cream! Where did you get it?" Darren asked as he slurped up his bowl.

"Little Man," Leigh responded. The Nobles were enjoying pumpkin chocolate chip, a new flavor of ice cream that Louisa and Leigh picked up after dance class.

"Can I have some?" Bunny asked from the living room. His voice is deep but cute. He has dirty white fur and is one foot seven inches tall. (Decent sized for a stuffed animal.) Bunny's favorite food is carrot bacon. He eats it non-stop and even has a lair full of it. We'll get to that later.

Miles sighed. "Bunny, can't you just have some carrots for dessert?"

The Rabbit made an awkward face but said, "Fine." Then he boinged to the kitchen. Yes, Bunny didn't hop or jump. He boinged, and if someone said otherwise, he would get mad. "Boing, a boing, a boing, a boing, a boing!" he made his usual noise and arrived at the refrigerator.

"I can't reach the handle!" Bunny protested.

"I'll get it!" Darren announced, getting up out of his seat.

"Thanks, Big Guy," Bunny remarked. (He had become accustomed to calling Darren this.) Darren handed Bunny his carrots, and Bunny ate the whole bag in under a minute. After the Nobles finished their ice cream they went outside.

Miles and Louisa were sliding in the backyard. You see, Miles had just finished an exciting baseball season, but he did not slide once in a game. Because of this, Darren insisted that he should prepare for his next season and practice. They even had an audience: Bunny. (He is a very rowdy fan.) However, Miles and Louisa's attention soon turned to their hula hoop.

Bunny knew that it was his chance. He thought, *I'm going to slide like they were.* True, Bunny despised exercise, but he felt that sliding would be worth it. While Bunny was sneaking outside, Louisa had an idea. "Something that involves my hula hoop," she told Miles.

Her idea was, well, a little sister idea. Louisa would put the hula hoop over her shoulders and run, pulling Miles in the wagon. "I grip the hula hoop and then you start pulling me while I am in the wagon?" Miles asked, confirming Louisa's plan.

"Right," Louisa responded. "Let's do it!"

Keep in mind that Louisa was 6 and Miles was 9, but he had no choice but to play along. Besides, it's not every day that your younger sibling wants to pull you around. After the hula hoop and wagon were all set up, Miles hopped in. At that moment, he realized something was wrong.

He asked Louisa, "Are you strong enough to pull me?"

"I think so," his sister replied confidently. Then she started to pull. But, as it turned out, Louisa was not strong enough.

Miles got out of the wagon. But Louisa didn't realize he had exited. She gave a massive tug to the now lightweight wagon, and it lunged forward, knocking her down. Then she tripped over Bunny, who had started his boing across the yard. Bunny also fell and started doing somersaults. Miles ran over to help Louisa get up, but Bunny was rolling straight for him, doing an impressive gymnastics floor routine.

Miles's moving leg kicked Bunny, who flung to the patio and crashed into Leigh. She tried to duck but instead banged her head into a patio chair.

She groaned, "Owwwwwwwwwwwwwwwwwwww!"

"Ow," Bunny said softly. That is what he usually did. (He didn't get hurt because he's stuffed.)

"Unacceptable! I think it's time for bed," Leigh shouted, rubbing her forehead. "Clean up this mess now!"

Miles and Louisa cleaned up the wagon and hula hoop, scolding Bunny for going onto the yard. He was about to go back inside, but Leigh stopped him. "You were misbehaving too, rabbit. So go clean."

However, Bunny was determined. He boinged right past Leigh, into the house, and toward the stairs. Darren was ready, though, and he followed Bunny. "Stop right there, Bunny!" He yelled.

"Stop right there, Big Guy!" Bunny repeated. He turned the corner and boinged up the slick stairs. He was about halfway up them when his rump slipped, and Bunny tumbled back down the stairs. Right at that moment, Miles and Louisa walked inside. Miles scooped up Bunny and walked up the stairs with Louisa on his side, passing their frustrated Mom and Dad.

The Noble siblings got ready for bed. By that I mean: Miles and Louisa messed around for thirty minutes until Darren finally got them to brush their teeth and put on their pajamas. After six minutes of *actually* getting ready, Miles and Louisa got in bed, and their parents came up to say goodnight. Leigh and Darren said goodnight to Bunny and Grey—Louisa's stuffed animal (who they didn't know was alive). Grey was the only stuffed animal to know about Bunny's secret of talking to humans. Luckily, he hadn't told any of the Stuffed Animal Squad yet.

You see, The Stuffed Animal Squad, or S.A.S., was the government of all stuffed animals. There are fourteen members, including Bunny. Bunny was one of the most essential stuffed animals on the planet. But for now, Bunny laid there in Miles's arms and fell asleep, dreaming about carrot bacon.

Okay, let's flashback again and revisit our good friend King Gewis.

CHAPTER
THREE

THE STUFFED ANIMAL SQUAD

King Gewis was delighted to find out that he could teleport himself.

He was walking slowly along the coast of Antarctica, thinking about the places he learned about that were similar to the cold, snowy, landscape. Alaska came to mind, and Gewis remembered how he used to dream about going there. He was so deep in thought that he didn't realize the swirling purple light: a portal.

Gewis looked around. The temperature was different, and there were many pine trees. *Could this*…he thought…*be Alaska?* Gewis looked around and spotted an iconic figure from his Alaska learning–Mount Denali. *It is Alaska!*

It took a while, but he found an old building on Denali that he turned into his castle and used his magic to turn real animals into stuffed animals.

The stuffed animal population grew, and King Gewis rose to power. But, although he should enjoy his power, he missed his son Rudy a lot, thinking he disappeared in the mist. But King Gewis was wrong.

When the curse swept through, seven-year-old Rudy escaped just like his dad. However, Rudy ran north, away from the curse. He still believed that his dad was alive somewhere. After walking north for a few days, he felt something inside him. It was the same feeling that Gewis got when the mysterious curse went through him.

Soon, Rudy turned stuffed too! He went through that hour of pain, and when it was over, he was a stuffed dinosaur! Rudy was so surprised that he screamed. He thought frantically, *am I an extinct creature?*

Yes, sometimes animals become a different creature than before when turned into a stuffed animal. Rudy was a living turtle with a hard shell. Then he turned into a soft dinosaur. He was the same size, just a totally different form. The one thing that didn't change was Rudy's color. He remained green.

Also like his dad, Rudy now had magic. With this new power, he sensed his father. So, he went on a journey even longer than Gewis's, boating from Cape Town to New York City, taking the train to San Francisco, boating once more to Anchorage, and rode horseback for a few weeks until finally reaching Denali—where his father's presence seemed strongest.

He wandered the mountains before finding a large palace. When Rudy walked in, he was surprised to see many animals, stuffed and not stuffed, running around. There were also many beaver guards dressed in red, making sure the chaos didn't get too out of hand.

Rudy carefully waded through the crowd before finding what seemed like where his father was. He could sense it. He looked through a little peephole to see better. His expression grew grim when he saw his dad sitting in his red and golden throne looking all powerful. Rudy saw a huge silver plate on his dad's crown. It read: *King Gewis.*

Rudy was surprised. *That's his name now?* He thought. He knew that he needed to see his dad, so he walked around a circular hallway. Then, at the end of the hallway he saw two big doors. It was the entrance to King Gewis's royal throne room. But when Rudy got to the four beaver guards in front of his dad's doors, they pointed their spears at him and shouted, "Back off! You have already had your ceremony."

That was half true. Rudy had turned stuffed, just in a different way. He wanted to tell the four beaver guards this, but he knew that they wouldn't listen. However, the guards did the talking for him. They made a huddle, trying to not let him hear. One of them whispered, "Is it really the King's son?"

"But he's a dinosaur," another pointed out.

"He just doesn't seem like someone who had a ceremony," one of the guards said. "The only way that this dinosaur could have become a stuffed animal is through a ceremony...or just through genetics."

The second guard repeated, "But he is a dinosaur! He can't be the King's son." All of the three stuffed beavers turned and looked at the last guard. (So did Rudy, secretly listening into the conversation with his keen hearing.)

"Uh, I don't know," sputtered the fourth guard. "Let's just let him in to see the king." The four guards nodded their heads in agreement. They all turned to face Rudy, who spoke up. "Let me introduce myself. I am Rudy, King Gewis's son...."

The first guard interrupted him. "Yes, that is what the King told us your name was."

Rudy just stared at the first guard and then started again. "Thank you, but please do not interru–"

"Sorry," the first guard interrupted once again.

Rudy grumbled, but then continued. "You are correct. I am King Gewis's son. You have to let me in so I–"

"I just forgot! I have to be in a meeting," The first guard interrupted again.

"Yes, just go." Rudy said, trying to stay calm. The second guard nudged the first away. He left.

"Thank you for not interrupting me," Rudy said. "Anyw...."

"You're welcome."

Rudy gave the second guard a furious look. "I have had enough!" Rudy ordered. "Just let...."

The second guard screamed! "Spider, spider! It's a tarantula! Help!"

The third guard smirked at him. "It's just a daddy longlegs."

The guard with the spider on himself harrumphed. "How would you like a spider on you?" Then he put the daddy longlegs on the third guard, who had the same exact reaction. Eventually, they both ended up tackling each other on the floor. Rudy looked over to the last guard. She was the only one still in her assigned post. But she turned and ran away down the hallway.

Rudy clenched his fists tightly and mumbled, "My dad needs better guards." Then he stepped over the two guards on the floor who were still tackling and punching. Rudy pulled open the throne room doors with all his might, and for the first time in over two months, he saw his dad.

"Welcome son, I've been waiting for you." King Gewis said as he stepped off his throne. Then threw his arms out wide and smiled at Rudy.

"I need a hug."

RUDY RAN TO HIS DAD BUT SUDDENLY STOPPED IN HIS TRACKS. He eyed his dad. "What happened?" he asked.

King Gewis sighed. "It's a long story. I'll tell you later. I really missed you." He hugged Rudy tightly, then beckoned for him to sit down on a couch.

"How did you know that it was me even though I'm now a dinosaur?" Rudy asked as he sat down on a soft cushion.

"I felt it," Gewis responded.

Rudy told his dad that he could feel things too.

Gewis nodded and then grew serious. "I should probably tell you the story."

So he did, and Rudy sat and listened to the whole thing. When his father was done, Rudy asked, "So when the curse went into you it was for your protection. Now that you're stuffed and have a better life." He secretly made this a test.

"Yes, a much better life," Gewis replied. "I get to rule now! I have power!"

Someone just dropped a twenty-pound brick into Rudy's heart. "Yeah, um, definitely," he lied.

"Son," Gewis began. "We can rule together!"

Rudy couldn't believe his ears. "You're a bad guy now," he despaired.

"No, I am a king!" Gewis protested.

"A bad king."

The two kept arguing. Finally, Gewis cleared his throat and declared, "Join me. It will be for your own good!"

Rudy just shook his head. Gewis steamed with anger. His face turned from green to red. He shouted at the top of his lungs to his guards, "Get him!" And with that, father-son war started.

RUDY RAN AWAY. HE STARTED SPRINTING TOWARD A BIG WINDOW when twelve guards cut him off. These guards had metal armor and masks and seemed a lot more serious than the other four beavers guarding Gewis's throne room. More armored guards surrounded him. Soon, Rudy was cornered. He looked around for any exit. He could see none, and now he was fully surrounded.

Why not use my new magic? Rudy thought.

21

Gewis came over. He looked sad and frustrated. He sighed, then ordered, "Lock him up. Soon I will come to talk with him."

One of the guards looked puzzled. "Didn't you say that your son would join us? You promised he would."

"No! I did not promise. My son is a fool. If he doesn't join us, he has no future," Gewis screamed, now raging with anger.

But the guards didn't move.

"Well, what are you waiting for?" Gewis demanded. "ESCORT HIM!"

"Isn't he all-powerful like you? You said he could easily escape us," one of the guards noted.

King Gewis shook his head. "That's ridiculous! If my son was that powerful and magical, he would have done something by now. Take him to the dungeon!"

"We don't have a dungeon," one guard said. Gewis screamed in a high pitch that told the guards they should get out of there. They handcuffed Rudy and took him down a long hallway to the jail. There were twenty-seven guards, with twelve on each side of Rudy and three in front leading the way.

Maybe these guards aren't much more intelligent, Rudy thought. He knew that he could just turn around and run. But that wouldn't be an easy task. Rudy had to keep walking.

Eventually they passed an open window. The pane was fuzzy from the chill. *Why would someone open a window on a zero-degree day?* Rudy thought. He squatted down and then leaped high over the guards, who were not much taller than him, landing in front of the window.

Rudy jumped again and landed on the window ledge. He took one last look at the guards before swinging out the window. Finally, he had escaped the palace of evil. He ran down the mountain through the swirling snow, shivering. After a lot of running, so much so that the palace could not be seen any more, he spotted something unusual.

There, sitting under a tall tree, was a frozen squid and an icy dog.

Both of them had been turned into stuffed animals already, so they were luckily still alive. Rudy ran toward them and asked, "Are you guys okay?"

Of course they weren't. "I mean, do you need help?"

Of course they do, Rudy thought.

The helpless dog just nodded his head desperately. His lips were frozen together so he couldn't talk. But he didn't have it nearly as bad as the squid, who's whole body was frozen and couldn't move.

Rudy picked up the squid, the dog barely limping after them. "Is this squid even alive?" Rudy asked the dog, who just shrugged in response.

The three traveled far across the Alaskan ice, Rudy about to turn into a popsicle. But then they stopped at a tree. Surprisingly enough, it was flourishing in the middle of the blizzard. It was taking up the only bit of sunlight for miles, and warmth surrounded it. But the craziest thing about this tree was its color: purple.

Rudy gasped. On the wide branches were some very large pears that were also purple, except for a few black spots. Rudy was starving and he figured that the others were too, so he marched forward, plucked off one of the pears, and took a deep breath. *I'm not sure what's wrong with these pears, but if I don't have one now, I'll probably die from starvation.* Rudy thought. He looked at the pear and then took a small taste.

Blackberries.

Coffee.

Chocolate.

Bland cotton.

Rudy tasted all of these things as he felt his body unfreeze a bit. All the flavors were delicious, except for the bland cotton, of course. He took another bite, and slowly all of the snow and ice on him melted away. He felt even more magical now. It made him feel good. Although the last part of the bite was bland and didn't taste good, it made Rudy feel the best. Every time he tasted that bland cotton flavor, more snow melted off him and made him feel warmer.

Soon, he had finished the whole purple dotted pear, feeling like he was in Miami. He knew that in order for the squid and dog to survive, they had to also have a pear. Rudy walked out of the sunlight and over to them. The dog looked at him with a surprised expression. Rudy waved his hand towards the tree, and the dog followed. Then, with his full strength, Rudy pried open the dog's mouth. He plucked off another pear from the tree, this one even bigger and gave it to the dog. "It will make you feel better."

The dog looked over to his friend for approval. The Squid couldn't move, but he gave a look that said: *trust this dinosaur. Just eat the fruit.*

The dog bravely took a small bite. Then he took another bite and repeated the same process that Rudy had done with the pear. After two minutes the whole thing was gone, including the core, which was also edible.

"My name is Rodger." Rudy turned to see the dog smiling at him and wagging his tail.

"Your name is Rodger?"

"Yep."

Rudy looked at the dog. He had thick black fur covering the top of his body, but his legs, paws, belly, and lower head were all brown. Rodger was a few inches taller than Rudy.

"I owe you something. Uh, what's your name?" he asked.

"My name is Rudy."

"Nice name," Rodger exclaimed. "Thank you so much. I was freezing, but then you came wandering down and helped me and Squiddy."

Rudy looked over at the chunk of ice the squid, Squiddy, was stuck in. Squiddy gave another look. This time it was a look saying: *could you two please hurry up. I'm in a bit of a situation here.*

Rudy looked at Rodger. "We should help him." Rodger nodded in agreement, and Squiddy gave a look at Rudy saying: *thank you.*

Rodger went over to Squiddy and picked him up. He set his friend down by the trunk of the magical tree, and then went to go find a rock. Soon he came back with a pointy rock in his mouth. He dropped it in Rudy's hands. "Uh, you can smash the ice," Rudy said, wiping away the saliva.

Rodger then picked up the rock and then slammed it onto Squiddy's block of ice. The ice broke quicker than expected and the sharp point of the rock hit Squiddy right in the chest! But the squid didn't say anything because he was too cold to talk. Rudy was sure that if Squiddy wasn't a stuffed animal, he would have frozen to death or at least experienced serious frostbite.

Soon Squiddy finished the purple pear and exclaimed, "Thank you!"

Rudy smiled, "You're welcome."

Rodger went over and patted his friend's head. "This dinosaur's name is Rudy."

Squiddy nodded, "Nice name."

"Thanks, uh, you too. Squiddy is, um, a very creative name," Rudy said sheepishly.

Squiddy sighed, "I know, I don't really have the best name."

"Well, I guess my dad was named Turtle before he was King Gewis." Rodger and Squiddy looked at each other and then at Rudy.

"Wait, your dad is King Gewis?" Rodger asked in disbelief.

"Uh huh."

"Wow!"

Then Squiddy and Rodger started asking a bunch of questions. *Why not just tell them the whole story*, Rudy thought. So, just like his father had earlier, he told them his story, about his early days as a turtle, then how the curse soon swept through Africa. He told them how he got split up from his dad, but how he still sensed that Gewis was alive.

Finally, he told Squiddy and Rodger what had happened just before he met them.

"My dad, King Gewis, is evil," he said sadly.

"That all really happened?" Squiddy asked.

Rudy nodded.

"And I was born in Fairbanks," Rodger murmured.

"I don't have much of an exciting life, unlike you," Squiddy told Rudy, who understood that some stuffed animals wanted his crazy life.

"One thing that is better about your life is that you are not always going from place to place and doing crazy things. You get to just cozy up and enjoy life."

Rodger shook his head, "I want adventure."

Squiddy looked down at his eight tentacles. He was pink and small. The only thing on him that wasn't pink was his white eyes. (With black pupils of course.)

There was a moment of silence. Rudy examined Rodger.

"You're fluffy for a Rottweiler," he blurted randomly.

Squiddy and Rodger looked at him. "Rodger doesn't like it when beings call him cute and fluffy. It embarrasses him," Squiddy said.

Rodger blushed, "But it's okay. I'm used to animals saying that."

"Well, I guess I'm a weird-looking turtle," Rudy said.

All three of them laughed. And just like that the three became best friends. The pears gave Rodger and Squiddy magic. Then they started fighting against King Gewis.

AFTER A LONG WAR, THEY WON. IT WAS A HARSH FIGHT, BUT they survived and beat King Gewis.

Of course, they didn't beat him and his thousands of allies by themselves. Rudy formed an entire army of stuffed animals who realized the evil of Gewis. Although outnumbered and not as powerful, they won with strategy. During the battle, Squiddy, Rodger, and Rudy all met a small Giraffe. Since Squiddy was named Squid with a "y" at the end, that's what they named the Giraffe.

Giraffey.

When Rodger first ran into Giraffey as a baby, he immediately took him back to their base. Giraffey was a medium sized stuffed animal. He was brown with black spots like a real giraffe, but he was nothing close in height. He was only a foot tall. But soon he was old enough to fight against Gewis. Once he took the battlefield, everyone gawked at him. Giraffey was, well, fiercely aggressive.

The Stuffed Animal Squad (or, as Rudy proposed, the S.A.S.) of Rudy, Rodger, Squiddy, and Giraffey believed in peace throughout all of their kind. King Gewis believed in power, and he forced unfair rules on everyone. His most famous quote was probably, "I am the best because you are the worst, and the worst is not the best."

He wanted all stuffed animals to join his side. Rudy was upset about how his dad had changed, but he didn't let this get to him. The squad kept fighting, persevering through the Alaskan weather. Then one day, Rodger got a crazy idea.

In the middle of the night, he snuck into Gewis's castle and led many of his soldiers, who were forced to fight for him, to freedom. Unfortunately, he was caught by Gewis himself and imprisoned.

Although most of the soldiers were freed, Rodger was not, and when Rudy awoke the next morning to find Rodger missing, he searched desperately for him, eventually finding him in the castle jail. Rudy knew that the cells were magic constraining, so Rodger couldn't use his magic from the purple pear tree.

Rudy talked with Rodger about how to get him free, but nothing seemed to work. Gewis had a very secure jail. A few weeks later, Squiddy led an attack on the castle with Rudy and Giraffey by his side. All of their soldiers charged to King Gewis's castle.

"We're outnumbered!" Gewis had shouted, frightening the small remainder of his army.

The Stuffed Animal Squad won the battle and took the castle. That day, something very mysterious happened. Rodger had crafted a special metal weapon. Fearing Giraffey's strong magic ability, he convinced the young stuffed animal to put some of his magic into the weapon. (That is why, to this day, he does not have as much magic as the rest of the leaders.)

The weapon was called the S.A.S. Weapon. It was very powerful and could electrocute stuffed animals. On that day, April 6th, 1881, the S.A.S Weapon made Gewis, and his remaining army literally disappear. Giraffey had whacked the weapon on Gewis's head, and in a yellow mist, he and the army vanished!

Giraffey told everyone that his weapon was just very powerful, though there was one thing suspicious.

A soldier named Ruth Demor had held onto Gewis when he disappeared. She managed to convince the whole army to grab hold of each other. They complained about how awkward it was but held on. It was as if Ruth Demor had told them something important earlier. And then, right as Giraffey struck, Ruth bit Gewis!

His last word before disappearing was, "Owww!"

The S.A.S. celebrated their victory, and right away Rudy got the keys to the jail and walked down the hall to finally let Rodger out. But he wasn't there. Rudy, Squiddy, and Giraffey – the first three members of the Stuffed Animal Squad – gasped. They spotted a window beside the cell of Rodger that was smashed, and waited, but Rodger never came back.

CHAPTER

FOUR

AMADAY

Years passed, and the squad grew.

They ruled over stuffed animals, but in a fair way, much different than Gewis had. The next member to take the place of Rodger was Grey. (The same dog that Louisa got over a century later.) Grey and Rudy became the two main leaders of the S.A.S., because of their magic and leadership ability. Giraffey, Squiddy, and a new dog, Bo Bo, became the secondary leaders. These three were each in charge of a different thing. Giraffey is in charge of Fighting Allies and all the battles and missions. Fighting Allies are the stuffed animals who are called in by the S.A.S. if they ever need help or backup.

Bo Bo is leader of the fairy godmothers, who are small little stuffed animals that are responsible for making all bigger stuffed animals. (They are the only ones other than Gewis that have that power.) So really, instead of some company, it's them who are the ones you should thank for your stuffed animals.

Squiddy is in charge of security and the squad's base. The base is on a tall mountain called Amaday just outside of Denver, Colorado, where the Nobles live. (The leaders used their magic to make Amaday invisible to humans.)

The S.A.S. was forced to move to Amaday when Gewis's castle was burnt down in a forest fire, but now they live and work there happily. In fact, Miles and Louisa had found Grey only because the entrance to the Amaday train was through their house. The Amaday train is the train that zips from Denver to Amaday underground. Originally, the Noble's house was in a park that had a secret entrance to the train, but the park was destroyed and houses were built. So, as it turned out, the S.A.S. and other stuffed animals had to sneak through the Noble's house to use the Amaday train.

Anyway, one downside to the new location is that the bad guys' base is right across from Mount Amaday. There are some things you need to know about the bad guys. First of all, they don't get a cool name like the Evil Squad, or something. They simply don't deserve that. Also, notice that their name is not capitalized, unlike the S.A.S. One thing is for sure, the bad guys are pretty lousy.

One more thing about Amaday. A few miles away is a large city of toys. A while back, Grey was minding his own business when he found a stick. Despite his power and seriousness, he couldn't resist the stick. (As he puts it, once a dog, always a dog.) Grey picked it up in his mouth and sat there for a while until an angry person appeared and told him to drop it. Well, maybe Grey was just feeling wild that day, but he didn't listen.

The person with the voice came over and tried to pry the stick out of his mouth, only to fail. For hours, the tall figure with purple robes and a gold mask tried to pull the stick out of Grey's mouth until finally saying, "I'll make a deal. You will give me that stick, and I will make you even more of them." Grey whimpered in agreement (remember, he was pretending to be a real dog as humans couldn't know that stuffed animals were alive) and dropped the stick without saying anything.

The figure kept their promise and picked up the stick, tucking it in his pocket, and zapped another nearby stick alive. "Bye," The figure said, leaving Grey behind to face the stick menace. But, as it turned out, the living stick was friendly, and it went around tapping toys and making them alive.

All these toys turned alive and migrated to Toy City, a safe place for them outside of Amaday. Eventually, after nearly 70 years, the magical stick got run over by a car, devastating Grey and the toys, but Toy City still runs and, like stuffed animals, toys live forever until they get seriously hurt.

Anyway, back to the S.A.S. It was just Rudy, Squiddy, Giraffey, Grey, and Bo Bo for a while until they decided that more members were needed as the Stuffed Animal population had grown. (The fairy godmothers were busy.) Rudy sent out Giraffey to recruit some more members. After a week, Giraffey returned with Tuskey, a young, talented inventor who, after training, became the sixth member of the S.A.S.

Giraffey continued doing this until the leaders decided that 14 members, the present-day number, was enough. (Plus a few Fighting Allies who we'll meet later.) The members of the S.A.S, in order of when they joined, are Rudy, Squiddy, Giraffey, Grey, Bo Bo, Tuskey, Albert, Flatbeak, Pink Nose Guy, Alfredo, OHM (Orange Hairy Monster), Bunny (yep, he's back), Piggy, and Pecan.

THERE WAS A KNOCK AT THE DOOR. THEN TWO MORE.

"Maui, Maui, Maui," someone's voice said on the other side. This was the password to get into Amaday.

"OHM!" Giraffey called. Orange Hairy Monster (or, as he preferred to be called, OHM) is a stuffed animal monster. His job is to open the door. Yes, this may sound like a weird job, but it was important, and he helped assist in the security of Amaday. In order to do this, OHM had to look through a slot. He put his face up to the slot and peeked through to see if the knocker was safe to enter. It was Bunny!

OHM opened the door for his fellow squad mate. "Hi everyone!" Bunny exclaimed as he boinged in.

Not paying attention, he bonked into Tuskey, the inventor, who was carrying a box of mechanical supplies.

Tuskey fell over and whatever was in the box shattered. He sighed, "Hi Bunny."

Tuskey is an elephant. He was named after the two tusks on the front of his face. Pecan, who is an emu (and the newest squad member) came over and helped Tuskey clean up that shattered glass. But Bunny was rude again and ignored Tuskey's problem. Soon he passed Albert, who waved. Albert is another dog. He was the seventh member to join.

Grey passed Bunny and gave him an awkward smile. "Good morning, Bunny," he said before walking back to his office. Bunny was now passing Piggy's office. She is the chef, and an interesting species called a monster pig.

"Bunny, Saren is here, if you want to have a plopping contest," Piggy informed him while frying up some eggs for the squad's breakfast.

"Yeah, but Saren always wins the plopping contests," Bunny replied.

Saren and Bunny both loved to plop, challenging each other, but usually Saren won. He once was a national plopping champion, therefore being pretty hard to beat.

Anyway, Bunny sat down at a table and watched Tuskey carry all of the supplies that he dropped earlier. Bunny sighed, feeling guilty about how rude he had been.

Tuskey walked back to his office, and was met by Alfredo and Pink Nose Guy, his unofficial partners. Alfredo is a moose and Pink Nose Guy is a rabbit. They are both super small stuffed animals. "What happened?" Pink Nose Guy asked when Tuskey came running into his office.

"Oh, Bunny is just being annoying again," Tuskey responded, who usually didn't complain or talk like this.

"Ah, I see," Alfredo said. "As usual."

The three were currently working together to create a flying ship. They were at the step of attaching bombs, which they would use to drop over the bad guys' base. (Don't worry, it's not as violent as it sounds. Tuskey makes bombs out of slime, so the base is damaged but stuffed animals are not.)

Alfredo looked over his shoulder and saw the beautiful sunset showing through the window. A lot of times squad members complained that Tuskey had the best office because it was the only one with a window.

"Squiddy's office has one too!" Tuskey would argue.

"A smaller one," someone would shoot back.

But, yes, Tuskey was grateful. The only problem with his office was that it was right next to the jail where the squad holds captured bad guys.

Usually, the squad didn't treat their prisoners badly. They gave them three meals a day, except, of course, if you were a super bad guy, you would get a punishment of eating only plain oatmeal for a week. Although there were only thirteen bad guys, the jail was almost always occupied.

With his screwdriver, Tuskey nailed in a part of the bombships' wing.

He worked for a few minutes before telling Alfredo, "I want you to go spy on the bad guys and see what they're up to."

Alfredo gleefully hopped down from his spot next to Pink Nose Guy and saluted.

"Alright!"

Alfredo left the room.

"Great," Tuskey said, then continued working with Pink Nose Guy.

Soon he exclaimed with excitement, "It's almost ready!"

Pink Nose Guy rubbed her hands together.

Meanwhile, Alfredo had started running towards the platform where the squad kept their plane, but Rudy stopped him.

"Meet me in my office," Rudy said. "It will be quick." Alfredo sighed but followed Rudy to his office. The door was closed, and they sat down.

"Alfredo," Rudy began.

"That's me!" Alfredo interrupted.

"Yes, I know." Rudy sighed. "You, Alfredo…"

"That's me!" Alfredo said again.

"Please, I am trying to speak."

"Oh."

"Anyway, you are the one I trust most to spy on the bad guys," Rudy said.

"I am?" Alfredo replied doubtfully.

"Yes," Rudy explained. "And now I want you to go on a spy mission for me."

"That's funny," Alfredo told him. "Tuskey just asked me to do the same thing."

"Okay," Rudy said, a little surprised. "If this is too much for you to handle, that's fine. But I need you to grab something from Room Decor."

Room Decor is the bad guys' boss.

"Okay sir," Alfredo replied, happy to have another task.

"Room Decor stole our only map to the purple pear tree," Rudy said solemnly.

"What!" Alfredo exclaimed.

Yes, this is the same magical tree in Alaska that gave the leaders their magic.

Rudy continued, "Now the bad guys are able to find it and become magical themselves."

"But isn't the tree guarded?" Alfredo asked.

"Yes. But we can't risk them getting past," Rudy looked firmly into Alfredo's eyes. "I trust you to receive this map before it's too late."

"I will. You can count on me."

Rudy told him that he was excused, and without any more questions, Alfredo left the office.

The pressure's on, he told himself. He always liked a good challenge. OHM opened the door for him, and Alfredo trotted onto the platform outside. He walked over to the squad's plane and hopped inside.

Then, after typing in a code, Alfredo started the engine. The plane had a small cockpit, and, in the back, there were about twenty seats.

Alfredo was sitting in the pilot's chair and chanting, "I'm on a spy mission! I'm on a spy mission! I don't know who I'm talking to but I'm on a spy mission!"

He pulled a lever, and the plane roared to life, taking off toward the bad guy base!

CHAPTER

FIVE

ALFREDO'S SPY MISSION

Alfredo flew the plane over a narrow canyon and landed it in front of the bad guys' base. The nice thing about the squad's plane is that it doesn't need a runway to take off or land. And it was super quiet.

Alfredo hopped out of the cockpit and snuck inside the base. (This was pretty easy because the bad guys had an open screen door.) He made sure the coast was clear before tiptoeing down a dark and skinny hallway. He stopped at a door that had voices on the other side. He carefully looked inside.

Yes! Alfredo thought. The bad guys were having one of their "secret" meetings.

Spying missions were always the best when this was the case because the bad guys always gave out a lot of information. Alfredo listened to the discussion from outside in the hallway with a close ear.

"Yes, I have a plan!" Room Decor was saying, who, if you remember, is the boss of the bad guys.

"I have great plans!" Lizhat shouted. He's a green Lizard, with yellow stripes, and is the assistant to the boss.

Room Decor snapped her fingers. "Yeah, yeah, but this time I have a better idea."

Room Decor is a unicorn and technically not a stuffed animal. She's basically a pillow and is meant to be room decoration. (Where her name comes from.) She sat at the table with an evil grin, her trademark purse hanging on her shoulder.

"Well then, smarty pants, what's your plan?" Lizhat asked her.

Room Decor stared at him, then continued, "My plan, Lizard..."

"My name is Lizhat."

Room Decor shook her head. "Very well, Lizard. You can call yourself that."

Lizhat burned with anger, "Just tell us your plan! What is it? Your plan of failure!"

Room Decor sighed, "We have never succeeded. And do you know who comes up with all of our plans? Our plans that fail? Yes, you. I wouldn't say a word about failed plans, you hear me. I'm the boss, so deal with it *Lizard.*"

Lizhat didn't know what to say. He gulped, "Go on."

"My plan is this," Room Decor then told her plan to the twelve other bad guys listening.

Then Room Decor heard a sound from behind the door, and she whirled around in surprise. She walked over to the door and opened it, but nothing was there.

Alfred had acted quickly. He dodged getting caught by jumping onto the doorknob and then launching himself to the top of the open door, and walked unsteadily across the top of the door before realizing that Room Decor was closing the door and he would be squashed!

Luckily, in the last second, Alfredo leaped across the room and grabbed onto a chandelier above the meeting table. He pulled himself up and decided to listen to the meeting from above. Somehow, no one had noticed him.

Anyway, Room Decor sat back down in her seat. The other bad guys were paying no attention to the conversation. One of them even fell asleep, drool going down their chin. Finally, Room Decor finished her plan.

One of the bad guys asked, "Can you just summarize it in one sentence, please?"

"Yeah, sure," Room Decor responded. "The owl will fly over to the Amaday and eavesdrop with our special eavesdropping machine."

The owl raised a wing.

"Yes?"

"Um, why can't I just eavesdrop the regular way with a glass cup?"

Room Decor thought about this question. "Because Amaday has rock walls that are two feet thick."

"Oh."

Room Decor continued, "The owl will eavesdrop on the good guys, as they are probably up to no good, and the rest of us, all except a guard that I will choose to stay back, will be waiting at the entrance of Amaday with a walkie-talkie. The owl will tell us through the radio what they are up to."

Everyone nodded.

"If we're lucky, we can ambush their base."

Whispers came from around the room, most of them agreements.

"An okay strategy," Lizhat pointed out, "But not as strategic as my plans."

"This plan is a lot better than yours!" Then everyone started chanting (except for Lizhat and Alfredo), "Room Decor! Room Decor! Room Decor! Room Decor!"

"Alright, alright, that's enough," Lizhat demanded. "This will be the one time that someone else besides me will come up with a plan."

At this remark, everyone booed at Lizhat. Even Alfredo.

He quickly covered his mouth. *Darn it!* he thought.

A few bad guys looked up at the chandelier where Alfredo was sitting but shrugged and then started booing again.

"Remember Lizard's egg plan?" one of them screamed.

"It's LIZHAT!"

Room Decor shushed everyone, "Okay, we better get on with our plan."

She led the line toward the bad guys' plane: *The Bad Buster.*

"On our way to Amaday!" they chanted.

The owl scooped up her walkie-talkie and flew out the door heading for Mount Amaday. The other twelve (remember, there was a guard staying at their base) walked to the takeoff zone. They hopped into the bad buster.

Room Decor stepped into the front seat and was about to propel the bad buster on its way, but then, one of them, a dog, spotted something.

"Glis!" He shouted. "Pop! Pop! Sim ago!"

The other bad guys in the bad buster turned to look at him.

"Huh?"

"Pop! Pop! It Glis!" He furiously pointed at the squad's plane parked right there!

Another one of them saw it too. "I recognize that," she said.

"What?" Lizhat asked.

"It looks like..." she recalled what it was. She had seen it once, during a battle against the S.A.S.

"That is property of the good guys!"

Room Decor smiled casually and pressed a button that released a robotic arm. It picked up the squad's plane with a frightening amount of strength, and the engine of the bad buster roared to life.

Alfredo gasped. He helplessly watched the bad buster take off, carrying his plane along with it. Soon, it was just him and the guard, who walked away.

Fortunately, Alfredo knew that even without his plane, he could radio Amaday and warn them of the attack. But then he realized the problem. He had forgotten to bring his walkie-talkie!

Oh boy, Alfredo thought, starting to panic. He watched the bad buster recede into the distance. Sure, the bad guys usually didn't win the battles, but Alfredo admitted that they had a decent plan.

He took a deep breath.

I can do this, he told himself. *Just one step at a time.*

Alfredo looked around the bad guys' meeting room, wondering where Room Decor hid the map to the purple pear tree. He hopped down from the chandelier and landed with a thud.

Alfredo quickly ran to the entryway and looked to make sure the coast was clear. It was, so he turned and ran down the hallway, looking for a room that was heavily guarded or secure.

There was one, and Alfredo found that it had a strong lock.

He tried to pick it but couldn't.

"Hey!"

Surprised, Alfredo dropped the paperclip in his hands and turned to see the bad guys' guard staring at him.

"What are you up to?" he demanded.

Alfredo didn't see the point in lying. "I'm trying to break into this room and steal one of your valuables," he said.

"Oh, uh, okay," the guard replied. "That was pretty straightforward."

There was an awkward silence before the guard laughed. "Well then, here you go!" He tossed over a key to Alfredo.

"What? Are you on my side or something?"

"Um," the guard said. "No, I mean, um, I guess."

Alfredo frowned.

Something's not adding up here, he thought. He looked at the key in his hands, then back at the guard.

"Sorry," he said, then dropped the keys.

"Come back here!" the guard shouted as he chased Alfredo.

They ran throughout the base, but although he was faster, Alfredo eventually ran out of breath.

He slid inside a small room.

"I see you!" the guard called.

Suddenly, Alfredo spotted something. *The map!*

He ran forward and pulled out a large sheet of paper. Sure enough, it showed the location of the purple pear tree.

"You're cornered," the guard snickered as he entered the room.

"I can see that," Alfredo responded, gripping the map in his hands.

The guard's expression changed quickly.

"P-put that down!" he stuttered.

"Make me."

Then Alfredo bolted out of the room, speeding right through the guard's legs, out the open screen door, and outside. (The guard was a tall dog, so it wasn't too hard for Alfredo, being an extremely small stuffed animal, to fit under him.)

Now he just needed to escape.

Alfredo frantically looked for something, a miracle, that could transport him back to Amaday before the guard caught up with him.

He rummaged through storage boxes but couldn't find anything before the guard appeared.

"Can you just surrender right now," the guard asked. "It would really make my job easier."

"Sorry."

Alfredo spotted a handle poking out from behind a wall and ran over to it. *This must be the gas tank.* He thought, wondering if maybe it could be used for something. But then he realized how silly this idea was. But when he turned around to walk away, his tail swished and hit a button.

The gas shot out like a tsunami right at Alfredo!

He tried to dodge it, but the gas still knocked him in the back, and he went flying over the railing. Luckily, he quickly grabbed onto the ledge. He pulled himself up and tried not to look down below. It would only hurt a bit because he was stuffed, but still…

Alfredo looked into the horizon. He had been at the bad guy base longer than he thought. The sun was setting. Nighttime attacks, he knew, were always sneakier. The gas was still shooting out from the tank, and Alfredo thought of a very risky idea. Still clutching the map, he grabbed a stick, a rock and a roll of duct tape.

The guard started running toward him, but Alfredo jumped in front of the shooting gas just in time…and he was launched into the air. If you were watching from farther away, you would start panicking and ask, "Is that a missile?"

Yes, that's how fast Alfredo flew through the air. Now the *Bad Buster* and the poor owl flying desperately beside it, were in view. Quickly, Alfredo ripped off a piece of duct tape. The rest of the roll fell to the ground far below.

Next, he made his slingshot. Holding the map in his antlers, he taped both sides of the duct piece to the two forks of the stick.

Alfredo picked up his handmade slingshot and aimed.

The owl, or the bad buster? he thought to himself. *Which one should I hit?*

But he didn't need to choose.

Unfortunately for the bad guys, the bad buster was about to run out of gas, so they had to turn around and race back to the gas tank at their base. Inside the cockpit, Room Decor grumbled and zoomed over Alfredo, making him spin in circles.

He now had one option. He would aim the rock at the owl. Alfredo hoped that he would hit his target, although dizziness would not make it easier.

Alfredo pulled back his slingshot and was about to pull out the rock that he had grabbed but was surprised to find that it was missing.

Great. Just great. I dropped it, he thought, extremely annoyed. Then he realized something. *How am I still in the air?*

True, the gas had shot him pretty far, but he should have been falling by now. Alfredo looked down. He was sitting on top of a Bald Eagle!

The eagle was flying beside another one, who had a fish. They both cawed at each other and flew side by side. These two eagles were real animals, not stuffed animals.

The male (without Alfredo) had a fish for them to share, and they started flying lower toward their nest.

Alfredo acted quickly. He brainstormed a quick plan, and then, without thinking about the outcome, he snatched the fish from the other eagle.

Somehow, neither of them noticed. (Just the true nature of a spy.) Then Alfredo put the fish in his slingshot. He pulled it back, and launched it at the owl, who was flapping her wings helplessly a few yards ahead of them.

The one Alfredo was riding saw the fish first.

"A flying fish!" she exclaimed in eagle language. (All Alfredo heard when she said this was a screech.)

"That's impossible," the other one said. "I mean, I'm smart enough to know that they can't get this high."

"No, look!"

The male looked ahead. "You're right!" he said, very surprised. "It looks like the fish that I am holding right now."

He looked at his talons, but nothing was there.

"What the…" Then he realized something was on the other eagle's back.

He pointed with his wing at Alfredo.

"Rodent!" They both screamed at the same time.

Alfredo sat there hoping he wouldn't become an appetizer. The two eagles whirled their heads back and forth from Alfredo to the fish. "Fish! Rodent! Fish! Rodent! Fish! Rodent!"

Finally, they decided, "The fish smells better. It's also bigger."

The two flew after the flying salmon swiftly, which had missed the owl by a few feet.

Alfredo was disappointed that his plan didn't work. However, the eagles were determined to catch that fish, and were now flying close to light speed.

Suddenly, they pointed their beaks downward. They dove, and Alfredo tried to not lose his grip on them or the map, still tucked tightly in his palm!

He looked back and could make out the bad buster in the distance, refueled, and in the air again. According to what Tuskey always told Alfredo, it would take an approximate seven minutes until they reached Amaday.

Meanwhile, the eagles were nearing their prey.

"Get out of the way, slow owl," they called.

Alfredo closed his eyes as they crashed into the owl.

She fell to the ground spinning in circles, a dazzle of feathers littered in the air.

The eagles grabbed the fish, and they flew to the other side of the canyon and perched on a rock. The male only got in a few bites because he didn't want to disappoint his mate.

"You're next, scum," he told Alfredo, who didn't understand what the eagle was saying, but still knew that it wasn't good.

Quickly, knowing that he needed to alert the squad, Alfredo got an idea. He would pick up the fish again and throw it toward Amaday. That way he could get a free ride as the eagles flew after it.

Yeah, there's no way that they will forget the fish and eat me instead, Alfredo told himself.

He bent over and stole the fish from the eagle's beak, throwing it as far as he could towards Amaday.

"What do you want, rodent?"

Alfredo pointed at the salmon, but they shook their heads.

"I guess eagles don't like to play fetch," Alfredo said. He hopped off the eagle's back before it was too late to realize his mistake.

She lunged forward!

Run!

Alfredo sprinted up a little hill away from the eagles, who seemed to be in no rush.

"Slow poke," they teased.

Although he did not understand them, Alfredo was getting annoyed with the eagles.

"Pick on someone your own size," he said, putting his hand up to one of them.

"Whoah, little moose. A brave one you are," the eagle responded before leaping forward at Alfredo.

Suddenly, the other eagle screeched.

The owl, who seemed to be in decent shape from when the eagles crashed into her, smacked both of them in revenge, not seeing Alfredo.

Not meaning to, a bad guy had just saved him.

Then the owl flew off. "That's payback!" she shrieked.

"Dead meat!" The eagles growled, and the owl realized that she should never mess with a fully grown *real* eagle. Quickly, she turned around to fly away.

"I'll get you for that!" The eagle roared after her. He spread his wide wings and followed the owl, his mate joining the chase.

"Pick on somebody your own size," Alfredo called. "Like her!"

Then he rushed back to Amaday.

CHAPTER

SIX

THE BATTLE

The S.A.S. huddled into their meeting room, which was under Leader Grey's office. It was locked, and Grey had the only key. (As you can see, it's much more secure than the bad guys' meeting room.)

Once every member was tucked into their spot, Alfredo walked into the middle of the room and gave the purple pear tree map to Rudy.

"Thank you," Rudy said appreciatively, tucking the map behind him.

"What's that? A coloring page?" Bunny asked.

Rudy sighed, "No, it's a map to the purple pear tree."

"The what now?"

"The purple pear tree. Remember?"

Bunny scratched his chin. "Oh yeah…the one that gives you magic?"

Rudy nodded.

Alfredo watched Bunny and Rudy impatiently. "The bad guys will be here any minute."

"Yeah, you can say that" Bunny said. "But it always takes, like, an hour or two."

"Bunny," Rudy stated. "Please let Alfredo continue."

"Alri…"

"Anyway," Alfred said assertively. "I will try to explain this quickly."

Then he took a deep breath and told the squad what the bad guys were planning.

Afterwards, there was a moment of thought until finally, Rudy spoke up. He was the oldest member of the squad at 147 years old. But he still looked like he did when he first turned stuffed. Dark green fur. Even darker spikes that were used as powerful weapons, and finally, small coal black eyes.

Anyway, Rudy told his plan. "Either me or Grey will go into the main room, closest to our walls, so that the owl can hear us clearly."

Alfredo raised his hand, and Rudy nodded at him.

"Um, when I left from the mission, their guard saw me leaving. He probably alerted the rest of them."

Rudy thought for a while.

"But he was also pretty startled and could be speechless," Alfredo said.

"Most likely not," Grey told him. "You probably didn't escape with that much style." (Alfredo frowned.) "But those bad guys are always in a hurry. They probably didn't listen to their guard."

Rudy nodded in agreement.

Giraffey scribbled something in his notebook.

"What are you writing?" Flatbeak asked. He is a penguin stuffed animal, black and white with a cute orange beak. He is the nurse for the squad and has the amazing ability to float like a balloon!

"I'm making a chart of how many times the bad guys attack and who wins each time," Giraffey replied. Bo Bo rolled her eyes. He was always making charts like that.

"So far we've won 43 times, and the bad guys have won once."

"May I continue?" Rudy asked.

"Oh, yes."

Rudy cleared his throat. "Grey or I will stand in the middle of base. Then we will call out 'time for bed' or something. All of you must say yes, and pretend you are going to sleep. The bad guys will think most of us are asleep, when we are really in ready positions. Once they enter, we will ambush them, while Pink Nose Guy will pilot our mini bombship."

It was settled. The squad had their plan, and the bad guys had theirs. The fight would soon begin.

"TIME FOR BED," RUDY CALLED OUT. IT WAS DECIDED THAT Rudy would say this because he was better at pretending.

"Wait, but aren't we ambushing them?" Bunny asked.

Rudy glared at him. "Remember..."

"Oh yeah," Bunny replied. He remembered now.

Squiddy was giving signals and pointing, telling the squad members where to go. He signaled for Bunny to go in the back of the ambush line.

Bunny plopped down next to Pecan and stretched.

"Touch your toes," Pecan whispered.

Bunny looked embarrassed. "I can't."

"Shhhhhh," Tuskey said from ahead of them. "Get ready."

He was holding a remote that would help track the bombship Pink Nose Guy was in. There was a big red button that Tuskey would press to drop the bombs on the bad guys' base.

However, Rudy told him to make sure that no bad guys were still in the base. (Although the bad guys were the sworn enemies of the S.A.S., they didn't believe in exploding each other.) Tuskey realized that if he was in the middle of a battle, it would be very intense to press the button on the remote, so he got up and moved back into his office.

The squad waited for a little while. Rudy had to say his fake bedtime lines a few more times.

This feels like I'm in preschool, Bunny thought.

But finally, there was a bang at the door! Everyone advanced in battle positions.

"This darn thing isn't breaking in!" A familiar voice called.

"I guess we'll need a new door," Pecan whispered to Bunny as there were a few more bangs.

Finally, the door was knocked down and Lizhat revealed himself, leaning against the doorway. He yawned, putting his hand up to his mouth. Behind him were the rest of the bad guys, except the owl (who, Alfredo grimaced, hopefully had escaped the eagles).

Room Decor was holding a gigantic ax!

Lizhat finished yawning and then saw that the good guys were actually right there in front of them. He couldn't believe it.

"Amaday-A-A-A!" Squiddy cried out. (This is the battle cry of the S.A.S.)

Lizhat shouted out the bad guys' battle cry. "They tricked us! Ahhhh, I can't believe it. Scramble, no I mean, attack!"

Squiddy looked at him awkwardly and shrugged. Room Decor, who had been surprisingly quiet, started yelling out commands, but most of the bad guys ignored her and just ran to fight. They jumped forward, trying to punch everything in their sight. (Including one another.)

Lizhat targeted Squiddy. Squiddy ducked, and Lizhat fell to the ground. Giraffey picked him up and shouted, "I know martial arts!" Then Lizhat was thrown to the floor. I hope you can tell that Giraffey loved to fight. He moved on to beat up some other bad guy, and after he succeeded, he pulled out his electric guitar from a closet and started to play a rock song that he wrote.

Someone playing heavy metal in the middle of a battle was pretty intimidating to the bad guys. However, while he was singing the lines, "Knock 'em out till tomorrow," two bad guys lunged at him from behind and tackled him to the floor, a string snapping on Giraffey's guitar.

While that was going on, Lizhat recovered from the faceplant. He looked around the base of the S.A.S. and realized that the bad guys were clearly losing. (As usual.) But Lizhat was determined to beat them this time! But first, he needed some backup.

"HEY YOU!" He shouted to the nearest bad guy, who scurried over, looking very frightened.

"Yes?"

"Fly back to our base in the bad buster and pick up the guard we left there."

"Yes sir," the bad guy responded, running out of the squad's base. Almost immediately, the owl flew into the base. She hovered in the air, watching the other bad guys get tortured.

"Well, what are you floating around for?" Lizhat screamed at her. "Fight!"

She nodded, then flew toward Flatbeak, who was also in the air.

But Flatbeak couldn't fly, he could only float. This meant that the owl had an advantage. She snuck up on him, knocking him out of midair! Acting quickly, Flatbeak puffed his chest, and spread his flippers out on both sides. Just before touching the ground, he floated back up to face the owl.

With a very powerful punch, he nailed her in the face!

She shrieked. "Ooooooooooooooooooooooooooooowwwwwwwwwwwwwwwwwwwwwwwwwwwwww! I'm in pain!! I want to say bad words, but I won't! Ouch! A lot of pain, I'll tell you…" The owl kept moaning and groaning, but then realized she wasn't actually hurting. She delivered a punch right back at Flatbeak.

Over on the other side of Amaday, Rudy walked smoothly into Tuskey's office. Inside, Tuskey was sitting on a blue bean bag. Because the bean bag matched Tuskey almost exactly in color, Rudy didn't see him at first. Next to Tuskey was Pink Nose Guy, tucked inside the mini bombship, looking ready for action. The ship was only about the size of a remote-control drone, and Pink Nose Guy and Alfredo were the only two that could fit in it. But, despite this fact, the bomb inside was super powerful, and Tuskey had been working on it for months.

"It is time," Rudy said. He spotted the familiar black remote sitting on a counter next to him. His hand made it only halfway there.

"Wait, this is just a facsimile," Rudy noticed with his magical sense.

"Yep," Tuskey said. "The real version is here."

"Good grief, Rudy," Pink Nose Guy complained. "Why do you have to use so many fancy words?" Rudy shrugged.

Tuskey pulled the original remote from behind his back. "That one is just a model in case any of the bad guys discover it, probably from Bunny telling them, and come looking."

Rudy nodded, "I know you're not that fond of Bunny at times, but don't judge him. Still, the idea of having a fake is smart."

"I'm ready!" Pink Nose Guy called. She gave a thumbs up sign to Tuskey.

"Banana banana monkey?" He asked her.

"Banana monkey monkey," Pink Nose Guy responded.

"That's our secret code for asking if someone's ready," Tuskey whispered to Rudy. He leaned back into his bean bag and started tinkering with controls on the remote. The bombship lifted into the air. The engine made a tiny squeaking noise, but besides that, the ship was completely silent.

Outside there was a growing noise of wings flapping, and suddenly, the door burst open! The owl screamed. Flatbeak yelled at her. They were now in a huge boxing match, except in the air. Flatbeak snarled and lunged. However, the owl was prepared this time. She launched a wing smack right back at him. Flatbeak hurled through the air toward Tuskey who wasn't paying any attention.

"Look out!" Flatbeak shouted.

"Huh?" Tuskey said. He looked up. Luckily for him, he jumped out of the way just in time. But unfortunately, Tuskey was about to press the launch button for the ship, so when he jumped to the right, he also moved the little steering wheel on the remote. This swerved the ship to the right, and Pink Nose Guy was now going straight for the wall.

"Ahhhh!" She screamed. "I'm going to crash!" Although stuffed animals don't feel much pain, they could if it was bad. Rudy watched Pink Nose Guy fly toward the wall. If someone didn't do something soon, the ship would surely crash, and break and she would get hurt. Quickly, Rudy put his hand in front of him and with a blast of green light, his magic, he moved the bombship away from the wall, and Pink Nose Guy drove it out of the office shouting, "Thanks!"

"Why didn't you tell me to get out of the way?" Tuskey asked Flatbeak once she was gone.

Flatbeak pouted, "I did."

"What was that ship?" the owl asked.

"Uh…" Tuskey and Flatbeak exchanged glances.

"Now now, don't be nosy little girl," Tuskey said.

"I demand an answer!" the owl shouted. "And also, I am *not* a little girl."

"Well, it's none of your business," Flatbeak told her.

The owl growled. "Since you aren't telling me what that ship was, I figure its top secret. I'm going to follow it."

Tuskey shrugged, "Suit yourself."

The owl was surprised to not see anyone panicking about her following the ship. "Well," she said, "if you think that the ship is too small for me to track, then you're wrong!" She pulled out a little gadget. "This can track metal."

Rudy, Tuskey, and Flatbeak showed no expression. "So?"

The owl was getting flustered. "I, uh, well either way, I will find that ship." Then she flew away.

Tuskey high-fived Flatbeak. Of course, the owl couldn't keep up with the fast bombship of theirs, even with her gizmo device. "Well, we pretty much won the battle," Flatbeak said with excitement.

Rudy watched them with disappointment. "Don't get your hopes up."

Tuskey frowned at him. "I guess you're right, but I don't see how the bad guys can defeat us."

"True, but you never know," Rudy said. "I'm going to keep fighting."

"Sure," Flatbeak replied. "I can drop heavy things on people's heads from the air."

"I'm just going to track Pink Nose Guy and celebrate once she bombs their base," Tuskey said.

Rudy sighed then started to walk away. "We're still in the fight, so don't celebrate yet."

Outside, Giraffey was on a roll. He smacked all of the bad guys onto the floor a few times each, then, using the S.A.S. weapon – the same one he used to make Gewis disappear – he whacked them.

Bunny was not having as much of a time. He didn't necessarily enjoy the battles, as he was more of a peaceful rabbit. He sat there watching the fighting until there was a sudden flash of black spots. A bad guy, the same one who had spotted the squad's plane earlier, was sitting on top of Bunny.

"Could you please get off me," Bunny said impatiently.

"Urg," they responded.

Bunny took that as a no. He stayed in that position for a while, no one bothering to help. So, for entertainment, Bunny watched some of the other fights going on.

On the other side of the room a bad guy, who was, ironically, a Care Bear, approached Bo Bo.

"Hello," she began.

Bo Bo rolled her eyes. (She liked to do that.)

"I love you," the bad guy continued. "But for some reason I am forced to fight you."

Bo Bo rolled her eyes again then said, "Farewell." She kicked the Care Bear as hard as she could, and they went flying and landed outside on the platform. Bo Bo turned around and was surprised to see Lizhat standing there.

"I've got ya!" he shouted before punching her. Piggy saw this and started running over to help her friend, but Bo Bo used magic to throw Lizhat off.

He grumbled then ran forward again. But something stopped him...there was a loud boom in the distance. Pink Nose Guy had exploded the bad guys' base!

Lizhat just shook his shoulders. "Ignore the noise."

The bad guy sitting on top of Bunny got bored, so Bunny boinged up and yelled, "Yay, Pink Nose Guy exploded..."

Fortunately, Squiddy used his magic to create a sound bubble (the soundproof bubble that comes out of his tentacles) around Bunny, so no one outside of it could hear what he finished saying.

"Exploded what?" someone asked.

The bad guy who spoke the weird language said, "Grr la tod sico grrr im."

Squiddy sighed, gave Bunny one of his famous looks, then released the sound bubble. No one was too suspicious, and the fight continued. Over in the corner, Room Decor watched the battle closely. Surprisingly enough, no one paid her any attention. And even more surprisingly, she wasn't taking part in the fight. Like usual, her mysterious purse hung on her shoulder, the contents inside unknown.

Anyway, the fight raged on, but soon most of the bad guys were pinned to the ground by the squad. Finally,

Squiddy had the chance to use a sound bubble on someone else besides Bunny. He focused very hard, and a large bubble popped out of one tentacle, capturing the bad guys inside. Since a few squad members were holding down the bad guys he had to make a small hole in it so they could get out.

Lizhat tried to escape too, but Squiddy quickly closed the gap. Although most of them were captured, a few bad guys had fled when the fight got out of hand.

"We win…" Giraffey smiled. "Again." Grey turned to the sound bubble of bad guys and, in a flash of yellow, tried to use his magic to lift the bubble.

It didn't work.

Usually, Grey would be able to lift the weight by himself, but for some reason Rudy had to help him this time, and even with the two strongest leaders the sound bubble could barely be lifted. After a minute of using all their strength and magic, Grey and Rudy moved it over to the squad's jail. Squiddy popped it and the bad guys inside were trapped in the large cell. This meant the fight was over, and for the forty-fourth time in a row, the S.A.S. won.

LIKE I SAID BEFORE, A FEW BAD GUYS HAD ESCAPED.

When they reached their base, or what was left of it, they were horrified. One of them asked, "What happened?"

"Lightning," said another. "It destroyed our base with a powerful strike."

"Yeah," the first agreed.

"What, no!" Room Decor barked. "You guys are clueless! Lighting isn't that powerful, and anyway, look at the sky."

The bad guys looked up. The sky was perfectly blue. "Uh, there's a lot of clouds over there."

"Those aren't storm clouds," Room Decor muttered. "But I don't care about our base anymore." She put down a brief case that she was holding and held up a map.

"They stole this from us, and without anyone realizing, I took it right back!" she exclaimed.

"Where does it lead to?"

"Oh, just to a tree that gives you magic." Suddenly, they heard a noise and all three of them looked over their shoulders. One of them gasped.

"It was her!" they bellowed. "That good guy bombed our base. Oh, they will pay."

Pink Nose Guy was flying back to Amaday in her ship. Room Decor didn't care, but the other two started snarling and complaining. Soon she had enough. "Silence!" Right at that moment, the owl, who had chased after Pink Nose Guy's ship, landed on the ground next to the remaining bad guys. Well, this infuriated the two bad guys.

"Why didn't you stop that ship?" they screamed at the top of their lungs.

"I don't know," the owl said. "This metal-tracking device didn't work. Apparently, someone stuffed a cracker where the batteries are supposed to go."

Room Decor stormed away from the three.

"You guys are nothing like my boss!" she shouted, clenching the map and briefcase in her hands. The three other bad guys exchanged glances. None of them knew which boss Room Decor was talking about.

CHAPTER
SEVEN

THE GAME OF SATALUA TAG

"**O**h, oh, pick me, pick me!"

Mrs. Keller had just asked a question. "Um, Gus," she said.

Bunny sighed. "Darn it."

Miles was doing remote learning, and Bunny decided to join. (Off screen, of course.) Every time Mrs. Keller asked a question, Bunny raised his paw, even if he didn't know the answer. Besides, she wasn't going to call on him anyway. The Nobles would keep the fact that they lived with a stuffed animal that talked a secret.

"Bunny, do you know what 140 x 21 is?" Miles asked him.

"Uh, two hundred?" Bunny guessed.

Miles shook his head. "If you don't know the answer, don't raise your hand!"

"My paw," Bunny corrected.

"Right...your paw."

"Wait," Bunny started again. "I have the right answer this time."

Miles took off his headphones. "What is it?"

Bunny thought for a moment.

Finally, he exclaimed, "New Orleans!"

Miles sighed, "I don't know what Louisiana has to do with math."

"Neither do I."

Miles kept going, trying to ignore Bunny. Now, if you're not familiar with remote learning, let me tell you that it's not fun. Miles didn't mind the fact that Covid made school online, but Bunny shouting nonstop wasn't helping. After an hour of Bunny blurting out wrong answers, Miles finally had enough. "Bunny, you're a good rabbit and all, but I need to focus," he said. "Can you go somewhere else for now?"

"Fine," Bunny said, and, although he didn't want to, boinged away.

He boinged into the living room where something caught his eye. It was the newspaper on one of the spinning chairs. The headline read:

Explosion On Mountain

Investigators think old mining dynamite went off Tuesday. Although no mines have been reported in the area, researchers will investigate further.

Bunny concluded that when Pink Nose Guy exploded the bad guys' base, humans thought it was some old mining dynamite. The battle had already been six days ago, and the S.A.S. figured there wouldn't be any more for a while unless the bad guys in jail escaped somehow. Bunny kept boinging around the living room thinking about how bored he was. Over at the table, Miles was still working. Bunny wanted so badly to raise his paw when a question was asked and blurt out the answer.

Owner needs to focus, he told himself.

But Bunny couldn't help it.

"The answer is twenty-four!"

Even with headphones, Miles heard Bunny loud and clear. He glared at the rabbit and then kept typing.

Leigh came out of her office for two reasons. Firstly, Bunny had said, "the answer is twenty-four!" in a very dramatic voice, so she wanted to see what the fuss was about. Secondly, she needed a refill on coffee.

Leigh poured herself some espresso then told Bunny, "You need to be quiet. I'm on an important meeting." Bunny grumbled and tromped up the stairs. (Or whatever you call tromping for a rabbit that has legs too thin he can only boing on his rump.)

Once upstairs, he boinged into Louisa's room.

Nothing stood out at first, but Bunny could smell something. He followed the scent and found some carrot bacon tucked in the corner. There must have been hundreds of pieces!

"Ho ho!" he shouted, then leapt forward. He landed in the pile before realizing that something wasn't right. It definitely wasn't carrot bacon!

Suddenly, Sweetie burst out from behind a rocking chair! She rolled onto the floor, laughing and pointing at Bunny. "You actually fell for that!"

Bunny groaned. He should have known that it was Sweetie who put the paper carrot bacon there. In frustration, he boinged right on top of her!

"Hmmmp!" she said from underneath Bunny's rump.

Bunny sat there, even when Sweetie started pounding and biting him. Eventually he hopped off and she was not happy. Sweetie, as you just found out, is a huge prankster. She always wears a pink baby suit, is about a foot tall, and is Miles and Louisa's favorite doll.

"So," Sweetie asked. "Wanna play a game?"

Bunny was about to say yes, when he remembered something. "Sorry," he told her, "But I have to study."

Sweetie frowned. "Okay."

You see, Bunny had stuffed animal school too, but sometimes he skipped class to be with Owner. (He loved human school much better.) But still, studying had to be done, so Bunny boinged away, into the Noble's basement. He went down the hallway, then, making sure the coast was clear, opened a closet door and boinged to the back where a secret trapdoor waited. He pushed it open and entered the Amaday train station underground. Then he boinged into a car and zipped off to Amaday!

A FEW HOURS LATER, BUNNY WAS SITTING AT HIS DESK, STUDY-ing. Luckily, there wasn't too much work, but, as usual, he was starting to regret skipping stuffed animal school again. It was true, though, that Bunny had a good excuse. But he didn't dare tell his teacher about remote learning with Miles. Bunny yawned. It was almost midnight, but he kept going.

Who cares what gives the leaders their magic? he thought after reading a question. "I heard that," Squiddy said as he walked past on his tentacles. (Or whatever you would call that.)

"You did?" Bunny exclaimed. He didn't know that Squiddy could read minds.

"Yeah, you must be getting tired." Bunny quickly re-alized that Squiddy was talking about his yawn, not the thought he had.

They were the only two awake and Bunny had no idea how Squiddy could do it every night. He was always the overnight guard.

"How do you get your magic?" Bunny asked.

Squiddy sighed, "That's one of the questions, isn't it?"

"Uh, no. I'm just wondering," Bunny lied.

"Very well," Squiddy began. "I think you should know this by now, but we leaders get our magic from eating the Purple Pears." Squiddy stopped for a moment before real-izing that Bunny wanted to hear more. "They are rare and only grow in one tree on a tundra in Alaska."

"What's a tundra?" Bunny asked.

Squiddy cleared his throat, "They are treeless areas of land, usually very cold. Which is one reason the Purple Pear tree is so special."

"I get it," Bunny said, scribbling down the answer on his study sheet.

Squiddy peeked over his shoulder. "So that was a question."

Bunny quickly covered his paper. "N-n-nothing."

Squiddy sighed and noticed a little cart full of books parked beside Bunny's desk. "Where'd you get that?" he asked.

"My teacher lent it to me because, you know, I have noodle arms."

"Good of them, huh?"

Bunny grumbled at Squiddy. "I just wish I didn't have to do stuffed animal school at all."

Squiddy nodded.

"I have been going to school, just a different kind. It's much better," Bunny blurted out before he could stop himself. Squiddy looked suspiciously at Bunny, and if he had an eyebrow, he would have raised it.

He thought for a moment then announced, "Meet me in Rudy's office tomorrow at six o'clock sharp."

"Alright," Bunny replied.

Squiddy patted the Rabbit on the back. "I think you should sleep," he said. "You have a long day ahead of you."

THE SUN SHONE BRIGHTLY THROUGH THE WINDOWS AND THE curtains, glowing on Miles and Bunny, who were sleeping in bed.

Suddenly, Darren walked into the room. He went over to the curtains and slid them open. When this happened, Miles yanked the covers over his head. He claimed that the sound of the curtains being drawn, and the shades being pulled up was his least favorite sound.

"Come on!" Darren clapped his hands and said, "Time to get up."

Miles groaned loudly and clenched his fists. Louisa, who had just woken up, jumped straight out of her bed on the other side of the room.

"Today's gonna be a great day!" she hollered.

Miles groaned again and stayed right where he was, snuggling Bunny. Louisa and Darren walked downstairs to make breakfast. Miles stayed there for five more minutes, but eventually Darren called him down again. He shuffled out of bed and got ready, groaning the whole time.

Bunny, however, laid in bed until he was ready to wake up. He was in a decent mood because stuffed animal school was off for the day, so he could have some free time. Bunny woke up a few hours later, ate some carrot bacon, and boinged to the basement, careful not to distract Miles from his remote learning. Once downstairs, he boinged to the back of their closet and was met by Saren.

If you don't remember, Saren is a Fighting Ally who is plopping enemies with Bunny. The two got along pretty well. Bunny boinged up to him. Saren was blasting salsa music and didn't hear him.

"Hola!" Bunny exclaimed.

The music stopped. "Oh, Hola," Saren said, turning around. "¿Cómo estás?"

"Uh…" Bunny didn't know Spanish.

"¿Hablas español?"

"Uh, I guess so."

"Bien," Saren said. "¿Qué estás haciendo?"

"I don't speak Spanish!" Bunny shouted.

Saren looked puzzled. "But you just said that you did when I asked you if you spoke Spanish," he said, really confusing Bunny.

"Uh…"

"Never mind. Let's just speak English."

"Thank you," Bunny replied. "Anyway, I'm wondering if you can come to Amaday with me."

Saren smiled. "Sure thing! I actually have a break now." Just then, another Fighting Ally walked into the room, beckoning for Saren to leave.

"Come on," he told Bunny.

Together, they hopped onto the Amaday train, pushed some buttons, and sped off towards Amaday. The train ride was fast and soon they arrived. They hopped out and were met by a large fountain. Bunny boinged to the lower part of Amaday. This was where many of the Fighting Allies worked and the public section of the base. Only one door connected to where the squad worked, but it was off limits for most stuffed animals.

Bunny and Saren entered and immediately saw Sweetie.

"Sup' dudes," she said.

"Hi, Sweetie," Bunny responded. "Do you want to play with me and Saren?"

Sweetie's face lit up. "Sure!" She exclaimed. "Want to play satalua tag?"

"¡Seguro!" Saren said.

"I'll take that as a yes," Sweetie replied. Then she started running around the base with her eyes closed, so of course she ran into one of the leaders.

"Sweetie!" Grey shouted. "What are you doing?"

She opened her eyes. "Hi! Wanna play satalua tag?"

Grey sighed, "I guess."

"Yes!" Sweetie exclaimed as Bunny and Saren caught up with them.

You see, this is why many stuffed animals loved Grey. Even though he is a leader, he's not too serious and takes breaks to have fun. So, the game started. Satalua tag was much different than regular, human tag.

Satalua stood for *Stuffed Animals and Toys Alive Led Under Amaday.* You see, it could often get violent, which basically tells you that Sweetie made it up. There are two teams. It was decided that this time they would be Bunny and Grey vs. Sweetie and Saren. Each team got a slow player. (No offense to Bunny and Saren.)

Okay, here's how you play Sweetie's version of tag: There must be two or more players per team. One player is the tagger, and their job is to tag the players on the opposing team. The tagger's teammate tries to slow the other running team down. (Usually this is by wrestling or something violent like that.)

Whoever is tagged first on the other team will be 'it' the next round. However, the current tagging team must touch all the opposing players before switching to running. Once all the players on the retreating team are tagged, the teams switch roles. The player tagged first on the other is the new tagger, and the teams keep switching roles until the time runs out.

There is a timekeeper, usually Sweetie (who often cheats if she is also playing), and whichever team has the most time running wins. Okay, that was a lot, and if you understand, great. If not, well, game instructions have always been confusing.

Anyway, Bunny, Sweetie, Grey, and Saren were ready to play.

"Ah, wroof wroof wroof wroof," Grey barked as he sped away from Saren, the tagger.

Sweetie knew that this was her chance. She stopped wrestling Bunny and snuck to the corner of the couch and when Grey rounded the corner, she jumped on top of him!

This gave Saren time to run and tag him.

Sweetie jumped off of Grey shouting, "He's it for the next round!"

"We have to catch Bunny now!" Saren said.

Yikes! Bunny thought, trying his best to get away from Sweetie but it was no use.

"Run!" Grey told him.

But Bunny was no match for Sweetie, and soon she stopped him just in time for Saren to tag him. "Okay," she said, checking her stopwatch. "You guys have been running for 49 seconds. Yeah, we can win this thing."

The teams changed roles now and Grey was it. He and Bunny usually made a decent team. With Bunny's big body, he could slow down Sweetie and Saren. And Grey had incredible speed, making him the best tagger. It looked like things would go pretty smoothly this time. Grey tagged Saren in under 20 seconds. He high-fived Bunny, "Good job. Now, let's get Sweetie."

Sweetie was a fast runner too. Not quite as speedy as Grey, but close. The chase was on. Grey and Bunny ran (and boinged) after her, when Grey got a sudden idea.

"Bunny, you stay here. Get ready to chase Sweetie into the closet."

"Okay."

They were playing in the empty cafeteria, and Sweetie had just started running away, ducking and jumping past tables meant for large feasts hosted by the S.A.S.

She stuck out her tongue and said, "Can't catch me!"

Grey jumped up over a table and landed in front of her.

Sweetie looked up. "Oh, hi Grey. Sorry but I am in the middle of…"

Grey cleared his throat.

"Wait a minute!" Sweetie cried. "I forgot! You're the tagger."

Grey sighed. Sweetie could be forgetful at times. She barely dodged his paw before turning around and heading towards Bunny.

"I gotcha!" Bunny shouted.

Sweetie barely dodged him, and he grumbled. *Boing!* Bunny leaped into midair and knocked her over. Of course, there were no fouls in Satalua tag, so this was legal and a good strategy.

"Ha!" Grey yelled, rushing toward her.

Well, even though he had already been tagged, Saren could still help. He jumped in front of Grey just in time.

Startled, Bunny let go of Sweetie and she bolted away.

Quickly, Grey yelled, "timeout!"

Just to add on to the 1,000 rules, each team got three timeouts that they could use. Bunny boinged over to Grey and they huddled next to each other, Saren standing next to them eagerly.

"Let's gameplan in the bathroom," Grey told Bunny.

This was a weird thing to do, but the other team couldn't hear their strategy, so they walked into the bathroom and locked the door.

"Okay, we only have a minute, so let's make this quick," Grey said.

"I called this timeout mainly for a break, but just to be clear, I'll go after Sweetie. You just hold back Saren. Kapeesh?"

"Uh," Bunny replied. "Do I say kapeesh or kapash?"

"I don't know. So, are you ready?"

"Yes!" Bunny boinged in excitement. However, when he did this, he knocked Grey into the toilet!

"Whoops!" Bunny cried.

"Are you okay?" Sweetie asked from outside the door, hearing all the ruckus.

"Yeah, I'm fine. But Grey's not." Bunny tried to pull him out of the toilet. He finally managed to do this and picked up the leader, who was soaking wet.

"Thank..." Grey was saying when Bunny slipped on a puddle and dropped Grey back into the toilet! Well, Grey had kept his anger under control at first, but now he was about to blow!

"Oh, sorry!" Bunny exclaimed. He definitely didn't want to be the one who made Grey mad. He was still on the floor, so in order to get up, he gripped the toilet. But unfortunately, it was the wrong part of the toilet.

The flusher.

It was too late for Grey to use his magic, and the water started sucking him to the bottom of the toilet. If he was any smaller, he would have gone straight down the pipes. Luckily, he was big enough to not get flushed, but this also meant that Grey clogged the toilet.

Water started leaking everywhere.

Bunny thought of the trouble he would get into but took a deep breath. He just needed to rescue his friend.

He stuck his hand inside the toilet. *Gross!* Bunny patted around inside the toilet until he found Grey's paw. He tugged hard on it, thinking that Grey was wedged in there. But actually, he wasn't.

Bunny pulled him out *way* too hard, and Grey sailed through the air straight out of the toilet. His nose slammed right into the door. Now, like I said earlier, stuffed animals do not often feel pain, but when a part of them is hard and non-stuffed – like Grey's nose – it hurts. On top of that, something strange happened, where Grey's whole body started hurting. All a sudden, he just started shaking, and he tried not to howl, but couldn't help it. Soon it stopped, and the leader was furious. He unlocked the door, and stormed back into the hall, toilet water dripping from him. Bunny followed, feeling extremely guilty. Sweetie and Saren came over to see the commotion.

"What happened?" Sweetie asked, her voice on edge.

Grey didn't respond.

"It's time for the meeting," he told Bunny, then walked away without another word.

CHAPTER

EIGHT

THE PROPHECY

Bunny boinged into the squad's base, passing through the secret door that connected it to Amaday. He was usually happy to be at the base, but for the first time in a while, he was scared.

OHM happened to be on a break when he walked by.

"Hey, Bunny! What's up?" he asked.

Bunny was about to say what he usually said, "Well, a lot of things, in fact. The ceiling, the sky, the clouds, and space are all up," but today he decided not to.

When OHM didn't receive a response he said, "Not much, eh?"

"Yeah," Bunny said sadly. He went farther into the base, checking a clock on the wall. It was 5:57 PM, meaning that the meeting Squiddy called would start in three minutes.

"Hi Bunny," Pecan said.

"Oh, hi," Bunny responded, trying to sound cheerful, so he wouldn't make her feel bad.

"Wanna have dinner with me?" She asked.

"Sorry, but I'm busy," Bunny told her.

"Oh," Pecan said disappointedly. "Well, maybe to-morrow."

Then she skipped away to eat dinner by herself.

Lucky, Bunny thought. He imagined himself having a delightful meal with Pecan, going deep into thought and chewing the air. But soon reality came back. Bunny stood in front of the squad's meeting room. Slowly, he knocked on the door.

"Come in," came Rudy's voice. Bunny opened the door and was met by the five leaders, all looking very serious.

"Sit," Bo Bo instructed calmly. She beckoned for Bunny to sit in the spot next to her. Bunny boinged over and plopped down next to her, too anxious to make his usual, "plop!" sound.

Grey watched Bunny in silence. (He seemed to have dried off reasonably fast, given that the toilet incident was only 15 minutes ago.)

"Let this meeting begin," Rudy announced. "Now Bunny, first we will talk about you and your school grades."

Rudy started lecturing on how Bunny, as a member of the S.A.S, should get much better grades, blah blah blah...

Unfortunately, Bunny was covering his ears and not paying any attention. *La la la*, he thought, not realizing that Rudy had finished a minute ago.

Finally, Squiddy cleared his throat. "Bunny?"

"Yes? What?" Bunny responded.

Rudy sighed, "Are you ready to continue?"

"Oh, um, yes."

"Alright, now…"

"Thank you, Rudy," Grey interrupted. "Now I will talk."

Rudy was startled by his fellow leader's attitude. "Okay, Grey," he said. "Go on."

"Bunny, I'm disappointed in you for countless reasons," Grey began.

Bunny fiddled with his paws, thinking how much Grey's mood had changed since when playing Satalua tag. Grey continued, "One reason I am very unhappy with you is, well, what happened earlier today."

Grey looked at the rest of the leaders. "Bunny, knocked me into the toilet." Then he added, "On purpose!"

Bunny was about to protest, but Grey shushed him. "At that moment, I decided something. I'm so sorry Bunny."

Suddenly, there was a knock on the door.

"Who is it?" Grey grumbled.

"It's me, Albert."

"What?"

"The sheep dolls. They just got here," Albert said from outside the meeting room door.

Rudy sighed and walked towards the door. "Continue, without me," he said.

"No, no," Grey replied. "We will wait."

Rudy nodded and left the meeting room.

The other five sat awkwardly until Squiddy saw a fly. He stood up from his chair and walked over to a desk, picking up a jar and attempting to catch the fly.

"I'm getting some snacks," Bo Bo announced. Then she, like Rudy, left the room.

"I'll come too," Giraffey said, following Bo Bo.

Grey took this opportunity and leaned in next to Bunny. "I am going to share your secret," he said, smiling wryly at Bunny.

"OPEN THE DOOR, PLEASE," RUDY TOLD OHM.

"Yes sir," OHM responded, who had just finished his break.

"I've told you many times that you can just call me Rudy."

"Right, sorry," OHM said. "I won't forget. Uh... probably."

There was a sudden banging on the door.

"Hurry up in there and open this bleepin' thing!" someone shouted.

Rudy sighed, "I will discuss with them."

OHM unlocked the door, and Rudy walked outside. There were six dolls. Excuse me, sheep dolls. (They hate it when they're just called dolls.) Sheep dolls have the 'power of prophecy' and get their name from their ability to hypnotize sheep. Using this special magic, they put a spell on a sheep, receiving the ability to control them! There are many groups of sheep dolls worldwide. Each group travels around trying to tell fortunes and make outrageous trades.

Rudy looked at them then turned to OHM.

"Call the Fighting Allies," he said. "Tell them to keep the sheep dolls out next time!" OHM nodded and closed the heavy door. Rudy turned back to the sheep dolls, who hadn't heard him.

"Hello, and good day," he said, trying to hide his annoyance.

"Me name's Alice," the group's leader said. (Rudy hated it when people used incorrect grammar.)

Anyway, she shook Rudy's hand.

"Now, kind sir, please take us to your leader, uh, what's his name, Rudy?"

Rudy grumbled, "I am Rudy."

Well, this startled and disappointed Alice. "Wow," she said. "You're much older and weaker than I thought."

"I beg your pardon," Rudy stamped his foot.

"I thought you would be like this muscular lion who gobbles up enemies. And anyway, aren't dinosaurs extinct?"

Rudy glared at her once more, "Be careful lady, or *you* will become the enemy that I gobble up." Rudy knew that, although all stuffed animal schools teach their students about the S.A.S., sheep dolls were homeschooled by their group mates and didn't learn things about the S.A.S. Think of the squad as the government. Stuffed animals worldwide learned everything about them in school. In fact, the Stuffed Animal Squad might be more powerful than the government, as the stuffed animal population is similar to the human population. Rudy never really thought twice about his power though, and, as you can tell, the squad lives a pretty normal life.

"Now, before we trade," Alice continued, "We must have a fortune telling session." She sat down, legs crossed, her fellow sheep dolls following.

"Please make this quick," Rudy told them, sitting down too. He knew that the sheep dolls were just a bunch of baloney. Alice saw how he was sitting.

"Ah ah ah," she said. "Criss cross applesauce."

Again, Rudy grumbled, changing the way he was sitting. He thought back to the last time his fortune was told – "You will eat ham when the world is desperate" – and he wondered what his silly fortune would be this time.

Alice pulled a globe out of her backpack. "Let's begin."

Oh no, Rudy thought. Every time the sheep dolls came by, they always started with this silly introduction.

"Abracadabra is not the magic word," Alice said, waving her hands ominously. "It's only part of the magic paragraph. Now, hup hup, shepherds, watch out for us. You might as well get onto the bus. We, the sheep dolls, no one stands in our way." There was a pause to this slow chant. "Except piiiiiiieeeeeee."

The sheep dolls behind Alice were humming along in a solemn tune.

"Sheep are our core. We don't ask for anymore." Alice took another pause. Then, the melody turned into a cheerful country song!

"Sheep, sheep, sheep, sheep, yee haw, giddy up! We trust you. One knows why. But we don't know where that one is." A third pause. "So, we trade and trade, find items that will help us get to them! Yee haw!"

The song was over, and Rudy was sure that it was the cringiest thing he had ever heard. When it was done, the globe flashed a brilliant white. Alice put both her hands on the side of it, and closed her eyes, focusing intently. The other sheep dolls behind her were closing their eyes too, so Rudy decided to follow. The silence went on for a while. Suddenly, a few minutes later, the globe went black!

Rudy opened his eyes, along with the five sheep dolls behind Alice. Confused expressions spread across their faces. Soon, Alice realized that something was wrong, and she looked as well. Rudy saw her face, and he immediately knew something wasn't right.

Her face was pale white, and Rudy started to feel something in his magic.

"Y-your, uh, fortune is, um, is…" she stammered. "Nothing."

Cue the dramatic music: *dun dun dunnnn!*

However, Alice had some more to say, "Wait. Never mind."

Then, to Rudy's horror, she floated into the air and a ghost with long, flowing hair came out of her mouth. "Bless the ones who will save the worlds," the pale ghost said ominously. "The first battle will not be the last. Once the portals are opened, three worlds will unite, and only then will you really start to fight. When it is not clear on the planet so blue, but despair is deep, and an ancient wizard has since long stopped his urge to weep, a hero with much before but nothing behind will rise and save two worlds as one. And when time comes close, they will have a choice, and in the end, they must save what matters most."

USUALLY, RUDY WOULD NOT THINK MUCH OF IT, BUT SOMEthing in his wise mind told him that this prophecy was true. He had an idea of who he would have to give magic to, as the fortune instructed. You see, leaders have magic. They usually keep it for themselves, but in an emergency, they can give some of their magic to another stuffed animal, and, sometimes, a toy. This act is called magic giving.

Anyway, Rudy's faithful magic was almost screaming in his head: *Bunny. You must give magic to Bunny!* Alice, the sheep doll's leader, had crumbled to the floor, but Rudy used his magic to give her strength. Slowly, she rose, her face the color of paper.

"Bye," Alice told Rudy. The leader watched them leave and realized that the fortune explained a lot. Everyone had been wondering why the leaders kept having body aches. (The same thing that happened to Grey when he flew out of the toilet earlier.) It also explained why their magic had been weaker lately.

Somewhere, something – or someone – bad was stirring.

CHAPTER
NINE

KICKED OUT

After all of that craziness, Rudy went back inside. Once he got back into the meeting room, he met Bunny with carrot bacon, Giraffey with leaf bars, and Bo Bo with watermelon. (Their favorite foods.) Grey was sitting in his chair, smiling. Behind him, Squiddy had managed to trap that pesky fly in a jar.

"Sorry about that delay," Rudy said, sitting down. Then his eyes adjusted to the light, and he couldn't believe what he saw. Bunny was not eating his carrot bacon! Rudy's mouth opened, but before anyone saw, he closed it.

Bo Bo finished eating a slice of watermelon. She aimed its rind for the trash can, but like ten others on the floor, she missed. "Darn it," she said. "Air ball." Then she noticed Rudy's expression.

"It's crazy, huh."

Rudy nodded.

"For the first time ever, Bunny is actually refusing to eat carrot bacon," Bo Bo said.

Rudy just shook his head and clapped his hands. "Let this meeting resume."

Everyone settled in.

"Grey, you may continue," Rudy said. As he listened, he waited for the right moment to give magic to Bunny.

"Now, Bunny," Grey said, "You are, well, a – *cough* – amazing member of the S.A.S. But everyone makes mistakes. Even me and Rudy. But, um," he shook his head. "You make the most, I'm sad to say."

Bunny tried to be angry at Grey, but he couldn't. It was true.

"This year, you made the largest mistake of your life. The largest mistake in the history of mistakes," Grey was getting into it.

Why does he have to be so cruel? Bunny thought. *He's enjoying this! I really thought we were friends.*

Grey continued, "Man, I wish the whole squad was here!"

"They're busy," Giraffey said.

Grey tried his best to act sorry. "You're right," he said. "I'm just really pumped for a T.V. show tonight."

Of course, this was a lie.

"Okay…" Squiddy said.

Grey continued. "This mistake was against stuffed animal rules. You have changed history, Bunny, but in a bad way." He scratched the back of his head. "Now, I know that..." Grey thought for a moment.

Using this time, Bunny got up and although he didn't want to, dumped his carrot bacon in the trash!

Rudy watched him with concern.

"Anyway," Grey started again, "let me just cut to the chase." He started patting his legs. "Drumroll please!"

No one followed his lead.

"Oh well," Grey smirked. "The secret's out, Bunny. You have talked to humans."

Bunny waited for a reaction, but there was just silence. Rudy was focusing hard on something. His eyes were closed and was trembling and pointing at Bunny.

After about a minute of silence, Grey started scratching his neck. "It's getting hot in here," he said. "Talk about awkward silence." There were no reactions, so he decided to get some laughs going.

"Knock knock?"

No one responded.

"Who's there?" Grey asked himself sarcastically.

"Bye."

"Bye, who?"

"Bye Bunny!" No one laughed. It was a rather mean joke. (And one that didn't make sense at all.)

"Can someone just say something?" Grey asked. It seemed as if he was all alone in the room.

Finally, Bo Bo asked, "What?"

"I know, crazy, with all these weird things going on. The aches, and battles, and just life. But let me explain." Grey did just that. The only stuffed animal who didn't hear him tell Bunny's story was Rudy. He suspected as much from Bunny, being the type of stuffed animal who talked a lot.

It must be hard to not talk to the humans who are with you for half the day, Rudy thought. Although he had never been snuggled, or even touched by humans, he understood. But Rudy did not focus on that. He was almost done giving magic to Bunny. Now, all he had to do was stab Bunny with one of his spikes, his source of magic. (This may seem cruel, but it's just how magic giving works.)

You see, Rudy's spikes could shoot out before quickly reappearing, a useful fighting strategy. Rudy got up from his chair. He scooted over to Bunny, who barely noticed because of Grey's explanation about him and the Nobles. Rudy leaned forward and whispered in Bunny's left ear, "I'm sorry." Then he shot one of his spikes right into Bunny's ear.

"Yodely!" Bunny shouted, boinging into the air. "What was that for?"

He yanked the dark spike out of his ear and threw it at Rudy.

"I'll explain later," the leader replied calmly.

Bunny wanted to plop on Rudy, but he knew that the wise leader would never do something like what he just did unless it was for a good reason.

Meanwhile, Grey was saying, "I found this out by…" when he stopped and looked at Rudy. "Yes? Do we have a problem?"

"Sorry," Rudy told him. "Go on."

Grey looked suspiciously at him but continued.

Rudy walked back over to his chair, feeling much different. He was missing some magic, meaning that the magic giving session had worked.

Bunny felt different, like he had magic.

Hah, he thought. *Ridonkulous. Besides, I don't even know what it feels like.*

But it was true. He did have magic.

Bunny was feeling really bad and decided to start thinking positive.

I can still live with the Nobles.

"Bunny, you will not be able to talk to humans ever again. Which means that you cannot live with the Nobles," Grey said.

I knew that was coming, Bunny thought.

"Now, we will decide your punishment," Grey told his fellow leaders. "Let's kick him out."

"What?!" Bo Bo shouted, who was defensive of Bunny.

"Yeah, just get rid of him."

Rudy sighed. He would never let a decent member of the Stuffed Animal Squad get kicked out of Amaday. But, of course, his magic told him that he had to give in to what happened that day.

Quietly, he said, "I agree."

Well, Bunny heard this, and he looked down at his feet, not believing it. The other leaders didn't hear, though.

"What?" Bo Bo asked.

"I agree," Rudy repeated much louder.

Bo Bo, Bunny, and Squiddy, and Giraffey looked at Rudy. Now that the two most powerful leaders agreed, there was not much they could do.

"Okay Bunny, this is not official...yet" Grey said. "But how about you just leave while we, uh, discuss some leader-only things."

Wobbling a bit, Bunny stood up from his chair. He was suddenly feeling very dizzy. He arrived at the door, opened it, and boinged away. Behind him, Squiddy closed the door, feeling extremely guilty. The meeting was his idea after all.

Now that Bunny was gone, Grey showed his excitement. He was happy with Rudy for agreeing with him. He ran over and rubbed Rudy's tummy. "Who's a good Dinosaur, who's a good Dinosaur?"

Rudy narrowed his eyebrows, realizing that Grey was acting strange. But he didn't think much of it, mostly because of how guilty he felt. He sighed, then turned to face the other leaders. "Alright, does anyone have anything to say?"

Squiddy raised his tentacle.

"Yes?"

"I just want to say that, well, kicking Bunny out is just not..." Squiddy stood up. "A dance-worthy choice!" he shouted before starting to break dance on the floor.

Rudy looked around at his fellow leaders. They were all acting like Grey now, jumping up and down, and saying ridiculous things.

Oh no, Rudy thought, realizing that something definitely wasn't right.

BUNNY DECIDED TO SAY GOODBYE TO ALL OF HIS FRIENDS IN the S.A.S., so he walked out of the meeting room, and into the main area of the base.

OHM and Albert spotted him first. They were having dinner together.

OHM was eating garbage and Albert had a pear sandwich. (As you may have figured, stuffed animals have interesting appetites.)

With a mouth full of food, Albert asked OHM, "What do you call a cow with three legs?"

"Har har har!" OHM laughed. He did not understand that the funny part of a joke was not the question.

"No, not har har har!" Albert said. "Guess again."

"Har har har!"

Albert shook his head and took another bite.

Bunny already knew this joke. The answer was: a cow. But Bunny did not say the answer. Instead, he said, "Bye."

OHM whirled around to face Bunny. "Oh, you're leaving."

"Yep."

"See you tomorrow."

"I'm not coming back tomorrow," Bunny said.

"Oh, have a fun break!"

"No, I'm leaving…" He gulped. "Maybe forever."

"Well then, have a nice life," OHM said.

Albert dropped his sandwich in astonishment.

"Har har har!" OHM laughed at him. Then he thought for a moment about what Bunny just said.

"You're leaving forever?" he asked.

"Yes," Bunny told them both. "Probably."

"Hi," OHM said. "I mean, bye."

Albert looked very sad about this, when suddenly he started panting.

"Heh heh heh heh heh."

This time Bunny narrowed his eyebrows.

"Bye, Watermelon," Albert said.

"Bye, Thomas Edison," OHM said.

"Uh, bye," Bunny said, and that's basically how he ended up saying goodbye to everyone.

Next, Bunny walked over to Pecan, who had just finished eating some butter pecan ice cream.

"Hi," Bunny said.

"Hi," Pecan replied.

"I'm leaving."

"Hi."

"Maybe forever."

"Hi."

Maybe Pecan had too much sugar, but Bunny suspected it was something more. By now he had strong suspicions. He moved on, and the same thing happened with Flatbeak, who came running out of his office yelling odd things like, "Ahhhhhh! Buffaloes!"

Okay, Bunny thought, watching him through the base. *This is getting even weirder.* He boinged to the kitchen, where Piggy was pouring milk on her head.

"Bunny, help!" She exclaimed.

Quickly, Bunny boinged over to help his friend.

"I can't stop doing this!" Piggy shouted, milk running down her face. "My arms have a mind of my own!"

At least she's not saying weird things, Bunny thought.

"Go go ga ga," Piggy said. Then she added, "I can't help that either!"

Bunny yanked the milk jar out of Piggy's untamed hands, but she ran to the refrigerator and pulled out an egg carton. Bunny watched her – in slow motion – open it up, pull out two eggs, and crack them against the sink.

The yolk fell into her hands.

"Help me!" Piggy shrieked.

But it was too late for Bunny to help, so she gulped down two raw eggs.

I wonder how sick she'll get, Bunny thought. But he didn't want to find out. He ran over to her and tried to get around her legs that kept kicking him.

"Sorry!" she told him.

Bunny quickly grabbed the carton.

"Thank you!" Piggy said.

Outside the kitchen, Bunny put the egg carton and the other hazards (mostly blades) on the floor.

But at that moment, Flatbeak ran by, and when he saw Bunny, he yelled, "The Buffaloes have got me!"

"Bye Piggy," Bunny called for the last time. He boinged away from the kitchen, toward Tuskey's office.

He arrived and bumped his rump on the door.

Tuskey opened it and smiled.

"Come in…" *Phew*, Bunny thought. "For the party!"

Bunny sighed, but walked inside the inventor's office, which was usually messy and full of inventions. That day was no different, except, of course, it was one hundred times worse! There were books scattered everywhere, rotten food on the floor, and the office was muddy. Worst of all, Tuskey's inventions were ruined.

I can't believe this, Bunny thought to himself. *Tuskey has worked so hard on all of these.*

"Now, what do you want to do?" Tuskey asked. "Pin the Pepperoni on the Pizza, or Eat Donkey Tails?"

"How about none of the above," Bunny responded.

"Nah, you gotta have fun in life!"

Bunny grumbled, "Fine, are there any other options for games?"

"Oh yeah!" Tuskey shouted, his face lighting up. "Let's have some fuh-uh-unnn!"

Instantly, Bunny fled from Tuskey's office, knowing that he did not want to get involved in any type of "fun".

"Bye!" he shouted over his shoulder, and entered a closet, which seemed like the only safe spot on Amaday.

Once inside, Bunny closed the door and considered his options. He could finish saying goodbye to everyone, but with some trouble. Or he could go straight back to the meeting room and receive the consequences. (Which seemed like a better plan.)

Bunny thought for a while, *I could always escape to another country, like, maybe Chile, or...*

"Buffaloes!" Flatbeak screamed from outside the closet.

Suddenly, the door started to creak open, and as quick as he could, Bunny boinged behind a big crate. Two small figures entered the room. Once Bunny's eyes adjusted to the light, he saw that it was Pink Nose Guy and Alfredo! He ducked lower, wondering what crazy thing they would do.

Then he felt something. *Oh great,* he thought. *Of course I have to get a plopping urge right now.*

"Plop!"

Alfredo looked at the crate. "Who's there?"

"Uh, me?" Pink Nose Guy said, closing the door.

"No," Alfredo snapped. "I heard something else."

Slowly, they both walked towards the crate.

"It is crazy out there," Pink Nose Guy said.

"Yeah," Alfredo agreed.

"Yeah," Bunny said accidentally.

"Yeah...ahhhhhhhhhh!" Pink Nose Guy shouted, surprised.

Bunny boinged out from behind the crate, "It's just me."

"Oh," Alfredo said.

"Oh," Pink Nose Guy responded.

Alfredo pondered for a bit. "Why aren't you going crazy like the others?"

"Why aren't *you* going crazy like the others?" Bunny asked.

"Stop copying me."

"Stop copying me."

"I said, stop!"

"I said, stop!"

It went on and on, until finally, Pink Nose Guy interfered, "Come on guys, just stop."

Alfredo sighed, "Fine."

"I'm sorry." Bunny said. "This has been a rough day."

Pink Nose Guy nodded, "I understand."

"I've had a rough day too," Alfredo told them. "I spilled ketchup on my antlers."

"How is that even possible?" Bunny asked.

"Oh, well, I was in an argument with OHM. We were trying to see who is the strongest, so I flexed to show him my big muscles. But unfortunately, I was holding a ketchup packet…"

Bunny shook his head hastily, "My day was much worse." He told them everything.

"Wow," Pink Nose Guy said when he finished.

"That happens to me every day," Alfredo said. Bunny looked at him sternly.

"Well, uh, most days."

Pink Nose Guy nibbled her fingernails, thinking about what Bunny had said about Grey kicking him out. "What has gotten into Grey?"

"What has gotten into everyone else?" Bunny said. Suddenly, there was a cluck. Bunny paused. "I heard a Chicken."

"Where's Alfredo?" Pink Nose Guy exclaimed, looking around.

"The chicken has him!" Bunny yelled.

Suddenly, Alfredo jumped out from behind the crate.

"I have discovered a new species!" Bunny announced. "The Micken!"

"You know that's just Alfredo," Pink Nose Guy told him.

"Oh."

Alfredo ran around crashing into everything, clucking wildly, and flapping his arms like wings.

"I don't know why," Pink Nose Guy said. "But...cock-a-doodle-doo!"

Uh oh, Bunny thought. *Now I have two fowls to deal with.* (He had learned the word *fowl* in school with Miles.)

"Bye," Bunny said quickly.

"Bye-gock!" Pink Nose Guy responded.

Bunny opened the door, and boinged as fast as he could to the meeting room.

"Come in, Sam the Seagull," Bo Bo called.

"I'm not a Seagull."

"You are now."

Even the leaders are acting weird, Bunny thought. He plopped back down in his chair, and watched Grey chase his tail, Squiddy do somersaults, Bo Bo slam her head against the wall, and Giraffey nibble on his fingers.

The only other stuffed animal who wasn't going crazy was Rudy.

"Something is not right," he told Bunny.

"I've noticed."

Rudy thought about everything that had happened, trying to put all the events together. The leaders having aches. The sheep dolls fortune. Everyone going crazy except for him and...Bunny. *Wait a minute*, Rudy thought. *Bunny's not going crazy, probably because he has my magic. Could it be that...*

"So, am I kicked out?" Bunny asked, interrupting his thoughts.

"Yes and no," Grey replied, making Bunny look extremely puzzled.

"Just kidding, I've always *longed* to say that" Grey exclaimed. "So yeah, you're kicked out."

"Okay," Bunny mumbled.

"Now, git!" Grey shouted at him.

Bunny waved goodbye to Rudy, and boinged to the heavy door. Suddenly, he stopped. *I will not be gone forever*, Bunny decided. *After all, I am part of the squad!* He turned around to face the leaders. "I am leaving, but not forever."

Rudy tried to hide his smile. Something inside him said that giving magic to Bunny was the right thing to do. "Bye," Rudy told Bunny, nodding firmly.

"Yeah, merry Christmas," Grey said. Then he kicked Bunny in the rump as hard as he could.

"OUCH!"

"Don't eat goats," Grey slammed the meeting room door.

Bunny's boing to the door was quieter than usual. "A boing, a boing, a boing, a boing." It was strange to not have OHM there to open the door, and Bunny had to boing up there, unlock it, and yank the handle down. Once that was done, he turned back to look at Amaday. It was a mess.

"Buffaloes!" Flatbeak screamed as he ran by.

With a big sigh, Bunny closed the door. He boinged down the steps that led down to the Amaday train. There were no Fighting Allies in sight, but Bunny heard a laugh in the distance. They were probably going crazy too. He pressed a button that opened the train door automatically. He picked a seat and plopped down on it. He reached down, pulled a lever, and the train sped off.

Bunny Bun-Bun was officially kicked out of the S.A.S.

PART

TWO

THE RISE OF A NEW FRIENDSHIP

CHAPTER

TEN

A NEW FRIEND

The Amaday train screeched to a stop and Bunny boinged off.

During the train ride, he was thinking about all of the mistakes he made that got him kicked out of the S.A.S. But now Bunny stopped himself from thinking these things. "I have to show grit," he said aloud to the darkness of the train stop. "After all, I am a Rabbit. I am strong, I am smart, and I am courageous. I have G-R-E-I-T. At least I think that's how you spell grit…" He trailed off, realizing that talking to himself was pointless.

You see, Bunny wasn't allowed to talk to the Nobles, but he figured that if he was just careful, no one would catch him. He boinged out of the train station, through the secret door, and into the Nobles' basement.

Bunny decided that first, however, he would go to his lair. He boinged through the hallway and was passing the guest room when he heard a sound coming from inside. Bunny froze. But then he realized that the noise from the guest room must be Louisa and Miles playing one of their silly games, so he boinged into the room.

What? Bunny thought. Miles and Louisa were not there. He started to panic. If it wasn't Miles or Louisa who made that shuffling noise, then who was it? Bunny checked under the bed and looked over his shoulder when a thought dawned on him. *The closet!*

There was a small door next to the bed where the Nobles guests usually kept their stuff. However, if Bunny remembered correctly, it was also where Leigh kept things from her childhood. As quietly as he could, Bunny boinged to the closet. He imagined himself as a small mouse, skittering across the floor. He shivered. He did not like mice at all. Soon, he reached the door, its height towering over him, looking awfully frightening.

I am brave, Bunny convinced himself. So, without another thought, he boinged up and opened the closet door, closing his eyes.

"Uh, hello?" someone said.

When Bunny opened his eyes, a huge polar bear was staring right at him! He fell backwards before discovering that the polar bear was actually just a stuffed animal about his size.

"Wow," the Bear said. "Am I really that scary?"

They helped pull Bunny off his rump.

"Oh, uh, thank you," Bunny said. "But please get out of this house."

The bear frowned. "Why?"

Bunny did not want to be rude, but there was a stranger in his house! "Because, well...you know what, I shouldn't even be talking to you! You're a stranger, maybe even a dangerous one."

The bear frowned again. "But I've been in this house just as long as you!"

Bunny opened his mouth to protest, but he needed more information first. "You've been hiding this whole time?!"

The bear, once again, frowned. "Hasn't Leigh told you?"

Bunny scratched behind his ears, "What?"

"She hasn't!" The bear sighed. "Sorry, I'm being kind of rude. I'm Snow." They held out their paw.

That name sounds familiar, Bunny thought.

He held out his long ear, "I'm Bunny."

Snow hesitated, but then shook Bunny's ear. (Yep, just another normal handshake.)

"Are you a boy or girl?" Bunny asked.

"I'm non-binary," Snow replied. "You know what that is, right."

"Um..." Bunny thought. The word was familiar, but he forgot what it meant. "No."

"Do you know what pronouns are?"

"Yes."

"Okay," Snow began. "My pronouns are they/them."

"Cool," Bunny said. "Anyway, tell me how you got here."

"Alright," Snow responded. "I was in a toy store way back in 1881."

Bunny eyes went wide. "You're almost as old as Rudy."

Snow cleared their throat. "Excuse me. I meant to say *19*81."

Bunny nodded. That still seemed long ago, but it made a lot more sense.

"I lived there on a shelf for about two months. It was the worst. I could tell you the details, but that's another story."

"I've been on the shelf before, too, although I don't remember it," Bunny said. "I wasn't awakened by fairy godmothers yet."

It was true. Bunny had been found by some other stuffed animal rabbits and then been awakened. He lived with them for a decent amount of time before being found outside by a toy store owner and brought back into the shelf for only a day until Leigh bought him when she was still pregnant with Miles.

He had lived with the group of rabbits for about a decade, and he still saw them every once and a while, as their rabbit hole is outside of his lair! Anyway, after Leigh bought him for soon-to-be-born Miles, Bunny was found by Grey and brought to Rudy, who found an unusual spark of talent. But Bunny had never shown anything special, and he was sure the leaders regretted letting him join the squad.

"Anyhoo," Snow continued. "One day this guy with a cool hat plucked me off the shelf. He bought me for some low price. I remember being so angry because I felt so cheap." Snow paused as they recalled what happened next. "Oh, yes. Then I rode in a pick-up for about an hour. I couldn't see anything because the man planted my face into the seat! It reeked of salami."

Personally, Bunny was fine with the taste and smell of salami, and for a short period he called Miles and Louisa's Mom, Leigh, Mommy Salami.

Anyway, Snow kept going. "Soon we arrived at the man's house. Once he lifted me off the seat, I immediately recognized that it was on a farm. Two kids greeted the man as I surveyed the scene. For a farm, I guess it was beautiful. But nothing like New Zealand." Snow let out a dreamy sigh, and Bunny noticed a magazine behind them that read: *New Zealand, The Perfect Vacation.*

"Anyway, there was a girl and a boy. The girl looked about, maybe seven or eight, and the boy was about six or seven. I became the girl's favorite stuffed animal. Wanna hear her name?"

"What?" Bunny asked.

"Leigh."

Bunny was surprised. "So...you're Big Mommy's Stuffed Animal?"

"Yep." Snow told the rest of her story.

Leigh grew up and kept Snow. Even when she went to college. Then, after Leigh graduated, she met Darren. They got married and soon Leigh put Snow away in a closet because Miles and Louisa took up too much space.

Finally, the Nobles moved into their present house, and the whole time, Snow was with them. They finished their story and bowed.

"Now, I want to hear your story," Snow told Bunny.

Bunny cleared his throat dramatically, "I will tell you in a few decades, but first I'm going to tell you a secret."

Snow yawned, "But I don't want to wait a few decades."

"You just have to," Bunny said.

"Fine," Snow sighed. "But are you going to remember your story in a few decades?"

Bunny grumbled. "Of course, I will. Don't you know what a decade is?"

"Yeah," Snow said. "A decade is a time period of ten years."

Bunny snorted. "No, a decade is a second. The word decade is a cinnamon of a second."

"You mean synonym. And no, it's ten years," Snow replied.

"Whatever, just let me say something."

"Okay," Snow said.

"Alright," Bunny started. "Are you sure you're listening?"

"Uh-huh."

"One hundred percent sure?"

"Yes. Just tell me what you want to say."

Bunny nodded, then he boinged back to the door.

"Let me just make sure no one is listening," he said.

Snow waited patiently as Bunny checked the hallway and closet. Finally, he boinged next to Snow with a loud, "Plop!"

"Get cozied up," he said.

Snow sighed. "I am."

"Now, are you really sure you're listening to me?"

Snow stomped their foot impatiently, "Of course."

"Oh, by the way I like carrot bacon. Anyway…" Bunny leaned in close. He was like that for a bit. Then he sighed. "I forgot."

All that for nothing, Snow thought. "Can you at least tell me your story?" they asked.

"Sure, sure, sure," Bunny said. "Oh yeah! Now I remember what I was going to tell you. I'm part of the S.A.S."

Snow gasped. "Really?"

"Yep!"

"I know there's a member named Bunny, but I didn't realize you're *the* Bunny!" Bunny smiled. Despite being one of the most powerful stuffed animals in the world, very few stuffed animals knew him or remembered him from the lessons on the squad.

"Wow…" Snow said. They were almost speechless. "It's an honor."

Bunny sighed. "Yeah, but I don't really belong in the squad. I'm no more special than you."

"What's it like?" Snow asked.

Bunny didn't know what to say. "It's like…I don't know, it doesn't feel that weird. People really only pay attention to the leaders or the older members. It's almost like forgetting who's president."

Snow nodded. "I don't understand it either. Whenever I ask about you, most people just look confused. Anyway, can you tell me your story?"

Then he began telling his story, and when he told Snow that he was part of the Stuffed Animal Squad, their face lit up. And when he explained how he was kicked out, they frowned. He told Snow the whole thing, from when he was awakened by fairy godmothers to when he met the other rabbits who he lived with. He talked about the rabbit hole they lived in, and how he learned about the food carrot bacon. Bunny told Snow his passions: plopping, eating, and napping. He told them all the places he visited and the things he learned, just spilling it all out. Bunny was happy to share his feelings, from beginning to end. After the frustration of the whole day, this was what he needed.

And Snow was a good listener too. They were obviously still startled and fascinating to find themselves talking to an S.A.S. member, but they still listened to Bunny's stories, only talking to ask thoughtful questions.

Bunny moved on to when he got accepted into the squad. In fact, that was probably the only time he talked this much about his past. Then Snow asked what it was like to be in the S.A.S., and he explained that too.

And just like that, Bunny had a new friend.

CHAPTER
ELEVEN

BUNNY'S LAIR

The birds outside started chirping, waking Bunny up from his deep sleep.

He rolled over and stretched his noodle arms, yawning.

"Good morning," Snow said from the floor. (They were fine with giving Bunny the bed.)

Suddenly, Bunny felt a rush of excitement. Today was the day that he would reveal his top-secret lair to Snow. Of course, just yesterday Bunny had met them, but he knew that Snow was trustworthy. Or at least he hoped so.

The two new friends walked out of the room. "You're really excited for this," Snow said. "I mean, it's only 6:00 AM!"

"Yeah, I know," Bunny responded. "But I usually save my sleep time for a nap. Besides, aren't you excited to see my lair?"

"Yes," Snow told him. "But take it down a notch. Everyone else is still sleeping."

"Oh," Bunny had totally forgotten about the Nobles, and he realized that he was in the same house as them.

Slowly and quietly, they went up the stairs. Well, Snow was quiet. Bunny was more like, "Boing, a Boing, a Boing, a Boing!" very loudly. But they reached the top of the stairs without waking anyone up, and Bunny led Snow to a small shelf next to the Nobles' piano. He touched middle C, boinged over to the shelf, and whispered, "Bun-Bun."

It slid open to reveal a small room.

Snow's eyes went wide. "How do you have this technology?" they asked.

"Oh, I'll tell you later," Bunny replied. They both hopped into the small compartment. Bunny pressed an orange button and the trap door closed. Then he pressed another button, and the mini elevator creaked to life.

"Whoa!" Snow said.

They rode down for a few seconds and then the elevator stopped.

"Who made this for you?" Snow asked.

Bunny smiled, "It used to be a base for toys, but they found another one and gave this to me." He pressed the orange button, and the elevator doors opened, making Snow gasp. The elevator opened up to a humongous lair with shelves stocked full of food. The ceilings towered above and there were many rooms.

"I know. It's cool," Bunny said. "Now, do you like carrot bacon, carrot popcorn, carrots, carrot pie, carrot cake, or these strawberries?"

"My favorite food is strawberries," Snow told him.

Bunny tossed them the small bowl of strawberries, and his friend barely caught it.

"Uh, thanks," Snow said. Then they saw the train.

"I call it the Carrot Express," Bunny said proudly when he saw Snow gawking at it. The Carrot Express had a small engine and two cars, each painted to resemble carrot bacon with brown and red stripes and splotches of orange on the side.

"Boing in!" Bunny exclaimed. They hopped into the front car, and Bunny pressed yet another orange button. They waited. After a whole minute, Bunny grumbled. He smacked the control panel, but the train stayed in its place.

"Here, let me try," Snow said. They smacked the control panel a little harder than Bunny. Nothing happened.

Suddenly, the train made a terrible screeching noise! Bunny quickly covered his ears having no idea of what was happening. It blared on and on, like a screaming baby.

"What's going on?" Snow yelled over the noise.

"I don't know!" Bunny responded.

Finally, it stopped. Bunny rubbed his ears.

"What. Was. That?" Snow asked again.

Bunny shrugged.

Then Snow noticed the huge piece of medal on the track that was no doubt blocking the train. They heard a small voice coming from it but could not make out the words.

"Bunny, do you hear that?" Snow asked.

"Huh?" Bunny replied. "Oh, yeah."

Snow hopped off the train. They bent down to examine the metal thing. At a low volume, they heard a countdown.

"Two minutes and five seconds, two minutes and four seconds."

"It's a bomb!" Snow shouted. "We need to get out of here."

Bunny shook his head. "I can't let it explode my lair!"

"One minute and fifty-three seconds," the countdown continued, the voice much louder than before.

Snow grabbed Bunny and tried to pull him to the elevator entrance.

"We need to get back up!"

"No," Bunny protested. "Just hold on."

He boinged over to the bomb, and lifted it up, surprised to see how light it was. He turned around, and even though he knew it was a bad idea, followed Snow at a fast pace back to the elevator.

Once inside, Bunny pressed the orange button, and he and Snow traveled up the elevator again. Soon, it stopped, and the door opened up into the Noble's house.

"Three...two...one..."

Bunny chucked the bomb as far as he could. (Which wasn't very far.)

He and Snow turned around and ducked their heads. The noise that proceeded was way louder than the screeching train. Bunny and Snow covered their ears and thinking quickly, Bunny pressed the orange button. They were safe and the elevator traveled back down to Bunny's lair. Now that he thought about it, throwing the bomb in the Nobles house just so his lair wouldn't get damaged seemed like a terrible idea.

"Wow," Snow said. "Did you just explode their house?"

Bunny looked at his feet, feeling guilty. "I hope not."

But all they heard as they went down to Bunny's lair was the crumbling and shattering above.

ABOUT AN HOUR EARLIER, DARREN WOKE UP TO THE SOUND of his alarm clock. He got out of bed quietly, trying not to wake Leigh, and went downstairs. After reading for a bit, Darren decided to make his daily coffee. He dumped some coffee beans into the coffee machine, and then pressed a button. The coffee maker rumbled to life, making a ton of noise.

Well, Darren had thought. *That probably woke Miles and Louisa up.* So, he went upstairs, and opened the door to their bedroom.

As usual, Louisa was waiting, and she rushed right past him!

Miles was grumpy, of course, though Darren noticed he was grumpier than usual. Bunny had disappeared the night before, and Miles was starting to worry. It took him a while after Darren pulled up the shades, but Miles finally got out of bed. He got onto his hands and knees and crawled toward the closet.

"Miles," Louisa called from downstairs. "I'm already logging into my laptop for school!"

Yikes! Miles thought. He felt very rushed and put on his shirt inside-out. Miles heard Louisa yelling hello on her meeting, so he ran to the bathroom, brushed his teeth, and sped down the stairs. He whizzed past Leigh, who was on a phone call in her office.

He devoured a bowl of soggy cereal as fast as Bunny ate carrot bacon. Suddenly, just as he opened his laptop, Miles heard a rumbling. He always heard this peculiar sound when Bunny was nowhere to be seen. Whenever Bunny got back, he always told Miles that the rumbling was just the house shifting.

Of course, Miles knew this wasn't true, but he never paid much thought to this matter. As he logged onto the virtual meeting, he ignored the rumbling...until the bomb exploded. Its deafening sound ripped through the Nobles' house like a tsunami, shattering glass, cracking the floor, and breaking furniture. Miles covered his ears until it was over.

Darren came running into the room and led Louisa and Miles out of the house to find glass all over the yard! The patio doors had completely shattered, making the yard a dangerous mess.

Leigh ran out of the house too, with a shocked look on her face.

"What happened?" Darren demanded.

"I don't know!" Leigh responded.

Darren grumbled. "Who did this?" Then he carefully stepped back inside into the living room, where it was obvious that some sort of bomb had exploded. The Nobles followed him back inside, looking around for any clues of the culprit.

Suddenly, someone said, "Stay down, Snow." It was Bunny. He turned around to see Darren.

"Oh, hi Big Guy," Bunny chuckled nervously.

"What did you do?" Darren asked fiercely.

"Nothing," Bunny said, looking extremely guilty.

"I knew it was that rabbit!" Leigh muttered.

"What did you do?" Miles asked.

"Nothing," Bunny said again.

Darren glared at Bunny. "You're in huge trouble!" he screamed. (When this happened, Miles and Louisa liked to call him Mad Dad.)

"Get out of the house," Leigh snapped.

Louisa crossed her arms. "But then I will have no one to argue with."

"We don't like it when you argue. It's annoying," Darren responded.

"Do you have anything to say for yourself?" Leigh asked Bunny.

Bunny shrugged. "I like carrots."

"Alright, that's it," Darren said. "Say your goodbyes. You are officially kicked out of this household!"

"What!" Miles shouted. "Why?"

"Well, just look around," Darren told his family. "I'm sorry Bunny, but you must leave." Bunny solemnly boinged forward and gave Miles, Louisa, and Leigh a hug. They were all crying. Then he shook his rump at Darren and boinged away.

Miles followed him and whispered, "You can always come back."

They hugged each other and Bunny gave Miles one of his nose-kisses.

"We will meet again, Owner!" Bunny said, falling on his back. Then, with his ears, Bunny pulled himself across the floor. Of course, he ran out of energy, and decided to get up before boinging away.

Miles walked back into the destroyed living room, replaying everything in his mind. He couldn't believe what had just happened.

Meanwhile, Darren did some math equations in his head.

Getting new furniture will cost two million dollars. Repairing the window will be five hundred thousand. The insurance company will probably charge an extra million. Together, everything will cost eleven million. (He was much too angry to think straight.)

Louisa ran up to her room, crying, and Miles paced around the room, trying not to do the same. Darren picked up broken pieces of glass muttering, "I knew not to trust a talking stuffed animal."

BUNNY WAS NOW KICKED OUT OF BOTH OF HIS HOMES. HE boinged outside the Nobles' house in despair, breathing in the fresh air.

Who put that bomb in my lair? He thought. Then he remembered Snow. Bunny, even though he wasn't supposed to, snuck back inside the house, and when no one was looking, boinged over to the secret elevator. He pressed middle C, ducking behind the piano as he did.

Darren looked over his shoulder because he heard something but figured that his ears had just played tricks on him. Bunny quietly hopped into the elevator where Snow was waiting.

"What happened up there?"

"Oh, their living room exploded," Bunny told his friend. "That's all."

Bunny preferred to ignore the chaos that just took place. Snow, however, felt bad. "I should have known that would've happened," they said. "It's all our fault."

Bunny looked down, thinking that it was really just his fault.

"Who put that bomb in your lair anyway?" Snow asked.

"I don't know."

The elevator came to a stop, Bunny pressed the orange button, and they clambered out. "Well," he said sadly. "What should we do?"

Snow sighed. "You know what," Bunny said abruptly. "Let's just have some fun." Snow nodded, understanding how their new friend felt. They sat next to Bunny on the Carrot Express.

"Where are the seat belts?" Snow asked.

"There aren't any!" Bunny responded. He pulled a lever, and now that the bomb was gone, the train moved smoothly along the tracks, slowly gaining speed. Snow held on tight.

"Now, where should we go?" Bunny wondered aloud.

"It doesn't matter," Snow responded. "How big is this lair?"

"Pretty big," Bunny said. "Now, let's head toward the food shelves!" Snow liked Bunny. For a member of the S.A.S., he was funny, and, well, a little bit naughty. Snow had always figured that members of the S.A.S. were all serious and had many bodyguards. But Bunny was nothing like that.

Bunny steered the train to the right. "This is the non-carrot bacon section," he told Snow, who was surprised at how small it was.

There must be a ton of carrot bacon if this is just the non-carrot bacon section, they thought.

Soon, the two sped past a doorway. "What's in there?" Snow asked.

"It's my personal library," Bunny replied.

Snow got excited. They loved books. "Stop the train!" Bunny pulled a lever back, and the Food Express slowed to a stop. Together, they got off and went inside the library.

"Nice. This is as many books as…" Snow paused. "I don't know. It's a lot."

But once Snow got closer to the books, they were disappointed to find that most of them were about carrot bacon and how great rabbits are. There were many shelves, a few beanbags, and a high ceiling. Two shelves, however, surprised Snow. They picked up a book titled: *Section A, Part 2*. "What are all these about?" they asked Bunny, who was admiring a book about how to make carrot bacon on the other side of the room and didn't seem to hear Snow.

"Listen to this," he said. "It's the recipe for making carrot bacon."

"Okay…"

"Step one," Bunny began, "Pour carrot juice on the uncooked bacon. Step two: pour more juice. Step three: cook for fifteen minutes. Step four: take it out of the oven. Step five: do not eat it yet. Step six: I know it's tempting, but don't eat it."

Bunny paused. "Step seven: zest a unicorn on the bacon. Wait, what!" Bunny looked closer. "Oh, sorry. I meant, zest *a carrot* on the bacon."

"That makes more sense," Snow told him.

"Step eight: do a celebration dance. And step nine: serve the carrot bacon and enjoy!" Bunny put the book back onto the shelf, which allowed Snow to ask their question. But they had already forgotten it. However, this allowed them to ask a different question.

"Who makes all of your carrot bacon?" (Obviously, Bunny couldn't make all of it, based on how large his lair was.)

"Oh, my relatives," Bunny replied. "They, uh, share with me. We made a deal."

"Where do they all live?" Snow asked.

"In an extremely large rabbit hole attached to this lair."

"Are these the same relatives you used to live with?" Snow asked.

Bunny nodded.

"Can we meet them?"

Bunny sighed again. "Well, I heard Aunt Ducey is visiting."

Snow almost laughed. "Who?"

"Aunt Ducey," Bunny repeated. "She's the head of the family and is really bossy." Bunny and Snow stepped out of the library. While Bunny struggled to close the door, Snow remembered their question.

"Back in the library, what were those other books about?" they asked.

"Oh, just my relatives," Bunny said.

"You have that many?"

"Yeah, and not just my rabbit relatives. I'm related to about a third of Earth's population." Snow didn't really believe this. (Already, they knew that Bunny liked to make up untrue stories.) Anyway, the two hopped into the Food Express once again and took off at a swift speed. It sped past many shelves before making a sudden turn.

Snow almost launched out of their seat. "I told you that this train needs seatbelts!" they shouted.

"Sorry," Bunny said. "I forgot to warn you about that turn." It continued forward for a few seconds before Bunny pulled a lever and the train slowed to a stop.

He boinged off the Food Express, grabbed a handful of carrot bacon, then dumped it in one of the carts behind the engine. (After eating a few slices, of course.) "Want some?" Bunny asked Snow with his mouth full.

Snow didn't really, but they also didn't want to disappoint Bunny. "I'll try a slice." Bunny dumped a handful of carrot bacon into Snow's hand, who slowly broke a small piece. Then they bravely nibbled it. *Hmmmmm,* Snow thought. The carrot bacon wasn't half bad! Well, they definitely didn't enjoy it as much as Bunny, but it was pretty good. It was like regular bacon except with a sweet carrot flavor. Snow gave the rest of the handful back to Bunny.

"Decent," they said. Then the two took off again. One minute later, the Food Express arrived at a large set of doors.

"Alright," Bunny told Snow. "This is where my relatives live." He stepped forward and knocked on a door.

"Come in!" an unpleasant voice came from inside.

"That's Aunt Ducey," Bunny whispered. He boinged into his relatives' rabbit hole, Snow right behind.

"Welcome, Bonnie!" Aunt Ducey shrieked. "You're just in time. I need someone to do the dishes!"

"Where is everybody?" he asked, used to Aunt Ducey getting his name wrong.

"Oh," Aunt Ducey responded. "They all left." Then she noticed Snow. "Who's that?"

"Just a friend of mine," Bunny said. "But, back to my question. Where did everybody go?"

"Well, yesterday morning, this beaver carrying something that looked like a bomb came right to our rabbit hole and asked for most of us to come with him. When I asked why, he said that it was because there was a big triathlon happening," Aunt Ducey explained.

Weird, Bunny thought. But this explained the bomb. "What did the bomb look like?" he asked.

"Small," Aunt Ducey replied. "And...I don't know, gray?"

Bunny looked at Snow. It was the same bomb. "And you don't know anything else about it?" Bunny asked.

Aunt Ducey frowned. "Nope. Anyway, I agreed, so everyone left with the beaver." Bunny grumbled in frustration. He was so close to figuring out why there was a bomb in his lair! He sighed, then asked, "Can I show Snow around a bit? I'll do the dishes after."

"Fine," Aunt Ducey replied, scowling at Snow. "But be quick. You know I hate polar bugs."

"*Bears,*" Snow murmured as they walked away with Bunny.

"Sorry about her," Bunny said as he opened a door. "Here's the living and meeting room."

"Cool."

Then Bunny explained how the rabbit hole was the largest in the world. (Snow wasn't surprised. I mean, you hardly ever see rabbit holes the size of houses on Zillow.) Bunny showed Snow the bedroom's kitchen and finished the tour off with the indoor carrot farm.

"This is my favorite part," Bunny told Snow. "These carrots make my carrot bacon fresh and delicious."

"Well," Snow said. "That's not something you see every day. It's cool."

They walked through a hallway and popped back into the entryway.

Surprisingly, Aunt Ducey was not there.

"Quick," Bunny said. "Let's get out of here before she sees us." He and Snow ran out of the rabbit hole, clambered onto the Food Express, and sped off along the tracks.

"I'm going to take you through the fun part of my lair," Bunny said happily. "It has lots of sharp turns, though." (Snow held on tightly when he said this.) "But while we ride, I want to talk about something," Bunny informed his friend.

"Okay," Snow replied.

"But don't be afraid to have fun!"

Snow was alone in one of the many empty rooms that Bunny's lair had. (Bunny's part-time bedroom was next door.)

During the ride, Snow had listened to Bunny talk and talk about all sorts of different things. A few times, Snow was able to get a word in, but Bunny did most of the talking. That's when he brought up a totally different subject. "I want to learn how to ski," he told Snow.

Well, it happened by chance that Snow is an expert at skiing, so they agreed to teach Bunny. "My favorite resort is Winter Park," they said.

"Then let's go there!" Bunny exclaimed. It was settled. Once the Food Express came to a stop, they jumped off, went to their separate rooms, and started packing their bags. Snow stuffed a water bottle in the side of their backpack. Next, they put a pencil, notebook, and pencil sharpener inside. They were writing a book about stuffed animals.

Of course, Snow also had to bring a magazine about New Zealand.

Once they were done packing all of those things, they stepped out of the room they were in, and pretty soon, Bunny boinged out of his.

"Hi," he said. "All ready?"

"Yep," Snow responded. "Now, how are we going to get to Winter Park?"

Bunny had not thought of this. "I don't know."

"We could take a plane," Snow suggested.

"How about we dig a tunnel?" Bunny said.

Snow laughed. "That would take too long." But then they realized something. "There are buses that go up to Winter Park."

"You mean the stinky buses that smell like dead weasels?" Bunny asked.

"Um…"

Bunny sighed, "I guess that'll work."

"Alright," Snow said. "Let's pack some snacks." It turned out that they had to fit all the snacks in Snow's bag, because Bunny had overpacked.

"Why did you bring a tent?" Snow asked him. "You know, there's a secret hotel for stuffed animals."

Bunny shrugged, "I just feel like we will need it." Neither of them knew that Bunny's small amount of magic was kicking in.

"Then why did you pack broken crayons?" Snow wondered.

"Oh, I just like to look at them," Bunny said.

"Well, you have some peculiar interests." Snow stuffed five bags of carrot bacon, some strawberries, and granola bars into their backpack.

"Let's go," they said triumphantly!

"Hold on!" Bunny exclaimed. "I need to pack my plopping board!" He ran back into his room and returned with a small board in his backpack. *Yes,* Snow thought. *Very peculiar indeed.*

CHAPTER
TWELVE

BUNNY LEARNS HOW TO SKI

*W*e have to be there by now, Bunny thought. He was hot, uncomfortable, and the bus that they were in smelled like dead weasels. Bunny and Snow had barely caught the bus at a stop near the Nobles' house. They hopped in the back, and were squished together in a suitcase that Bunny had, uh, definitely not stolen from Darren…

Anyway, he regretted going along because this was not what Bunny had expected when Snow said they would "ride" a bus. The ride dragged on. "Is Winter Park in China or something?" he asked.

"No," Snow responded. "It's only an hour and twenty minutes away." Bunny sighed. But finally, after a few minutes, the bus stopped.

"We're there!" Bunny shouted with excitement.

"Shhhh," Snow reminded him. They waited for the sound of people getting off. But then the bus lurched forward again. This happened a few more times until Snow declared, "There's a traffic jam."

Bunny groaned.

EVENTUALLY, THE BUS ARRIVED.

People started getting off, and quickly, Snow led Bunny out of the suitcase. The trunk door of the bus opened, but no one was there to witness them hop out. Snow and Bunny rushed into the bustling ski resort of Winter Park. Well, Snow was fast, but Bunny was not. (Even though he wasn't the one pulling the suitcase.)

"I need a break," Bunny declared. Snow agreed and the two hid behind a large tree.

"This is the village," Snow told him.

"Ah," Bunny replied. "Then where is the ski resort?"

"The village *is* part of the resort. It's where all the shops and hotels are," Snow said.

"Oh, then where do we ski?"

Snow pointed up at the tall mountain. "There. That gondola will take us up the..."

"What about those things?" Bunny interrupted.

"Those are ski lifts," Snow said, getting impatient. "You can take a gondola or a ski lift to get to the top. But we need to rent skis from the secret stuffed animal village, and then we're ready."

After Bunny was well rested, they left the tree, making sure to stay out of sight of humans. They walked and boinged into a small building, which Snow explained was the stuffed animal village. They went through a hallway, and into a wide-open room. All of the doors and hallways reminded Bunny of a large mall. He read some of the signs above the doors.

A Duck Walked Up to A Ski Rental Store: Ski + Snowboard Rentals

Mr. Fred's Biscuits

The Fuzzy Jacket Clothing Store.

He sighed but kept following Snow.

"Okay," they said. "This is the hotel we're staying at."

The two friends walked inside a large set of double doors.

"Welcome," a Badger exclaimed from behind the counter. "To the dumpster hotel!"

"What?" Snow asked.

"Just kidding," the Badger chuckled. "I'm just messing with ya. Welcome to the Stuffed Animal Hotel! I'm the manager!"

Suddenly, a small dog burst through some doors behind the counter.

"Sir," she said. "The man in room 1,060,522 wants you."

The manager nodded. "Nice meeting you two," he told Bunny and Snow, before leaving the room.

"How old are you?" Bunny asked the smaller dog.

"I beg your pardon…"

Snow quickly changed the topic. "Please, show us to our rooms."

While the dog went behind the counter to get their keys, Snow whispered to Bunny, "Try to be nicer." Bunny nodded. Usually, most beings didn't tell him this, as they probably figured he wouldn't listen. But Bunny was determined to be kinder. Anyway, the dog reappeared, and she led Snow and Bunny up a flight of stairs. Fortunately for Bunny, their room was only on the second floor. (That saved him a lot of boinging.)

"Thank you," Snow said.

The dog nodded and then left. Snow turned to the door numbered *2,908,216,554,830.*

"How are we supposed to remember that?"

"No clue," Snow replied. They put the key in the door and it opened, revealing a luxurious room. Bunny immediately boinged inside and plopped on a soft bed as Snow closed the door behind them.

"Let's rest for a bit," they said. "But rent some skis later."

"Okay," Bunny replied.

Snow walked over to a large window and admired the beautiful view of Aspen Trees, though it was hard to enjoy the moment with Bunny eating carrot bacon in the background.

Snow sighed, "It's so…"

"Delicious!" Bunny interrupted.

"Well, that's not what I was thinking," Snow said. Then they turned around.

"Uh…"

Bunny had made a humongous mess! There were crumbs all over the bed and floor. Bunny sat there and gobbled up his last slice of carrot bacon before announcing, "I'm out."

Good, Snow thought. But instead, they said, "You should've packed some more. I didn't know you can eat that much."

"I'm still hungry," Bunny responded. He boinged back to the backpack and dug out his granola bar.

We will definitely need to get more snacks, Snow thought. Then they got an idea. "I am going back down to the lobby," they declared.

"Why?" Bunny asked. He tossed the granola bar wrapper in a trash can.

"This is a fancy hotel," Snow said. "There is probably a restaurant somewhere in the lobby." They set out, and Bunny agreed to stay out of trouble for one minute. Which, apparently, was a lot to ask. After Snow left, Bunny looked around the room. Once his eyes caught the lamp, well, Bunny just knew he had to try something. He boinged onto the dresser. Then he boinged to the lamp, but he was too rump-heavy, and it fell on the floor, breaking into pieces.

"Ahhhh!" Bunny shouted. "There's a piece of glass in my rump!" Luckily, it was just a large carrot bacon crumb. Bunny knew from Leigh that broken glass could be dangerous, so he cautiously boinged away. (It was physically impossible for him to walk or run, because his legs, which were also thin like noodles, and much smaller than his feet, could not hold up his body.)

By the time Snow came back the room was a total mess! "What happened?" Snow exclaimed. "This place became a pig sty!" Bunny looked around. He didn't realize how messy the room was.

"Well, there is a dining room, I found out," Snow said. "But before dinner, we have to clean this room up!" Just then, someone knocked on the door. Snow ran to answer it. There was a grumpy looking crocodile wearing pajamas.

"Quiet down in there, will ya," he said. Snow was about to apologize and explain, but the crocodile slammed the door. Snow walked back to Bunny and scolded him. He tried to protest, but Snow was strict. So, they spent the next hour cleaning the whole hotel room.

FINALLY, THEIR JOB WAS DONE. TOGETHER, THEY WENT TO the dining room back in the lobby. It was bustling and very fancy. When Bunny saw how many stuffed animals were in the room, and the fountain in the center, he knew that he had his chance to become famous.

"Hi," Snow said as they arrived at the hostesses' spot.

"Welcome," a duck said. "Table for one?"

Snow shook their head. "No. Table for two."

The hostess looked confused, "Are you meeting someone?"

"I'm here with my friend, Bunny," Snow replied. But when they turned around, Bunny was nowhere to be seen.

However, somewhere in the crowd there was a distinct "Boing, a boing, a boing, a boing, a boing!" Snow spotted

Bunny climbing up the big fountain in the center of the restaurant and started to run towards him.

"That'll be a twenty-minute wait!" the hostess called.

Snow rushed through the crowd and arrived at the base of the fountain. But they were too late. Bunny, surprisingly, had managed to climb to the top of the fountain. He cleared his throat, not noticing Snow.

"Me me me me meeeee," Bunny said.

Everyone in the dining room turned to look at him.

I'm in the spotlight now, Bunny thought.

Then he started singing a song.

"Go, Bunny. Go go, Bunny Bunny time. Yeah, me me! Hey hey, Bunny Bunny!" He expected everyone to applaud, but instead, the crowd stayed speechless. Bunny decided to try a different song.

"Get on the, get on the, get on the floor floor!" This time he danced, moving his rump in the air, and boinging around. A few stuffed animals clapped some. But, as Snow suspected, security arrived, and hauled Bunny down from the fountain.

"Our table will be ready in fifteen minutes," Snow told Bunny once he was back on ground level. Soon that time passed, and they were led to a small table. Everyone was still watching Bunny.

"I guess I'm sort of famous," he said. Snow sighed and looked at the menu the hostess had given them.

Bunny scanned the menu eagerly, but his face clouded up afterwards. "WHERE'S THE CARROT BACON?" he shouted.

"Shhhh," the same crocodile from earlier said. "This is a nice restaurant."

"Says the person who's wearing pajamas," Bunny shot back.

Snow kicked Bunny. "Sorry," they told the crocodile.

A toucan wearing a nice vest came to their table. *What kind of stuffed animal wears clothes?* Bunny wondered. "Hello," the Toucan said in an annoying voice. "I am Danny, your server for tonight."

"Well, I think we're still ordering," Snow told him. "But for a drink, I'll take the New Zealand kombucha."

"And you?" Danny asked Bunny.

"I'd like some carrot juice."

"Uh, sorry. We don't have that. But maybe you can have some orange juice."

Bunny sighed. "What kind of restaurant are you? I'll skip on drinks, then."

Danny looked offended. "Alright," he said. "One New Zealand kombucha, coming right up!"

Once he was gone, Snow said, "Remember, try to be nicer."

Bunny had forgotten. "Okay," he replied.

Danny came back, holding a glass of kombucha. He handed it to Snow and took out a little note pad. "Are you folks ready to order?" he asked.

"I think so," Snow responded. "I'd like the Swedish meatballs with the caesar salad." From the beginning, Bunny already knew his order. Although it wasn't on the menu, they probably didn't want to put it there because everyone would buy it. "Carrot bacon, please."

"Excuse me?" Danny asked. "What's that?"

Bunny tried to remain calm.

"I think the closest thing to carrot bacon would be collard greens. The chef makes them really delicious," Danny said quickly.

"I'll take that, then," Bunny said.

Snow knew that he wouldn't like collard greens. Danny wrote down their orders and walked back to the kitchen. "You know," Bunny said in his usual deep voice that Snow liked, "I just realized that a lot of stuffed animals' names end with a Y."

"Yeah," Snow agreed, a bit taken back by the randomness of the comment.

"Rudy, Giraffey, Grey, Bunny, which is me!" Bunny said.

"Yes, I know."

He went on and on. "Tuskey, Squiddy, Rudy. Wait, did I say his name already?"

Snow nodded.

"Sweetie," Bunny said.

"No, Sweetie ends in an E."

"Oh." Bunny didn't know that. No wonder Sweetie seemed annoyed when he gave her a hand-made birthday card.

Danny came back and handed them their food. "Mmm," Snow said. "I love Swedish meatballs."

Bunny looked at his food. "Yuck. That's edible?"

Snow sighed, "I can have your collard greens." Bunny dumped them on Snow's plate and watched them eat their food.

Finally, Snow finished. They looked at the menu again, and their eyes went wide. "What?" Bunny asked.

Snow showed him. Right underneath the word *Churros*, a more important word was written.

Carrot Cake.

Danny, once again, came back. Bunny was getting annoyed with him. "How are you enjoying…" Danny saw that Snow and Bunny's food was gone. "Oh, I see you have already finished."

"Yes," Snow said. "It was delicious."

"Please tell me that you have carrot cake," Bunny demanded.

"Why yes, we do…" Bunny boinged off his seat. "But it's sold out," Danny finished with a little smirk. Bunny plopped back down in his chair. Snow sighed.

"Well, what about churros?" he asked.

"We still have churros, yes." Danny responded.

"We'll take that, then," Snow said.

Danny walked away. Soon, he came back with churros, including a cup of a chocolate dipping sauce.

Snow thanked him and ate a few tasty bites.

"Mmm," he said to Bunny. "You should try some."

"No thanks," Bunny replied. The churros looked good, but he had suddenly grown tired. "When are we going to ski?" he asked. "That's the whole point we came here."

"True," Snow said. "We will head for the slopes tomorrow." Bunny couldn't wait. He was excited to try what Grey called a double black.

As it turned out, the first day was full of "green" runs. Which didn't make any sense because everything was covered in snow! Bunny told that to Snow. "Yeah, I know," Snow had responded. "That's how I got my name. Like you, probably, when I was first made, I was as white as snow. But all stuffed animals eventually get grimy."

Bunny had looked down at his fur. It was true.

Anyway, now he was practicing with Snow at the magic carpet ski lift. Suddenly, Bunny spotted an elephant snowboarding. "What's that?" he asked.

"Oh," Snow said. "A snowboard."

"Cool, can I get one?"

"Well, I only know how to ski, so let's stick with this for now," Snow replied patiently.

"Okay," Bunny said. Surprisingly, he was a fast learner. Earlier, he almost crashed, but after more practice, got much better.

"Remember, put your skis in the shape of a mountain to stop," Snow reminded Bunny.

"Why not carrot bacon?" he asked.

"Does it come in triangle shapes?"

"No."

Finally, it started getting dark. He could hardly believe that they had gone to the restaurant almost a whole day ago. Snow led Bunny to the bottom of the small hill. Together, they took off their skis.

"Great job!" Snow told him. "Tomorrow, we can maybe go down a longer path." Last night, as they had left the restaurant, Snow discovered that it had the option to deliver to your room. So tonight, that's what they did. Snow called the lobby, and soon, their food arrived.

"What's that?" Bunny shouted excitedly.

"They made more carrot cake, so I got us each a slice." Bunny would have liked a whole cake, but he was happy. Of course, he had to eat his dinner before dessert. Bunny had two large carrot sticks.

"Do you want to try some of my salmon?" Snow asked. Bunny shook his head, but Snow convinced him. "It's good," they said.

Slowly, Bunny tried a little bite, and the salmon actually tasted pretty decent! Bunny took a few more bites but eventually moved on and ate his dessert.

The next morning, it was day three of being in Winter Park. "Alright," Snow said as they strapped on their skis. (Stuffed animals

have straps rather than bindings on their skis because they don't want to wear ski boots.) "Are you ready?"

"I sure am," Bunny responded confidently. He was going to ride a gondola for the first time. Well, a stuffed animal mini version of a gondola. Together, they went into the little area where you got on. Bunny watched curiously as gondolas came down the mountain and did a little bump before circling around the platform, allowing stuffed animals with skis and snowboards to hop in.

Snow and Bunny made it to the front of the line. "Okay," Snow said. "When an empty gondola comes by, carefully jump – I mean boing – into it after me." Bunny nodded. He focused on the one that was almost in front of them. Next thing he knew, Snow jumped into the gondola.

It is just like plopping, Bunny told himself. He boinged into the gondola just before the doors closed. "Plop!" He landed next to Snow on the bench.

"Wait," he heard someone shout. The voice was awfully familiar. Someone suddenly opened the doors again, and a toucan wearing a nice vest hopped in. Then the gondola rumbled a bit, before slowly heading towards the top of the mountain. "Danny!" Bunny shouted. "What are you doing here?"

Danny brushed his vest. "It's my day off, if you don't mind."

"Well, I do..." Bunny stopped himself from being rude. "It's fine," he said calmly. He looked out the window. There were a few pine trees, but most of them were covered in snow. Bunny looked uphill. Another gondola station was waiting. He looked downhill. *Wow!* he thought. *We were all the way down there.* Many skiers passed by. Some speeding and others taking it slow.

"We will go down a stuffed animal run called Wigler. It is a green run," Snow said.

"Ha!" Danny said. "I'm going down a double black!" Bunny sighed. Finally, they arrived at the gondola station, so Bunny and Snow could get off. Apparently, the double black runs were all the way at the top of the mountain and Danny kept going up a different ski lift.

"Okay," Snow said after they had gotten off. "Follow me." Bunny steadily but slowly skied behind Snow, not expecting them to stop so suddenly.

"We're at the beginning of the run..." Snow was saying, but Bunny forgot how to stop. He started speeding down the mountain!

"Remember!" Snow shouted. "Point your skis together." Bunny tried to follow this advice, but instead he ended up tripping and tumbling down the mountain, crashing into other skiers.

"Go around me!" an old lady shouted.

Someone else angrily said, "Watch where you're going!"

"Sorry," Snow told the stuffed animals as they skied after Bunny.

"Just go to the side, you bunch of crazies," Bunny told everyone who yelled at him. All this did was anger them more. Soon the village appeared, and Bunny realized that he was heading straight for it! Behind him was Snow, followed by other shouting stuffed animals, who were pursued by ski patrol officers. Luckily, Snow was already an amazing skier. They pulled up alongside Bunny.

"Grab my ski pole!" Snow had poles, unlike Bunny, as he was a beginner. But that was not important. Bunny harnessed the purple pole, and Snow pulled him to his feet. "Now ski as fast as you can!" Snow shouted, looking over their shoulder to see the infuriated crowd only yards behind them. Bunny followed Snow's directions. If you did not know that he was being chased by a ferocious group of stuffed animals with metal ski poles swinging in the air, then you might have thought he was a professional skier. Bunny and Snow reached the bottom of the run, and without thinking, Bunny took off his skis, and boinged towards the hotel. Snow threw open the doors, and they burst into the lobby.

"I think we lost them." Bunny said. He was exhausted. But just to be safe, they went inside their room.

"Well, that was quite an adventure," Snow said, once they were safe inside.

"Yeah, I need a nap."

Bunny boinged in bed and closed his eyes, thinking of the Noble's. Snow had already become a good friend, but it wasn't the same now that he was kicked out of his family's home. And then he thought of the S.A.S. It had been three days since he was kicked out, and he already missed them.

But little did he know, his chance to see them would come soon.

CHAPTER
THIRTEEN

THE RETURN

Rudy was meditating. With all of these things happening, he needed to clear his mind.

So, there he was, sitting in his comfortable chair calmly. Everyone else had stopped acting crazy. They were all walking around the base wondering what happened and where Bunny went. Piggy had a bad stomachache from eating all those raw eggs, Flatbeak had stopped yelling, "Buffaloes!", and the other four leaders decided to have a meeting. Squiddy had an amazing memory, so he remembered a bit of what happened just a few days ago.

"Bo Bo, I think you kicked Bunny out," he said.

"What!" she exclaimed. "I would never do that."

"Or maybe it was Grey."

Grey panted in response. "Darn it!" he said. "Ever since we went crazy, I can't shake this – heh heh heh heh – habit of panting."

Anyway, after a not very productive meeting, Bo Bo, Squiddy, Grey, and Giraffey concluded that they had some-how lost sanity for a few moments. They all left the meeting room. Squiddy went back to his office. He said hi to Tuskey. "How are you doing with your office?" Squiddy asked him.

"All I can say is that it's still a mess."

"Well, good luck with the project."

"Thanks," Tuskey said. He walked away. Squiddy stepped into his office and ate a waffle. Then he worked on his computer a bit. But the whole time, he had something in the back of his mind that he couldn't figure out. It was something Rudy had told him a long time ago. Something that even Rudy had maybe forgotten. *Oh well*, Squiddy thought. He continued working.

Giraffey was talking with Albert by the entrance to the base. He told him what the leaders had concluded. "Al-bert," Giraffey said.

"Yeah," Albert responded slowly.

"I need you to go on a mission."

"Why?" Albert asked.

"Because we need to find out if other stuffed animals went crazy like us."

"We know that the bad guys did it," Albert said.

"According to Pecan, yes, who was guarding the jail."

At that very moment, Squiddy appeared. "I just re-membered something very important," he said.

"What is it?"

"Rudy told me, like, maybe a century ago or some-thing, that if you go crazy, it means that Gewis is near."

"Really!" Giraffey exclaimed, looking very frightened all of a sudden.

"Yes, I'm almost positive," Squiddy said. There was a loud bang on Amaday's main doors, and OHM peeked through the slot. Once he realized who was there, he fell back and fainted. Rudy had told everyone what Gewis looked like. So, with Squiddy's evidence, Giraffey knew in-stantly who was there. He sped for Rudy's office. Usually, you weren't supposed to interrupt the leader when he was meditating, but this was an emergency.

Rudy opened his eyes. He was startled. "What is it?"

Giraffey was panting more than Grey. "I think that Ge-wis is at the door."

RUDY'S REACTION WAS SURPRISING. HE BENT OVER AND grabbed a piece of paper off his desk. He scribbled down a note then said, "Find the nearest Fighting Ally. Tell who-ever it is to warn Toy City and deliver this note to Bunny."

"Got it," Giraffey said. He had no clue why Rudy was counting on Bunny! But he was in such a hurry that it didn't matter. Giraffey ran back out of Rudy's office and clam-bered out of an open window. He turned around. There were hundreds of Gewis's fighters surrounding Amaday. Giraffey was trapped. He figured they were all beavers, though there might have been a few other animals, but it was hard to tell what species someone was because they all were hidden in an outfit and mask of red.

Giraffey couldn't believe it. He pulled out his S.A.S. weapon. (The same one that he had used to make Gewis disappear.) Some beavers were on their phones. Others were lying on the ground and snoring. The rest simply stood there, shivering. It was a very chilly day. Giraffey remembered how terrible Gewis's soldiers were. *I guess it is still true*, he thought. But suddenly, one of them spotted him as he made his way through the crowd.

"GET HIM!" the soldier shouted, and no one was unfocused anymore. Giraffey was surrounded by Gewis's army. About half of them had stuffed animal weapons like books and sticks and stuff like that, while the other half had nothing.

Giraffey took a deep breath. *I can handle them.*

Gripping his weapon, he jumped into the air and took out six soldiers. Everyone else started to charge at him. Giraffey dodged a few books, sticks and rocks, before swinging his weapon at the soldier in front of him and kicking the soldiers behind him at the same time. Luckily, Gewis and the rest of his army hadn't noticed the scene yet. Giraffey picked up one of the books on the ground (the heaviest one) and closed it in a soldier's face. Its red mask clanked off, revealing not a Beaver but a Flamingo, proving Giraffey's suspicions. Gewis's army had grown.

At this point, things weren't looking good. Soldiers were charging from every direction, and this batch looked a little more talented. Although he never wanted to give up a fight, Giraffey reminded himself that the mission was to find the nearest fighting ally. Quickly, he ran towards the part of Amaday that was not the squad's base, knocking out a few soldiers with his weapon on the way. Finally, Giraffey figured that he could slow down a little. Looking back, he saw that no one was bothering to chase him. While he ran, Giraffey read the note Rudy wrote. It read:

Dear Bunny,

As you might know by now, Gewis, with his bigger than ever army, is attacking Amaday.

I am writing while I can. I know that we will put up a fight, but he will most likely win in the end. So, it is up to you and the Fighting Ally who delivered this note.

This is your chance, Bunny, to show everyone that you're very powerful. Which you are, because, yes, I gave you magic. It might seem hard at first, but you must learn how to use this magic to save stuffed animalkind.

I believe in you. Very sincerely,

Rudy

Giraffey closed up the note. He couldn't believe that Rudy had given Bunny magic. He ran into the lower part of Amaday, and while folding the note, his head banged against something hard.

"Ow!" he said, then looked up. Sweetie was hanging on the ceiling like a Bat.

"Oh, hi Giraffey!" she shouted. She was apparently the only one who didn't realize that Gewis was attacking Amaday.

"Wait, did your head just crash into mine?" Sweetie asked.

"Yes," Giraffey said, rubbing his scalp.

"Okay, then I have to cry."

"Noooooooo!" Giraffey said. But it was too late.

Sweetie started crying. Finally, after five minutes, she stopped. Sweetie's feet were now loose, and she fell from the ceiling and face planted. "Giggle," she said, then started crying again.

Giraffey sighed. *Maybe I should find another Fighting Ally. Sweetie is not trustworthy.* Giraffey kept running. But unfortunately, no one was in sight. He ran all the way to the grand fountain to find no one. He checked the doctor's office, which connected to where Flatbeak worked. Next, Giraffey looked in all the offices. No one. The base was fully empty.

Giraffey peeked outside. Everyone was fighting, like he assumed.

It was a big battle, between the S.A.S., and Gewis's army. (Who, unfortunately, was winning.) He sighed again. It would have to be Sweetie. When Giraffey reached her again, she was no longer crying. Instead, she was sucking on a lollipop.

"Tasty," Sweetie said.

Once again, Giraffey sighed. "Okay Sweetie, I have an important mission for you. Deliver this note to Bunny. You will have to track him down." Giraffey thought of something. "If you do this, you will become famous, and I will give you all the pineapple you want."

Sweetie looked at him. She bowed.

Giraffey handed her the note. "Gewis is attacking, so it will be up to you and Bunny once you find him. And try to convince Toy City to help, tell them that they are in danger too."

"Okay," Sweetie said. She started acting more seriously.

"Thank you," Giraffey said, surprised. "Now I have to go fight. But Gewis will probably capture us all." He led her to a secret back door. Giraffey still had his weapon. "You can have this," he told her. Sweetie smiled with glee and admired her new weapon. Giraffey hoped he wouldn't regret this, but before he had any second thoughts, he exclaimed, "Go find Bunny!" Then Sweetie ran out of the door as fast as she could.

REMEMBER, THE WEAPON THAT GIRAFFEY GAVE SWEETIE WAS the same one that everyone thought made Gewis disappear. But actually, it didn't. There is a stuffed animal legend called the Great Holder. No one knew who this mysterious monster was. On that day when Gewis and his army disappeared, so many years ago, it was actually the Great Holder who made them vanish. The legend was disguised as a beaver soldier, so nobody noticed.

The only stuffed animal that knew that the Great Holder was there was Gewis. He told everyone to hold on to each other. Some were hesitant, but they knew not to argue with their boss. So right when Giraffey struck his weapon, the Great Holder used *her* magic to turn everyone into a spirit and keep them in her magical purse. It's confusing and really weird, but true. Then, when the time came, the Great Holder released them.

Which is what happened one week ago.

Gewis was released in the ruins of his burnt down castle in Denali with his army. It felt so good to feel the warm sunshine on his face. Once he reappeared, the first thing he said was, "Fresh air is fresher than I remembered!" Then he thanked the Great Holder, who simply nodded, putting the magical purse she used to release Gewis and his army back on her shoulder.

After talking with Room Decor, Gewis walked to where the purple pear tree was. Yes, he remembered over a century ago when a mysterious human planted the tree. During the father-son war, he had forgotten about it, but now, he realized something. That purple pear tree was magical. It had supplied his son's friends with magic.

He led a siege and defeated the dozen guards posted up around it easily. Then, he used his dark magic to cut out its good magic. He went on a long journey to Amaday. Room Decor led him to her old base, where a few of the bad guys were still remaining from their last battle with the squad.

"I definitely want nothing to do with these idiots," Gewis declared when meeting them. "Now, you can help with the tryouts." You see, most of his army was the same from all those years ago. But the army was even stronger now. Partly because Gewis was more powerful than ever, and also because there were even more volunteers. Now there weren't just beavers on his side. (Gewis was glad. He was getting sick of beavers.) Room Decor had organized something almost like a draft. She had hung up posters all over in the largest stuffed animal hubs. This is what the poster said:

Stuffed Animal Triathlon Competition

If you are fit (meaning speedy, smart, strong, etc.), then you might just want to try out for this competition!

There will be 1st place, 2nd place, and 3rd place winners.

We are not exactly sure how long it will last, but bring multiple tents if you can. (If not, that's okay! We will have extras.)

Tryouts start 12/13 (fold paper over for map of where to go)

Competition host: Lewis the Turtle

There are only 100 spots, so try to get there early!

P.S. Thank you to our sponsor, the Stuffed Animal Squad, for being so willing to help.

So sure enough, over a thousand stuffed animals flocked to the mountain with the remains of the bad guys' base. It was all too overwhelming for Gewis, so instead of tryouts, he just picked the first hundred who showed up. "As long as you can hold a weapon or do something useful, you are qualified," said Gewis.

The peak of the bad guys' mountain was covered in tents. Although they were all empty because Gewis was hosting a meeting in the bad guys' base. The hundred new recruits for Gewis's army gathered in the base that had been recently demolished by the S.A.S. The lower sections of the walls had survived, but the ceiling had all collapsed. This made for a natural amphitheater, so Gewis was standing on a large chunk of ceiling, going over the rules of the competition.

"Alright everyone. When we arrive at Amaday, these special robots will come out. They look and sound exactly like the actual members of the Stuffed Animal Squad, but remember, they are not." While he was talking, some of the bad guys who had escaped the S.A.S. were passing out red armor: the official uniform of Gewis's soldiers.

Gewis continued, "They are specially designed by Tuskey, who we are very grateful for. There will be a race to Amaday, then you must try to defeat these bots, then race back to here. We will be closely judging to see who wins. And remember—it's not just about who wins but who fights the best."

He went over all sorts of rules and answered many questions. Finally, after what seemed like forever, Gewis said, "Well, thank you for joining this meeting. Now go get some goodnight's sleep because tomorrow is a big day."

RUDY WALKED TOWARDS THE DOOR. EVERYONE INSIDE THE squad's base was staring at him. The wise leader put his hand on the doorknob, took a deep breath, and slowly opened the door to reveal what was outside.

"Well, hi there son," Gewis said casually.

"Greetings, father," Rudy responded. Everyone in Gewis's army looked surprised. There were a few awkward glances as Gewis's soldier looked between him and Rudy.

Gewis cleared his throat. "I am now more powerful than ever, seeking revenge, and not filled with beans anymore! I mean seriously, you can get beans for $1.50 at Walmart these days." Everyone in the S.A.S., except for Squiddy, Giraffey, and Rudy were not as confident as usual. Rudy had told them so much about his father, but now being face to face, it turns out that they were not quite prepared. Gewis was almost as powerful as all the leaders put together. Plus, he had a gigantic army of nearly 200.

"What has brought you to Amaday?" Rudy asked.

"Oh, I have been waiting for so long, son. I'm giving you one last warning. I want you and all of your allies back there to join my side."

Rudy stared deep into his father's eyes. It had been about 150 years since the battle of Denali, the father-son war. The years when his father was just a regular Tortoise in Africa seemed so long ago. Finally, Rudy said, "We will never join your side. Besides, what's the point if we already rule all stuffed animals?"

Gewis smiled wryly. "Who said this was just stuffed animals?"

Rudy shook his head. "Do not even try, father. If you manage to beat us, you will not be prepared for modern day countries, the smallest with armies five times larger than yours."

"Use your intelligence, son. We won't fight them. We'll hide behind the scenes, use tactics to take over."

"The world's population has doubled and then doubled again. You stand no chance."

"Neither do you and your little helpers."

Unfortunately, Giraffey walked into the scene right when Gewis said the words, "Little helpers." And when Giraffey gets mad, he instantly starts fighting. "Attack!" he yelled.

So that's how the battle between the S.A.S. and Gewis started.

It was a quick one. Even Rudy and Grey were surprised at how powerful Gewis was, and he quickly overthrew the S.A.S. leaders. His army had some struggles, but in less than twenty minutes, the whole squad was locked up.

Now the fate of stuffed animalkind was in the hands of Bunny, Snow, and Sweetie.

PART

THREE

THE RISE OF A HERO

CHAPTER
FOURTEEN

THE JOURNEY BACK TO AMADAY

Bunny sighed. It was not the most entertaining day. Snow had left for a walk, and he was left in the hotel room with nothing to do.

So deep in thought, the door burst open, and without thinking, Bunny quickly grabbed a pillow and flung it at the person who was entering. The possibility that the person might be Snow did not dawn on Bunny.

"Whoops!" Bunny shouted. Fortunately, Snow dodged the flying pillow. "You're back already," Bunny observed. "I thought that it would take you longer."

Snow's expression was different. A very serious one. "Well, the dog down in the lobby told me that there was someone looking for you."

"And?" Bunny asked impatiently.

"So, I went to see this *someone,* and… it's a fighting ally."

"Who?" Bunny asked.

"She calls herself Sweetie."

"What! Why is she here?" Bunny exclaimed. He didn't know if this was good or bad. "Where is she?"

In the hallway, there was a loud grunt followed by a scream.

"Alligator!"

Bunny sighed. "Never mind."

SWEETIE QUICKLY RAN INTO THE ROOM AND SLAMMED THE door. "There's an alligator out there," she whimpered. Bunny figured this was the crocodile in pajamas who complained about his ruckus.

"Don't worry," Snow told Sweetie. "He's harmless."

Sweetie took a minute to calm down before asking, "So who is this fella anyway?"

"This is my friend, Snow." Bunny said.

Sweetie looked heartbroken. Bunny wanted to tell her that she never was his best friend, but, of course, that would be rude. Quickly, he said, "I have two best friends."

"Yay!" Sweetie exclaimed. "We're best buds."

"Yes," Snow responded, putting their hand out for the toddler. Sweetie grabbed hold of it and shook Snow so hard that it left them shaking. *She has even worse manners than Bunny*, they thought.

"Teddy bear, how ya doing?"

"Fine," Snow said plainly. "And I'm actually a polar bear."

Someone opened the door.

"Keep it down in here. I've already told you millions of times," said the crocodile wearing pajamas.

"Actually," Bunny corrected, "Only once."

"I didn't ask you, ya little mutt." *Yikes*, Bunny thought. *He does not know his animals.*

Sweetie let out another scream, and once again, "Alligator!" Then she hid behind the bed.

"Didn't you listen? I'm a crocodile," he snarled. "This is two strikes, one more, and you're out."

"We never got your name!" Bunny called out.

"Don't any of you ever listen? I never asked you, mutt."

"I'm a rabbit!"

"I don't care, mutt."

"Okay, I guess we'll just call you an alligator then!"

"Whatever!"

Snow, Bunny, and Sweetie waited in silence for a while. Finally, Snow spoke up. "So, Sweetie…You said that you had a message for Bunny."

"Oh, yeah." Sweetie rummaged through the backpack on her shoulder and pulled out a folded, dirty piece of paper. Bunny examined it carefully. "Well, read it already! I've lost my patience!" Sweetie exclaimed.

"Okay, okay." He slowly started reading the note. There was an awkward moment of silence, until Bunny looked at Sweetie. "*Gewis* is back?"

Sweetie looked surprised. "He is? I guess I wasn't paying that much attention. Oh wait...Giraffey wanted me to warn Toy City. Whoops."

Bunny sighed and handed the letter over to Snow. You see, there were very few stuffed animals who didn't know about Gewis. Although his reign was years ago, the subject was brought up in most stuffed animal history classes. "I can't believe it." Snow looked at the letter again. "Wait. Rudy said, *as you probably know.* We had no idea Gewis is back!"

Bunny shook his head. Was this really happening? Did he really have magic? Did Rudy trust him? "I guess that means he's doing a good job of covering it up."

"Wait..." Now Sweetie was reading the letter. "YOU HAVE MAGIC?"

Bunny didn't know what to say. "I guess so." He remembered when Rudy planted a spike in his ear. Although it healed right away, Bunny was super annoyed at the time. Now everything made sense. Bunny took a deep breath and announced, "We're going on a journey to save stuffed animalkind, I guess."

"Well, after we pack," Snow pointed out. The three brainstormed a plan, revising it and talking about it many times. Finally, when they came up with a decent plan, Sweetie yelped with excitement.

"We're going on a mission!" she exclaimed.

"You two pack," Snow said. "I'll go downstairs to check us out."

Once they left, Bunny started counting their bags, making sure they got everything. Sweetie was still wearing her mini backpack, and, to Bunny's surprise, she pulled out the weapon Giraffey gave her. "Is that the S.A.S. weapon?" Bunny asked in awe.

Sweetie smirked. "Yes." Then she started swinging it around in excitement. "We're going on a mission! We're going on a mission!"

Bunny tried to stop her, but before he could, she accidentally let the S.A.S. weapon slip free from her grasp. Outside, there was a loud thump. *Now we have really done it*, Bunny thought. He boinged to the door and peeked outside, where the crocodile in pajamas was on the floor groaning. "I think we better go," he told Sweetie. Quickly, they grabbed all of their bags and belongings, then got out of there!

"Alligator!" Sweetie squeaked as they ran out of the hotel room.

"I'M A CROCODILE!" the Crocodile shouted, slowly standing up.

"How did you get the S.A.S. weapon?" Bunny asked Sweetie.

"I'll tell you later," Sweetie replied. "We better go before the alligator gets us."

The crocodile lifted himself up, but they were already heading down the stairs. Bunny boinged as fast as he could, and they made it to the lobby, where Snow was about to head up the stairs.

"Why are you running?" they asked.

Sweetie handed Snow their backpack. "Well, it's a long story. But the point is, the alligator is after us!" Right on key, the crocodile came lumbering down the stairs.

"Good thing I already checked us out," Snow said. The three sped towards the door, through the lobby, and exited the hotel.

"Thank you!" Snow called out to the hotel manager, who was arguing with an employee about something.

"This time we can ride the stuffed animal bus," Snow told Bunny and Sweetie. "I found out where the stop is."

Finally, they halted to a stop. If the crocodile had followed them, they had probably lost him. After catching his breath, Bunny noticed many of the stuffed animals around them were whispering about something. Many of them looked disturbed. Snow walked up to a booth and pulled out some money.

"Sorry, but if you have not heard, Gewis has blockaded Toy City, so we cannot transport anyone there or to Amaday," the pelican at the desk told Snow. *It is worse than I thought*, Bunny realized that before now, Gewis hadn't told anyone of his return, but now, he was catching everyone off guard.

"Never mind about covering it up," Snow said. "It seems like he wants the world to know he's back." Something caught Bunny's eye. It was a stuffed animal newspaper. He pulled it off the rack and read the headline.

The S.A. Times

Gewis Returns: This Is Not a Joke

Gewis and His Army Battle the Stuffed Animal Squad to Victory.

Toy City Government Hiring Fighters to Aid the Stuffed Animal Squad. This

Is an International Disaster, But
Please Remain Calm.

So, this was why everyone was whispering.

"We need to make a decision," Sweetie said. Snow, and surprisingly Bunny, did not agree.

"There is no decision," Bunny spoke up.

Snow was impressed. "He's right. We have to hike to Amaday to save the S.A.S."

Sweetie looked at Bunny. "Really?"

"We have to do it for the squad."

"You sound like Rudy," Sweetie said. Bunny felt weird. He was proud, but also a bit sad. He was changing, and he wanted to believe that it was in a good way.

Sweetie shrugged, "Well, I'm fine with some exercise."

It was settled. They headed off for Amaday. You may think that a stuffed animal would not survive in the wilderness. Well, they are tougher than most think. The three friends kept a good pace. Or at least they tried to. Bunny started out with a burst of energy. He was leading the group for a while. But pretty soon he fell behind, and Sweetie took the lead. Snow was humming, Bunny was boinging and panting, and Sweetie was picking up flowers.

There was silence as they enjoyed the beauty of the Rocky Mountains. Snow was deep in thought, but after a few minutes of silence, they said, "Remember when you told me that you wanted to bring a tent?"

"Yeah," Bunny responded.

"Well, it turns out that you were right. We will need it."

Bunny thought about this for a moment. "Wait. We will need a tent?"

Snow sighed. "Remember how long the bus ride up here was?"

"Oh," Bunny said, disappointed.

"Yeah, this will take us a few days," Sweetie said, joining the conversation. Bunny absorbed this, but yet, kept going.

"Oh!" Snow shouted. "I forgot." They pulled a very interesting shape out of their pocket.

"What's that?" Sweetie asked.

Snow handed the thing to Bunny. "It's a weapon!" he exclaimed.

"Although I don't like violence, I think you will need this slapper for our journey," Snow said.

"Thank you," Bunny told his friend. He grabbed the slapper. It was like one of those slap-on bracelets that curl when slapped onto something. It fit in his paw perfectly and its rubber was smooth but painful if slapped hard enough.

"No fair!" Sweetie demanded. "How come I don't get anything?"

"Sweetie, you already have a very powerful weapon."

Sweetie turned her head around. "You mean this? The slinky thing. All this did was make Gewis and his whole army disappear. Besides, he somehow reappeared."

"Well, it hurt the crocodile."

"True." Sweetie looked at the weapon and smiled. "I guess you're right." Then, to Bunny's delight and Snow's horror, she hugged the S.A.S. weapon. *ZAP!*

"Giggle."

"Here we go again."

Sweetie started bawling.

No one expected the journey to be easy. But Bunny had no idea that it would be this hard, long, and tiring. They hiked on for a while. Eventually, Sweetie stopped crying and Snow was very grateful. Suddenly, Bunny heard something. "Stop!" he told his fellow travelers. He listened carefully and then heard it again. There was a small voice. Bunny looked up. He couldn't see anything but could tell that the voice was coming from high up in one of the tallest pine trees.

"I'm sorry Bluebush, but I've found no one," came the voice.

There was silence.

Whoever was talking sighed. Bunny knew that they must be talking to someone over the phone.

Sweetie was restless. "Can we keep moving now?"

"Shhhhh," Bunny gave her a menacing look.

"Wait!" the voice said. "There are three hikers. They must be tough, or they wouldn't be hiking through the woods."

It felt like hours, although only a few minutes. Bunny was sure that the voice had silenced.

"Sorry about that," he told Snow and Sweetie. They kept going.

"What was that?" Snow asked.

"I heard something," Bunny responded. There was a snap loud enough for everyone to hear.

"Was that you?" Bunny asked Sweetie. She had stepped on many dry sticks during the hike.

"No."

They all froze again. "I think that whoever I heard is following us!" Bunny exclaimed. But he was wrong. Emerging out of the bushes was a very large animal.

"Coyote!" screamed Sweetie.

They all ran.

CHAPTER
FIFTEEN

WELCOME TO TOY CITY

The coyote ran after Snow first. "You two, hide!" Snow told Bunny and Sweetie. You see, this was a *real* coyote. This story is mostly about stuffed animals, but don't forget, there are actual animals too.

Snow was speedy for their age, but still not fast enough. They knew that they couldn't outrun the coyote, so, from the corner of their eye, they spotted a tree. Of course, they were surrounded by trees, but this one was different. It was a spectacular climbing tree. Quickly, Snow ran to the base of it, and using their muscles, pulled up to a high branch where the coyote could not reach. There was some growling from the furious animal, but eventually, after Snow stared down the coyote, it moved on.

At that point, Sweetie had also climbed up a nearby tree and Bunny had hidden in a bush. The sharp branches poked him, but he tried to remain calm. Then there was some rustling to the left. Bunny sucked in his breath. So did Snow, who was closely watching. Sweetie clapped her hands in excitement. *Why is she so happy?* Bunny wondered. The rustling got closer. *Remain calm. Remain calm.* He couldn't help it. Bunny jumped out of the bush and screamed.

Snow sighed. With worried eyes, they looked at Sweetie. "We need to do something."

"Do you have a rope?" she asked.

"No. I wish."

The coyote was about to pounce on Bunny. Things were not looking good, until, suddenly, Snow thought of something.

"Bunny! Use the slapper!" they yelled.

Oh yeah. He stopped right in his tracks and turned around to face the coyote. The threatening animal snarled, bent its legs and...

SLAP!

Just like that, the coyote was no longer snarling. Now it was whimpering. Bunny didn't stop. He kept slapping it and no longer was the coyote after him, but Bunny was after the coyote.

SLAP!

Bunny used all of his arm power.

SLAP!

The animal was really whimpering now. It was so startled that it could not even move! Bunny pulled his arm back, then let out another attack of his new weapon.

SLAP! SLAP! SLAP! SLAP! SLAP!

"Alright, that's enough," Snow called from the tree. "Now you're just hurting it."

Bunny was satisfied with his work, and he boinged away. When the coyote was left alone, it ran away, back into the forest, with a lesson learned.

THEY HIKED FOR ABOUT A MILE MORE WHEN BUNNY DE-clared, "I'm getting tired."

"Me too," agreed Sweetie. It was getting dark, so Snow told them to clear the ground and help setup camp. Sweet-ie gathered all of the sticks, not to make a fire, but to clear a flat area so Bunny and Snow could make the tent. After all of that was done, the three of them sat on stuffed ani-mal-sized lawn chairs and ate granola bars and salad.

"You were pretty heroic when you slapped that coy-ote," Sweetie admitted.

"Totally," Snow said. "I think that I picked the right weapon for you."

The three kept on chatting until they started yawning. Then they folded up the chairs, which took a lot of effort, so Bunny was super exhausted. He and Sweetie crawled into the tent. Snow stayed outside for a bit longer. Making sure that nothing would attract bears, they noticed that the stars above were slowly appearing. Then after five minutes of taking in the beauty of the night sky, they also went inside the tent.

Surprisingly, Sweetie had already fallen asleep on her sleeping bag, but Bunny was waiting for Snow. "What were you cleaning up out there?" Bunny asked in a whisper.

"Oh, just our food," Snow responded. "You know that I like it when things are tidy." (They didn't want Bunny to worry about the bears.)

"I've never actually paid much attention to the stars before, but they really are beautiful," Bunny said. The top of the tent was clear, so you could still see the stars from inside.

"You're right. Do you know any constellations?"

"What are those?" Bunny wondered.

"Well," Snow said. "They are shapes made by stars that humans imagined in the night sky."

"Cool." They gazed at the stars for a long time, and it was very comforting for Bunny.

"Today was a busy day," Snow said. "I'm sorry that we couldn't ski more."

"That's okay. Today gave me motivation. No matter how long it takes us to get to Amaday, we're not going to give up. I have to save my friends, and possibly stuffed animalkind." This was another statement that impressed Snow.

"What's that constellation right above us?"

"That's Orion," Snow informed him.

"What is it supposed to be? A chicken?" Bunny guessed.

"Not quite. It's a warrior."

Bunny studied Orion for a moment and then said, "I can see that."

Snow pointed out some of the other constellations. "Now it's really late," Bunny said while yawning again.

"Okay."

"Goodnight," Bunny mumbled.

Then he fell asleep. But Snow stayed awake and listened to the sounds of nature. Crickets chirping. The wind swaying the trees. Bunny and Sweetie snoring. The ferocious grumbling outside.

Snow sat up. They peeked through the door of the tent. Sure enough, a large black bear was sitting there, sifting through their food. Snow sighed. They knew that now the three would have to find food on their own. That would be tricky.

But Snow didn't worry about that right then. A few minutes later, after the grumbling stopped, Snow peeked out of the tent again. They were right. The bear had made quite a mess. They laid back down in their sleeping bags before being startled by a loud noise. Luckily, it was just a loud truck on the highway, which Snow had totally forgotten that they were only about one-hundred-fifty yards away from. This gave them an idea about how to get food.

Snow rolled around in their sleeping bag until they fell asleep too. This was the first day of an almost week and a half-long journey to Amaday.

THE NEXT DAY, THE GROUP WENT THROUGH EVEN MORE BEAUtiful scenery. They followed the same routine as the day before, hiking through the forest. However, when they set up camp again, Snow realized that there wasn't enough food to feed them all, thanks to the bear. When Snow broke the news to Bunny and Sweetie about the missing food, Bunny was upset, and Sweetie was worried about bears. Now she wouldn't take one step out of the tent without someone holding her hand.

Bunny thought this was ridiculous. "Scaredy Cat!" he teased her. Sweetie threw a fit in response. After that was over, Snow explained their plan about getting food.

"We will walk down to the highway, and since Sweetie is the most athletic..."

Sweetie flexed her muscles.

And crazy, Snow thought.

"... I will need you to jump onto a moving car."

"What!" Sweetie shouted. "Well, I mean it sounds fun, but on a highway? Isn't that kind of dangerous?"

"I know what you mean, but don't worry. Since we are in the middle of the mountains, the roads are bendy. And on the switchbacks, when the road turns almost eighty degrees, the speed limit is only 20 miles per hour. Sometimes, the careful people will go even slower. This is still pretty fast, but knowing you, I think you'll manage."

Sweetie seemed very excited about her mission.

"One more thing," Snow said. "If you find any food in the car, jump out immediately. If you can't, then just don't get separated from us. We will try to catch up."

Sweetie saluted.

Bunny was also excited, but mostly to get food. If he had to wait any longer, then he would eat poisonous berries. But Snow told them that the mission would be too dangerous at night, so he had to fall asleep with only a few cups of salad.

In the morning, Sweetie did some stretches before the three hiked down the mountain towards highway 40. "Yes!" Snow exclaimed. They had arrived right at a switchback. It was early Wednesday morning, so not many cars were on the road. Bunny and Snow hid behind a bush while Sweetie bent her knees, ready to pounce like the coyote almost had on Bunny.

A slow-moving car rounded the bend up ahead. Sweetie saw that there were three kids in the back seat. That was a good sign. A lot of kids meant a lot of food. As the car approached, she realized that it was moving very slowly. It was time for Sweetie to jump.

But Sweetie didn't have to do anything—the car rounded the switchback. Then it halted to a stop. One of the windows rolled down. "Alright, Justin, maybe some fresh air will help." A kid, about seven-years old, looking green in the face, rolled down a window. He was holding his stomach.

Once Sweetie realized what the kid was about to do, she turned away. "Ewww," Bunny said from the bushes nearby. The car kept going, but at five miles per hour. This was too easy for Sweetie.

"Hurry!" Snow called. Sweetie jumped onto the roof of the car like spiderman. Inside the car, the father asked, "What was that?"

"No idea," responded the oldest kid.

They started speeding up again. Thinking quickly, Sweetie hopped into the open window. There was a scream. Snow, watching from the bush, sighed. Four doors opened, and everyone hopped out.

"Talking baby!"

"Run!"

"It's an alien!"

A large, black and dirty pickup truck pulled over to where they were screaming. An old man hopped out. "What are ya kids screaming your heads off about?" he asked, yanking up his trousers.

"There's an alive doll!" one of them exclaimed.

"Ha," the man looked at their license plate. He noticed they were from New York. "I'm not talking to you city slickers."

He jumped back into his truck and yelled, "Jeff out!"

Then he sped away at fifty miles per hour.

Luckily, this had bought some time for Sweetie, who returned to the bushes with a large cooler. "Whew," she said, setting it down. "That's heavy." Bunny, Snow, and Sweetie headed off back into the woods, leaving behind the stunned middle-aged man and woman and their three kids.

Once the three friends were away from the highway, and they couldn't hear the dad yelling about "Jeff" and their missing food, Bunny opened the lid to the cooler. Inside was a rabbit paradise. The rest of the day was a success. Bunny's breakfast was so good that he had the energy to walk a whole fifteen miles! At the end of the day, they once again ate like beasts, and fell asleep right away.

Thursday was another average day. But they were pretty exhausted and only covered three miles. Friday morning was important because they had made it to the end of highway 40, and now arrived at interstate 70. As they were walking along the even busier highway, Snow told them about the town ahead called Idaho Springs.

"Idaho Springs...in Colorado?" Bunny asked.

"Yes," Snow explained. "It's weird. But anyway, we can go through it, or we can go around the town."

"I want to go through!" Sweetie demanded.

"Let's just play it safe and go around," Bunny suggested.

"Well, here's the thing. It would be cool to explore the town, but also risky," Snow said.

They thought it through. "If we get caught then we could just pretend to be non-alive," Sweetie said.

"No," Bunny responded, "We would be taken to someone's house. Or worse." All he wanted was to continue the journey. The group ended up listening to Bunny, until he realized that Idaho Springs probably had some good restaurants. He stopped. "We will most likely run out of food before we reach Amaday. Maybe Idaho Springs has some food where we can re-stock."

"You're right," Snow agreed, "Sweetie, I trust you."

Sweetie was on another food-finding mission. She returned nearly an hour later with a pizza box, and the group had food for their journey again.

On Saturday, they stopped to view a cool waterfall. On Sunday, they crossed a bridge over the interstate and headed toward Amaday. The whole time Bunny was thinking about Gewis and the S.A.S.

"How are we going to defeat him?" Bunny had asked Snow one night.

Snow shrugged. "We just have to believe. Maybe we can get toys from Toy City to help us." There was no need for them to alert Toy City about Gewis, as everyone knew about his return, but in order to get to Amaday, they had to pass through Toy City.

Anyway, it was Sunday night. They set up camp and sat down in their stuffed animal folding chairs. "We will get to Amaday tomorrow, if there's no trouble in Toy City," Snow said.

Bunny sighed when he opened up the cooler. "There's only enough food for one," he announced.

"That's okay, I won't eat any—"

"Actually," Sweetie interrupted. "I kind of like finding food. Snow, can you come with me?"

"Sure. Bunny, are you okay staying here and assembling the tent?"

"Yes."

With that, Sweetie and Snow left, and Bunny looked helplessly at the tent bag. Every night he helped Snow assemble it, but he doubted he could do it by himself. Bunny tried not to be a scaredy-cat like he called Sweetie, but now that he was alone in a forest, his ears picked up every single noise. A bird chirped, and he froze. Then a gust of wind blew, and he froze. This was time-consuming because the forest was full of eerie noises. In fact, it seemed to be screaming at Bunny. He kept picturing bears, which wasn't helping.

Not knowing how to set up a tent, surrounded by mysterious noises and images of bears, made Bunny tangle up the tent poles. Snow was speechless when they and Sweetie returned with potatoes. Bunny was just as much with a loss of words, although not about the unruly mess of a tent.

"Potatoes, that's all you got?"

"It's harder to find food than it looks, Bunny," Sweetie responded. "Besides, what happened to the tent?"

Snow helped him assemble the tent and they had a light dinner. Later, Bunny felt kind of sad. Snow could tell because he was not as talkative. Once they were back in the tent, Snow asked, "What's wrong?"

"I miss my old life with the Nobles," Bunny explained. "Also, the potatoes weren't great."

Snow understood. "I miss them, too."

"Already?" Bunny asked. "We just had potatoes!"

Snow sighed. "No, I miss the *Nobles*."

"Oh."

They talked it over for a while. "It's okay to be sad," Snow told Bunny. They both admired the stars and fell asleep soon after. In the morning, Bunny was not sad anymore. In fact, he was pumped up. He had only been to Toy City once, and that was a short trip with the S.A.S.

Like his owner, Bunny loved to learn about and explore new places, especially cities. After a breakfast of carrots, granola, and some more potatoes, Snow pulled a map of the big city out of their backpack. They smoothed it out on the ground and Bunny read the headline:

Toy City!

Population: 534,749

Area: 24 square miles

Founded: When Grey was playing with a stick, a mysterious figure swapped sticks, giving Grey one that was alive. This stick went around tapping toys and making them alive, and eventually, Grey founded Toy City in 1924.

They studied the map of the city. In the dirt, Snow marked an *x* to mark a spot southwest of the city.

"We are here," they said. Then they made a trail with their fingers until it ran into the map. "We will enter Toy City here." You see, although the city wasn't a kingdom or anything, it still was guarded.

"Knowing the situation," Snow continued, "Even if there are guards, they will let us in because they need all the help they can get."

"We can do this," Bunny said confidently.

Sweetie nodded. They packed up their stuff and headed north toward Toy City. After an hour, they arrived. Bunny and Snow gasped. It was about the only stuffed animal-made city that had a skyline. It was a super small skyline compared to New York City's but was still impressive.

"How have humans not discovered this?" Bunny asked.

"Well, the leaders put a magic force-field around it just like they did with Amaday. That's why Toy City is so crammed and packed," Snow replied. There was a 21-story building which is the highest stuffed animal-built building in the world. It was light blue and gleaming.

"What are you guys standing there for?" Sweetie asked. She had been to Toy City many times before.

"Oh, just marveling at its beauty," Snow responded.

"Once you're actually downtown, it's not as beautiful." This disappointed them. The three walked and boinged past a sign that read: *Welcome to Toy City.* There were posters on trees saying that the city's government needed volunteers to form an army.

"They don't realize how powerful Gewis and his army is," Bunny observed.

"Yeah," Snow said, "They need more than small posters to spread the word." There was an old run-down shop on the side of the sidewalk. (There are only wide sidewalks in Toy City—no roads.) Then, a few yards ahead, was a humongous mansion. It was painted white and grey, with a large fence surrounding it.

"Wait a minute," Snow said. "That's too big to be a stuffed animal house. That one is made by humans." They observed it for a bit more before deciding that it was slightly out of the magical force field, but it was still awfully close to Toy City. Another suspicious thing was that it was all so beautiful, except for a small little shed in the front yard. Just as Bunny was about to say something, the door to the shed burst open.

A blue wolf stuffed animal came out and yelled, "GET IN THE SHED! QUICK!" Bunny, Snow, and Sweetie ran inside, and the wolf closed the door.

"What's happening, and who are you?" Sweetie asked once they were inside the shed.

"Remember that voice you heard in the forest?" the wolf asked Bunny.

"Yeah…"

"Well, that was one of my associates. I guess I should say my only associate."

"So, you were the one he was talking to," Bunny realized.

"Yes, and, well, I think that we need to talk."

"Why?" Snow and Sweetie asked at the same time.

"You are trying to stop Gewis, right?" the Wolf said.

"Yes."

"Me and my friend, Bink, are too."

"Your friend and only associate is named Bink. What's your name?" Snow questioned.

"Oh, sorry. I'm Bluebush." Bunny looked at his bushy and blue tail. *That name makes sense*, he thought.

"I'm Snow, this is Sweetie, and this is Bunny," Snow said.

"I know that it may seem strange at first, but I need you to follow me," Bluebush announced. Bunny, Snow, and Sweetie exchanged glances. They all knew not to trust strangers that you just met, but...

Sweetie stepped forward. "Okay." *We have our weapons at least*, Bunny thought. They might need them, just in case. But Bluebush and Bink seemed pretty trustworthy. They all followed the wolf through a door, and then down a flight of stairs. He led them through an underground tunnel. As they walked, Bluebush explained everything.

"I live in this mansion with my owner" he said. "Bink lives in a closet, but he usually spends his time in the city. I wanted you to get in quickly because Gewis's soldiers pass every hour, and if they spotted you, that wouldn't be good."

"Wait," Snow told him. "Gewis has control of the city?"

Bluebush nodded gravely. "It turns out that only a third of his army was there to attack Amaday. The rest came to Toy City afterwards and captured the mayor and everyone with authority."

"But Toy City is so big," Sweetie said. "And Gewis doesn't have an army even close to being able to take over the city."

Bluebush shook his head. "I wish, but the citizens don't have much control here. Once the mayor and his officials were captured, the citizens couldn't do anything to fight back. Some have tried, but they're all in Gewis's prison now."

They arrived at another door. Bluebush opened it and they walked into a closet. Bunny explained all the details of how they had gotten there, with Sweetie and Snow helping too. Then he noticed that there was a strong beat coming from up ahead.

"That's Bink alright," Bluebush said. "Now it's time to get down to business."

CHAPTER

SIXTEEN

BINK THE OCTOPUS

They walked into a small and hot room. In the center, an octopus had headphones on and was humming to himself.

"Bink really likes music," Bluebush pointed out.

Bunny thought of Giraffey, who is an important member of the S.A.S. and a global rockstar. Bluebush walked over to Bink and tapped his shoulder. The bass beat that was blasting stopped. The octopus took off his headphones and turned around.

"Oh, hi there," he said.

Bunny recognized Bink's voice. "You're the one I heard in the forest."

"Yeah. You three are pretty impressive, battling that coyote and all. Especially you, although…"

"What?" Bunny asked.

"Well, I guess you're not as muscular as I remember."

Bunny sighed. "I get that a lot."

Bluebush introduced them to each other. Then they started getting serious. "Okay," Bink pulled out some blueprints. "I have planned out this mission."

"Wait!" Bunny exclaimed. "Aren't those blueprints of…" he paused and looked at them for a moment, "… my lair?"

"This is your lair?"

"Yeah."

"Pretty impressive," Bluebush said. "We got these blueprints in the mail from an ally of ours." Bunny had totally forgotten about his lair and how there had been a bomb planted there. This made him remember blowing up the Noble's house and he instantly felt guilty.

"I heard that Gewis has tried to block off all transportation to Amaday. I think he might have thought that this… uh, train in your lair was some sort of transportation to Amaday." Bunny was pretty upset about this. He recalled Aunt Ducey telling him about the beaver carrying a bomb that had come to her rabbit hole, and how she had allowed him to tour his lair. That must have been one of Gewis's soldiers.

"But why did we get your blueprints?" Bluebush asked.

"Well, we'll have to ask Ducklet," Bink responded.

"Ducklet!" Snow exclaimed. "She's my friend!"

"Yeah, she's been helping us lately."

"Suspicious," Sweetie whispered to Bunny.

Bink set that aside and took out some different and larger blueprints.

"This is a map of Amaday." Bluebush explained that the first step to their mission was getting to Amaday. "We might need to take the Amaday train, although it is heavily guarded."

"What's Gewis going to do with the S.A.S. anyway?" Bunny asked.

"I've heard that Gewis is planning to take over stuffed animals *and* humans." Bunny gasped. Surely Gewis couldn't take over the whole world.

"He wants to deport all of the humans on Earth to Mars." Together, they thought this over.

"Sounds stupid," Sweetie said.

"Sounds straight outrageous, and…"

"We don't even have the technology for that," Bunny said, finishing Snow's sentence. Everyone nodded.

"But you never know what Gewis is capable of," Bluebush pointed out.

Sweetie sighed then tried to understand their plan. "After we arrive at Amaday, we have to sneak in without anyone noticing us," she said, trying to sound very serious and important. But with the babyish voice she had, it didn't really work.

"Exactly." Bink put the blueprints in the middle of the table. They studied the map some more. "This is what we really need to figure out. How to defeat Gewis."

"If only one of us had magic."

Bunny's ears shot up into the air. How could he have forgotten? He had the magic that Rudy gave him! After Bluebush and Bink heard this news, they practically exploded with excitement!

"To celebrate, let's dance!" Bink turned on some music. Next thing after that, he and Bluebush were on the floor breakdancing.

"Bunny has magic!"

"Wow!"

"Bunny has magic!"

"Wow!"

"Bunny has magic!"

Neither Sweetie, Snow, nor Bunny wanted to ruin their fun, but Bunny wasn't sure how powerful his magic was yet. The music stopped.

"Hold on," Bluebush asked, "How did you get magic?"

"From Rudy," Bunny responded.

"What! You know Rudy, creator of the Stuffed Animal Squad?"

Bunny responded with frustration, "Of course I do! Don't you realize that I'm a member of the squad?"

"Really? Cool!"

You see, Bunny had always wanted to be famous, and you might think that being a member of the S.A.S. would make him famous, but it didn't. Everyone else got way more attention. It was as if he was just a regular stuffed animal, not even a Fighting Ally! He stormed out of the room. Bluebush, Bink, Snow, and Sweetie waited in silence for a while.

"What did I do wrong?" Bluebush wondered.

"Nothing, it's just that, well, let me go talk to him." Snow understood how Bunny felt. Snow walked until finding Bunny sitting in a bean bag.

"It's just not fair," he complained. "Why does everyone else get so much more attention than me? It's like I don't have any powers at all."

"Well, you can plop. That's a surprisingly strong power. You can ski. You are kind and smart, and you are clever. Also, very funny. And one thing I noticed is that you don't give up."

Bunny gave some thought.

"But you're right. I'm sorry," Snow said.

They made up and walked back into the room where Bluebush, Bink, and Sweetie were discussing plans. Bunny explained how he felt, and Bluebush apologized.

The three friends had officially made two more. Slowly, they were gaining more allies to help defeat Gewis. It was evening and Bink showed Bunny his sleeping bag. Snow and Sweetie were sleeping right beside him.

"I know that we all worked hard to get here, and today was a big day. So, I agreed with Bluebush that tomorrow will be a day off to relax. But we'll also try to find out more about what Gewis is planning.

"Okay. Goodnight," Bunny told his friends. This time, he fell asleep right away.

BUNNY WOKE UP AND CHECKED THE CLOCK ON THE WALL: *3:00 a.m.* Bunny heard another beat coming from the, what Bink liked to call, the music room.

He hopped out of his sleeping bag and boinged to-wards the beat.

"Boing, a boing, a boing, a boing, a boing." The music stopped playing and Bink answered the door to find Bunny waiting outside.

"What are you doing?" they both asked each other at the same time.

"Well, I heard the beat and wondered where it was coming from," Bunny replied. Bink motioned for him to go into the room.

"I know how you feel," Bink said after closing the door behind them.

"I have always loved making music. But no one ever noticed me. I got really mad and started, well, stealing things. But eventually Bluebush found me and convinced me not to do bad things."

Bunny nodded his head.

"Try not to get so upset about not getting more at-tention."

Bunny sighed. "I will try."

"Okay. I sure did learn my lesson that day."

They looked out the window. The lights along the Toy City skyline were beautiful. "Remember the *Bunny has magic* thing?"

"Yeah."

"Well, it inspired me to write another song." Bink showed Bunny the lyrics to the song called: Bunny has Magic.

"Wait, what do you mean by *another* song? How many songs have you written?"

"Just one other," Bink responded. "Or only one that I'm actually proud of." He showed Bunny the lyrics to the other song.

"It's about you."

"Yeah. Bink the Octopus."

"I like it," Bunny complimented.

Bink beamed.

Bunny yawned. "I'm going back to bed. But one more thing. Do you know Giraffey?"

"Yes, he's my idol."

Bunny wasn't surprised. "Well, I think you should meet him."

Bink nodded in response. "Hopefully we will find out what Gewis is planning tomorrow."

"Yes," Bunny said as he boinged back to bed. Little did he know, they had to find out what Gewis was planning soon because they were running out of time to save the S.A.S.

CHAPTER
SEVENTEEN

THE TRACTOR SHOW

Everyone was ready. Well, everyone except for Bluebush. (He had to stay home with his owner in the mansion.)

"Are you sure that you want to stay here?" Snow asked him.

"Yes. Besides, I'm going to be mission control." Then he pulled out some earbuds. "Put these in your ears. You can communicate with me when you spy on Gewis's soldiers."

Bunny's ears perked up. "We're going on a spy mission?"

Bink nodded. "It's the best way to get information."

The five sat down at a table and dug into a delicious lunch of eggs and BLT sandwiches, while Bunny (who was very happy to have bacon again) and Sweetie asked questions. They were the only two who weren't aware of the mission. "Where are we going to spy?" Sweetie asked.

"The ice skating rink in city square," Bluebush replied.

"Why there?" Bunny chimed in.

"Because Gewis's soldiers have complete control of downtown and they gather on the ice every night to discuss plans."

Bunny found this interesting. Along with the fact that he was going on a spy mission. He, the one that the S.A.S. never trusted to go on missions. He, the loudest member of the squad. Alfredo and Pink Nose Guy were always the ones who spied on the bad guys. Even the leaders laughed at the idea of Bunny going on a spy mission. But here he was.

"I'll try not to be too loud," Bunny told everyone. "But..." he got out of his chair and boinged around the table. "Boing, a boing, a boing, a boing, a boing!"

Sweetie laughed at him. "Is that how quiet you can be?!"

Snow sighed. "Well Bunny, I know you're not the most physically adept stuffed animal for a spy mission, but mentally, you're capable."

There were nods from around the table, although Bunny wasn't sure they were sincere. Everyone had slept in that morning, and Bluebush declared this a good thing because spy missions require energy. Their morning had been slow and mostly full of planning, and now it was almost 3:00

p.m. Gewis's soldiers would start gathering at the ice rink pretty soon.

Once everyone finished their late lunch, they huddled in a circle and put their hands together. "We *will* defeat Gewis and save all of stuffed animal, toy, and humankind," Snow said confidently.

Bunny really wanted to believe this.

"Three, two, one! Go team go!"

So that's how they started their day.

Bluebush walked away from the underground lair, out of the shed, and into the mansion to find his owner. The remaining four debated what to pack. They decided on a camera, some snacks, money, and sunscreen. (Not for sun protection, because they have fur, but Sweetie insisted it would come in handy.)

Then they had a silly argument about whose backpack to bring, and who would carry it. Eventually, they decided on bringing Snow's although Sweetie seemed upset by this.

The group walked down the hallway and up a flight of stairs. Bink opened the door, and they emerged from the shed. Bunny took in a deep breath of fresh air as he popped the earbuds Bluebush gave him in his long, floppy ears.

"Don't worry," Bink said. "We won't have to do much walking. Toy City is small and dense for its large population." They walked past a few more shops and stores, and then past a huge hill. Overnight, it had snowed a bit, so many toys and some stuffed animals were sliding down the hill. Bunny was a bit jealous, as it made him miss skiing, but he boinged ahead to catch up with the group.

"I'm surprised that no one is taking Gewis that seriously," Bunny noticed.

"Yeah," Bink explained. "I mean, the citizens can't do anything to stop him, so they might as well live their lives."

Something caught Bunny's eye. It was a billboard advertising a tractor show. "A tractor show?" he asked.

"Really?" Bink looked at the billboard. "Yes!" Sweetie, Snow, and Bunny looked confused. "Tractor shows are the best," Bink said. "Too bad Bluebush isn't here." When he saw that they were still puzzled, he added, "They do all sorts of tricks and acts."

"But shouldn't we focus on the mission ahead?" Snow reminded him.

Bink took a deep breath. "You're right. Hopefully I can see it after we defeat Gewis."

Bunny didn't know what to say about everyone's confidence. Being the only member of the S.A.S. (or the only former member of the S.A.S) he knew not to underestimate Gewis. Rudy, Squiddy, Giraffey, and Rodger had only defeated him, just barely, and that was with an army. *How in the world are we going to save the S.A.S.?* Bunny thought. *And I don't even know how to use my magic!*

Suddenly, there was a shout. Bunny snapped out of his deep thought and turned to see where the noise came from. There were three soldiers in red chasing after them. "RUN!" Sweetie shouted. They scattered, and the soldiers followed. They seemed to be in peak physical shape, unlike Bunny, who was already boinging slower than usual.

"Looks like the tractor show will come in handy," Bink said. "Follow me!" Bink led them through a crowd of toys, who yelled some rude words at them but stopped once they realized they were being chased by Gewis's soldiers. Now the toys united and took their anger at Gewis out on the three soldiers, who were greatly outnumbered. But the chase wasn't over yet. About a dozen more soldiers appeared.

"It's the rabbit Gewis wants!" one of them shouted. Bunny boinged as fast as he could. A large stadium loomed ahead of them.

"What exactly is your plan?" Snow asked Bink as they ran.

"I'm going to try to shake em' in the tractor show stadium!" They approached the entrance to the stadium where more soldiers in red waited. Fortunately, they hadn't been spotted yet, so they still had time to put on disguises. The soldiers pursuing them had been stopped by a traffic light, so this was their chance. (Although there are only wide sidewalks in toy city, the heavy population still calls for traffic lights.)

Quickly, Snow pulled Sweetie's backpack off their shoulders and started handing everyone things to disguise themselves with. Sweetie smeared sunscreen on her face. "I told you that this stuff would come in handy." Bunny tied his ears into a bun.

"Is everything okay?" someone asked. Bunny looked around wildly before realizing that the voice came from his earpiece.

"Sorry Bluebush," Bunny said, remembering that Bluebush was mission control. "We're disguising ourselves."

"Okay. Continue with the mission and let me know if anything's wrong." Bunny nodded before realizing that Bluebush couldn't see him. He sighed and put on some sunglasses.

"Groovy," Sweetie giggled. Bink yanked on a chef's hat and apron, while Snow put on a sun hat and some gloves. The soldiers behind them were still lost in the crowd at the traffic light, but it would be turning green soon. Quickly, Bunny boinged forward, his friends right behind. They reached the front gates of the tractor stadium.

The two soldiers looked at them skeptically. "Do you have tickets?"

Bunny turned around and realized that the traffic light had turned green, and the other soldiers were running towards them. They were trying to yell, "Stop them!", but their yells were muffled by the crowd.

"We'll just pay," Bink said hurriedly, spotting them too. The guards nodded, and Bunny held his breath. They hadn't recognized him yet.

Bink dumped some cash on the table and raced through the metal detector. Snow went in after him, and surprisingly, the backpack didn't alert the detector, even though the S.A.S. weapon, which was pure metal, was inside.

"Magic," Sweetie whispered as she and Bunny raced through. They were in the stadium! Bink asked a toy where their seats were, and he pointed to row one. Bunny followed his friends down the steps while admiring the stadium. It was probably the largest building in Toy City, an oval-shaped dome with thousands of seats. In the center sat a large track with all sorts of tricks and jumps. They reached their seats and Bunny plopped down.

Sweetie whistled appreciatively, although it sounded more like a quiet shriek. "These are the best seats in the house."

Bink glanced nervously back towards the entrance. "Yes, but we'll be more easily spotted." Suddenly, a large toy truck wheeled into the center of the open-roofed stadium. The crowd grew silent.

"Welcome everyone! Good afternoon," the announcer yelled. "It's December. And we all know what that means... what time is it?"

"It's tractor time!" the crowd echoed.

"Louder!" the announcer shouted. "What time is it?"

"IT'S TRACTOR TIME!"

Bunny's sensitive ears usually would have hurt, but since they were in a bun, he was fine.

"I think that you all know how this works. There are nine amazing tractors, all of which I will introduce soon. And they are here to entertain you with many tricks and flips, jokes and skits."

The gorilla sitting next to Bunny roared with excitement. A slow drumroll started, and the announcer raised her voice triumphantly. "And now, our famous tractors!" The crowd went wild, and the drumroll got loud. Bunny covered his ears, despite the bun.

The first tractor rolled out onto the track of many ramps and jumps. Keep in mind that these are toy-sized tractors, not actual tractors. Although he was the largest of the tricksters, even compared to Sweetie, he was super small. For this reason, Bunny was grateful for front row seats.

Then the next tractor rolled out and was introduced, and so on, until all nine of them were on the track. And then the show began. Despite being there just to avoid being found by Gewis, it was a rather fun show. Bunny sat there and watched them do all sorts of tricks. But then, towards the middle of the performance, one of the tractors turned directly towards Bunny and his friends and rode in front of their seats. Since they were sitting in the front row, Bunny went face to face with the tractor, who snarled.

"I may make a lot of money doing this, but I never mind a little more," the tractor said in a menacing tone.

Bunny paled as he realized what he meant. "There's a price on my head?"

"Yep," the tractor replied. "The reward is in the thousands! Good thing I overheard some of Gewis's soldiers talking about how you and your friends entered the stadium." With that, the tractor pulled out a radio. "They're in row 1, section 53."

Snow, who was sitting next to Bunny, jumped out of their seat. "We have to go!"

Sweetie and Bink were already on their feet too, and Bunny was already boinging up the stairs.

"They're on the run!" the tractor shouted into his radio. "They're on the run!"

"We're on it," someone on the other end replied.

For a while, the audience was too distracted with the other tractors, but now they looked curiously between Bunny and his friends and the tractor. Suddenly, some of Gewis's soldiers jumped in front of them, blocking the rest of the stairs. Thinking quickly, Bunny turned right and cut through a row of seats.

"Slow down!" someone exclaimed.

"Sorry," Snow told the people as they sped past.

"You're blocking my view!"

"You knocked over my soda!"

Bunny ignored the complaints and kept going, boinging as fast as he could. Behind him and his friends, Gewis's guards were chasing after them, provoking another round of complaints. They approached another set of stairs, but more soldiers in red were blocking the way up and towards the exit.

"I have an idea!" Bink yelled, taking the lead. He turned right again, heading back towards the track and the base of the stadium.

"Uh...Bink, that's just a dead end," Sweetie informed him.

"I know!" he replied as they raced down the stairs. "That's why I hope you all can jump."

Bink's plan became clear, and Bunny slowed down a bit. "Are you kidding me?" he asked.

"It's our only option," Bink responded.

Bunny turned around to find the soldiers closing in.

"I think he's right," Snow said.

Bunny finally grasped that this was true. He would rather charge through the track than get caught by Gewis. The squad depended on him. He followed Bink, who hopped the short barricade that separated the track and audience. He boinged as high as he could go and made it over with a few feet to spare. By now everyone in the stadium had noticed them. One tractor, who was doing a flip when they hopped the barricade, was distracted by them entering and face planted into the ground.

"Ohhhh, that looked painful," the announcer said. Then she realized what had distracted the tractor. "GET OFF THE TRACK!"

Bink didn't stop though, and he plowed through the dirt, passing the startled tractors. Apparently, fans had never hopped onto the track before. Sweetie was right behind him, then Snow, then Bunny. He was panting from all this running but kept going. It finally occurred to the tractors to try and stop them. As Bunny was passing the largest tractor, the tractor zoomed forward and rammed into him. The tractor was only half his size, but the force of his motor knocked Bunny to the ground.

"I was about to do a cool quadruple backflip!" the tractor complained. "But *you* interrupted the show."

Bunny quickly got to his feet. (Or should I say rump.) "We'll get out now."

The tractor gave him a hard stare. "You better." Bunny started to boing away, but now the tractor who had turned them in was gaining ground.

"Why didn't you stop him?" he asked the other tractor, who shrugged in response.

Sweetie and Bink were almost to the other side of the track and realized that they didn't have to run anymore. Sweetie ran up one of the jumps and did a twist in midair before landing on her head, which got a chorus of applause from the audience. Meanwhile, Bunny and Snow were struggling. They were running beside each other, desperately trying to escape the tractors. But there was no hope. They were just too slow. Bunny stopped with a triumphant plop and turned around.

"Get me my slapper," he told Snow, who quickly pulled the weapon out of the backpack. The tractors bore down on him. *I'm larger than they are,* Bunny told himself. But it wasn't enough. Right as they got near, he boinged out of the way with fright and tucked into a ball.

The audience gasped with excitement and shock.

"Nice move, Bunny," Sweetie called. Bunny thought she was being sarcastic, but it turned out that he was standing right in front of a wall that tractors tried to hop. But, unfortunately for the tractor going straight for him, he was on the opposite side of the jump and ended up smashing face-first into the wall.

Snow, who seemed to have realized this earlier, also stepped out of the way, although with much more style. Now they were running away, using the opportunity. Bunny boinged up and kept going. Now that the closest tractor was down, they had a head start from the others. He boinged even harder than before. Instead of his usual, "Boing, a boing, a boing, a boing, a boing," Bunny was more like, "Boing boing boing boing boing b-b-b-b-boing!"

Finally, he reached the opposite side of the track and hopped the barrier into the stands. Fans, who now seemed to think this was part of the show, high-fived them as they raced up the stairs. The entrance was near. But the two guards stationed at the front were blocking their path. Bunny, who was still holding his slapper, chucked it at one of them. It was a wild shot, but miraculously, it nailed the guard in the face, and he started jumping around, clutching his nose.

Sweetie yanked the S.A.S. weapon out of Snow's backpack, and it was too much for the last guard. He got out of there, leaving the entrance wide open. Bunny quickly grabbed his slapper, then looked at its shape. It was perfectly sized for fitting around his wrist. He slapped it on his fur like a real slapper bracelet and kept it handy there. Then he spotted two things out of the corner of his eye and raced towards them.

"Bunny!" Snow exclaimed. "What are you doing?"

"I need some souvenirs to remember this," he replied before snatching two toy tractors off the ground. He got back in line and admired them. They were both non-alive toys and the same size, although one was green and the other blue.

"We're fleeing an evil villain's soldiers and you're worried about getting souvenirs!" Bink told him. "Try to stay focused next time."

"Sorry, I will," Bunny said. "By the way, souvenir is a French word, right? It sounds French to me." Bink sighed and shook his head as they arrived on the bustling sidewalk. There were lots of toys and stuffed animals to hide in, but the stadium soldiers had probably called for backup. Plus, their disguises hadn't fooled the tractor, so others would probably see through them too.

"Where are we going?" Bunny asked.

"To spy on Gewis's soldiers."

Bunny had been so caught up in the tractor show and the chase that he totally forgot about the reason they had wandered into downtown Toy City in the first place: finding information about what Gewis was planning.

It appeared that Sweetie and Snow had forgotten too.

"Remember?" Bink asked. "We're going to the skating rink where Gewis's soldiers gather every night."

Bunny looked at the sky. It was almost night-time. December 22nd was coming to a close. Bunny couldn't believe how fast their journey had gone by. He was kicked out of the S.A.S. almost two weeks ago, he and Snow's ski trip over a week ago.

Now they had reached the city square. It was a large park surrounded by bustling sidewalks and tall buildings. Toys and stuffed animals were everywhere in the park–except for the ice skating rink. It seemed as though Gewis and his soldiers had claimed it. Soldiers in red swarmed the ice like an oversized colony of fire ants that decided to go ice skating.

Bink stopped and sat down on a bench. Bunny, who was still clutching the tractor souvenirs he had scavenged from the stadium, used this opportunity to stuff them in Snow's backpack.

"Alright," Bink said. "We'll give any information we find out to Bluebush. Other than that, stay silent and try to blend in."

"Do you have a plan?" Bunny asked skeptically.

"Er…"

"I do," Snow said confidently.

And then they got to work.

Bunny felt bad for Gewis's soldiers. Their red outfits and masks turned out to be extremely uncomfortable. After Snow had explained their plan, the group quickly snuck to the exit of the ice rink, where some soldiers were leaving the rink. They ambushed four of them and slipped into their armor.

Now Bunny, Snow, Sweetie, and Bink were disguised perfectly. As they entered the ice rink, not one soldier looked at them suspiciously. Without worrying about being caught, skating was quite fun. This was part two of Snow's plan: pretend to be a typical soldier and try to listen in on any conversation about Gewis. The third and final part of Snow's plan was to meet at the same bench in the park and discuss what they had learned. So there Bunny was, trying his best to skate. He was on his rump about 50% of the time, but he was getting better.

"I think you're a natural at winter sports," Snow whispered as they skated past gracefully.

"How's everything going?" Bluebush asked. Once again, it took Bunny a few seconds to realize that the sound was coming from his earpiece.

"It's going fine," he replied. "We're on the rink, trying to find out some information.

"Sounds good," Bluebush told Bunny. "But remember, don't act too suspicious."

"Roger that."

Bunny moved his noodle legs around, trying to skate as good as Snow. His legs were severely lacking muscle, so it took a great amount of strength to stay up, let alone move. Meanwhile, Sweetie was crushing some soldiers in a game of ice hockey and Bink was nowhere to be seen.

Suddenly, Bunny overheard soldiers talking. They were clumped by the wall, whispering, but with his amazing hearing, Bunny caught the word, "Gewis." Cautiously, he skated over to the soldiers. Or rather, he *tried* to skate cautiously. But he ended up tripping on the ice and sliding a few yards while also managing to bowl a bunch of soldiers out of his way. Red went flying everywhere, and the soldiers whispering stopped and they stared at Bunny.

He got up on his skates and flashed a smile like nothing had happened. "What's up?" Bunny could almost hear the soldiers rolling their eyes through their masks. Fortunately, they didn't find Bunny's wild skating suspicious and continued their conversation.

"Yes, she has completed it," one of the soldiers was saying.

"Who?" Bunny asked casually.

"Room Decor," the soldier replied. "Gewis calls his machine the S.T.L. Please tell me you know what that stands for."

"Er..." Bunny paused before telling the truth. "No."

The soldier eyed him suspiciously. "It stands for Sleep Then Listen."

Bunny shivered. "That doesn't sound good."

The soldier gave him an even more suspicious glance. "What do you mean? This weapon will give us control of the squad! It seems as though you don't support our cause."

"What!" Bunny exclaimed nervously. "Of course not!" He figured that he had asked enough questions, so he skated away from the group. He left the ice rink through a gate, took off his skates, and shed his red outfit behind a tree. *Finally*, he thought to himself. Fresh air hit him as he boinged to the bench where his friends were waiting.

"What took you so long?" Sweetie asked impatiently. She, Snow, and Bink were sitting on the bench, discussing what they had heard.

Bunny plopped down on the bench. "Plop! So, what did everyone learn?"

"Well," Bink began. His voice was on edge. "I found out when Gewis is going to strike."

"When?" Bunny asked but not really wanting to hear the answer.

Bink sighed. "December 23rd. Precisely midnight."

"But that's tomorrow!" Bunny exclaimed.

Bink nodded. "Yes. We have limited time."

There was a moment of silence. It felt so wrong that Gewis was plotting something during so many holidays. It was right before Christmas, Hanukkah, Kwanzaa!

The silence went on until Sweetie said, "I learned that Gewis has a machine that makes you listen to his every command."

Bunny put two and two together. "And I learned that Room Decor made him a machine called the S.T.L...Sleep Then Listen!"

"Hmmmm," Snow said. "So, this machine must make you fall asleep, then become attuned to Gewis's commands.

I found out that he's planning to take away the leaders' magic and add it to his own."

"That would make him ultra-powerful," Sweetie pointed out.

This made Bunny recall that *he* was given magic by Rudy. He needed to figure out how to use it... and fast.

"Okay," Bink said. "I'll tell Bluebush all–"

"You're not telling anyone anything," someone yelled.

Bunny whirled around to find the soldiers he had been talking to surrounding their bench. The soldier that seemed to be the leader smirked. "Too bad Gewis gave us a voice recording of what your voice sounds like. You acted pretty suspicious, so we listened to it after you left, and the voices matched."

Bunny shrunk in their glare as four soldiers pulled out handcuffs. But before they could get closer, Snow shouted, "Run!"

Thinking quickly, Snow pulled the sunscreen bottle out of the backpack.

"I guess you're right, Sweetie," Snow said after squirting two soldiers with it. "This sunscreen does come in handy!"

"I'll get you for that!" one of the soldiers shouted.

"Thanks! I needed the extra sun protection," the other said. (He appeared to be the least competent.)

"It's six o'clock in the middle of winter, you fool!" the leader told him before chasing after Bunny. Snow tossed the S.A.S. weapon to Sweetie, who started to take out soldiers with it. Soon the soldiers seemed to realize that Sweetie was too scary, and Bink was too fast. So, they let them run off and instead focused on Bunny and Snow. Just like at the tractor show.

Bunny kept going, however. The leader launched some rocks at him, but they went wide, shattering an expensive vase beside the sidewalk. Now Bunny left city square, boinging into the streets of downtown Toy City. Buildings over ten stories tall soared into the air. (Keep in mind that ten stories high is extremely tall for a stuffed animal.)

Toys gathered on the streets. Up ahead was a gleaming blue building which Bunny recognized as City Hall. He kept boinging, but the soldiers were slowly gaining ground. On the other side of the sidewalk, Snow was struggling even more. Suddenly, Bunny got an idea. He knew how upset the citizens of Toy City were about Gewis. He had blockaded their city and overthrown their government! Bunny hollered at the top of his lungs, "Help! Gewis's army is trying to hurt me!"

The crowd of toys and stuffed animals suddenly silenced as they watched Bunny and Snow race down the sidewalk, followed by soldiers in red. They seemed unsure about what to do, afraid of the punishment for helping Bunny.

But then Sweetie started booing Gewis and his army, "Booooooo! Booooo!"

This was all it took. The crowd started booing and surged forward, towards the soldiers.

The soldiers, who realized they were outnumbered, quickly ran away with fear. But the crowd wasn't fast enough to save Snow: a large truck zoomed down the sidewalk and two soldiers hopped out before shoving Snow in the back of the truck. One of the soldiers pulled out a walkie-talkie. "We have the enemy's friend and best asset, which should deter him enough. But just in case, close up the borders. If anyone sees a large rabbit and an annoying baby, arrest them. The octopus has no worth to Gewis."

Then the soldiers hopped in the cab and Bunny watched in shock as his friend was whisked away.

BUNNY LAY IN BED. AFTER SNOW WAS CAPTURED, HE, SWEET-ie, and Bink had trekked back to the shed and informed Bluebush about what happened. On the bright side, they had found out a decent amount about what Gewis was planning, but there were still things they weren't sure about. And, obviously, Snow had been captured.

Tomorrow's a big day, Bunny thought. Bluebush and Bink set up a plan to rescue Snow and then head to Amaday.

So many thoughts were going through Bunny's mind. They only had one day left to save the S.A.S., to save stuffed animalkind. But he was super tired, so he drifted off to sleep without another thought.

ON THE OTHER SIDE OF TOY CITY, SNOW WAS STILL AWAKE, finishing their dinner of stale oatmeal. They sat in Gewis's jail, thinking that all hope was lost. However, somebody else in a different jail was thinking the exact opposite.

"BUT SIR…"

"I have made my decision."

The S.A.S.'s jail was dark and scary, but Lizhat turned away from his fellow bad guys (the ones the S.A.S. captured before Gewis came along) and marched through the room to Rudy, who was in deep discussion with Grey.

"Lizhat?" Rudy asked, surprised. His face was wrinkled and dirty, same with everyone in the dusty room—S.A.S. and bad guys alike.

"I want to make a truce," Lizhat said at once. To his dismay, Rudy was not taken aback at all. Grey, however…

"You?" he laughed. "A truce?!"

"Grey," Rudy said calmly. "Let Lizhat talk."

Lizhat took a deep breath. "I don't like Gewis either, you know. And we've been locked up in here for even longer than you; I'd do anything for fresh air. Please…trust me, we can escape and defeat Gewis together—just this once."

"Ah, yes…" Rudy began.

"I know what you're going to say," Lizhat interrupted. "'You are going to tell me to put my faith in Bunny. Every time someone has come up with an escape plan you just tell us to wait for Bunny."

Rudy frowned. "I know Bunny better than anyone in this room, and I'm almost certain he'll come back."

"BUT WILL HE?" Lizhat shouted, not meaning to raise his voice. At this point, everyone was watching him. "YOU'VE TOLD US THAT FOR WEEKS AND

LOOK WHERE HE IS – SOMEWHERE PROBABLY MILES AWAY!"

Rudy sighed. "Alright, you don't have to believe me. But let's focus on this truce."

"I still don't trust him...or Bunny," Grey whispered.

CHAPTER

EIGHTEEN

HELP FROM SOME FAMILIAR FRIENDS

B unny woke up with a yawn. Outside his window, there was a few feet of fresh snow. *Wow!* he thought.

Bunny remembered that the day was going to be a big one. First, he'd join Bluebush, Bink, and Sweetie in the rescuing of Snow. Then they would leave Toy City to confront Gewis! Bunny got out of his sleeping bag. He boinged into the small kitchen where a surprise was waiting for him – carrot bacon! The last time Bunny had his favorite food was way too long ago. You see, he preferred to have carrot bacon *at least* once every day. This had been one of the longest breaks without it.

"You woke up early," Bluebush said. It appeared that he was the one who made breakfast.

"Well, today's a big day," Bunny replied. "Thanks for making breakfast." In truth, he woke up early with nerves. Once again, Gewis seemed too powerful. How would they stop him? And Bunny was also worried about Snow. What if they couldn't rescue his friend?

"We need to get pumped up," Bink said, walking into the kitchen. He turned a knob on a radio, and it crackled to life and started playing Journey's *Don't Stop Believin'*. Sweetie came into the room, and everyone sat down at the table. The carrot bacon wasn't as good as his own, but Bunny enjoyed it, along with a large fruit salad and orange juice.

Afterwards, he and Sweetie made sure their backpacks were all packed and ready to go. "Good thing Snow gave me my weapon before they got captured yesterday," Sweetie said. Bunny had been using his slapper weapon as a bracelet, and now he looked down at it. Yes, good thing he didn't give it to Snow either, because Gewis's soldiers had probably confiscated the backpack.

Bunny put a backpack on his shoulders and stepped outside. A few seconds later, he was back inside, shivering.

Bluebush laughed. "Good thing we have extra winter coats." The four of them put on the stuffed-animal sized jackets, got themselves together, and walked outside once more. Bink locked the door behind them.

"M-m-maybe I will c-c-come back here again," Bunny said, his teeth chattering from the cold.

"We hope so," Bluebush agreed. "You are our friends, and you know where to find us." They set off towards Gewis's jail in the intense cold. Once they were closer to downtown Toy City, they were met by a surprise! The number of soldiers wearing red had tripled. The streets were swarming with them!

"Quick, hide!" Sweetie said. They ran into a bakery, but some of Gewis's soldiers were having brunch. Sweetie led them outside again, and this time they ran into an alley. But it was a dead end! Some soldiers were coming toward them holding trash bags.

They haven't spotted us yet, Bunny thought.

"Hey!" a soldier yelled. "I've spotted them!"

Out of nowhere, two small stuffed animals appeared from a trapdoor beside them and exclaimed, "Get in here!" Bunny didn't question the orders. He boinged into the trapdoor followed by his friends, and the small stuffed animals closed the hatch just in time.

"Come back here!" the soldier's muffled voices came. There was some banging on the trapdoor. Luckily, it held up.

Bunny recognized the two animals that helped them. "You're fairy godmothers!" he said.

"We are indeed," the first replied. She explained how all of the other fairy godmothers had either been captured by Gewis or ran away in fright. These two, however, decided to fight Gewis. (Remember that fairy godmothers are the tiny, magical, and rare stuffed animals that make larger stuffed animals. Bo Bo is their leader.)

"We're here to rescue our friend Snow," Bunny told them.

"It will be hard," one fairy godmother warned.

Bluebush nodded. "Let's hurry, then."

They followed the surprisingly quick fairy godmothers through a secret tunnel that led them to the jail where Snow was prisoned.

FOR ONCE, THE STUFFED ANIMAL SQUAD DIDN'T THINK RUDY was being wise. He had always been known as the wisest leader, the one everyone went to with questions and concerns. But now, here he was in jail, being laughed at by the squad.

"You really think Bunny will return?" Grey asked tauntingly. "To begin with, there's a very little chance he *knows* about Gewis's return. And now you're expecting him to go on a journey to rescue us?"

Rudy sighed. "You don't have to believe me. But who else can we rely on? Who else will save us."

"The fighting allies?" Piggy suggested.

Rudy shook his head. "My father has probably taken care of them. In fact, he probably took care of them before he took care of us."

Pecan sighed. "Well maybe we're just helpless, then. Maybe the Stuffed Animal Squad is no more." Everyone had thought of this, of course, but the fact that it was said aloud made the mood even more grim. Even Rudy knew it could be true.

Meanwhile, on the other side of Amaday, Gewis was reclining in his son's office and talking to Room Decor again. "Tomorrow we will take all of the leaders' magic, and then use it to take over the world!"

"What time, sir?"

"Precisely midnight," Gewis responded. "Go get a good night's sleep."

Yes! Room Decor thought.

"No," Gewis said with a chuckle. "Why would I let you do that? Wake up at six and make sure the S.T.L. is in good condition."

Room Decor sighed. She was loyal to Gewis, but he could be strict sometimes. Then she walked out of the room and headed to bed, the last time she would do this.

AS THEY WALKED THROUGH THE TUNNEL, BUNNY REALIZED something. "We know that Gewis is planning to take away the leaders' magic and that he has an army of two hundred but is that really enough to take over the world?" he asked.

"You're right," Bink agreed. "Maybe the S.T.L. is a superweapon."

"Well," Bluebush said. "Whatever it is, I know that we can handle it."

"I'm just counting on Bunny's magic," Sweetie chimed in.

"Hurry it up!" one of the fairy godmothers called. "We're almost there!"

Bunny was exhausted and the tunnel was cramped and hot. Quickly, he shed his winter jacket and left it on the side of the tunnel.

"Don't worry," Bink told him. "The jackets were cheap."

Then the fairy godmothers instructed everyone to be quiet because if they talked, guards from above could hear them. The ceiling of the tunnel looked fragile and breakable. Every once and a while it creaked, so it made sense that it wasn't very soundproof.

Finally, the group arrived at another trapdoor. "This will lead us into the staff room. I have a feeling that it will be swarming because Gewis's soldiers are lazy," a fairy godmother explained.

"Wait, the jail has a staff room?" Bunny asked.

"Yeah. It's supposed to be for a few guards having lunch. But that's not really how it works out."

The fairy godmothers apparently forgot how privileged they were to be small and how easily Bunny, Sweetie, Bluebush, and Bink would be spotted. But by the time they realized this, it was too late. They emerged from the trapdoor and every soldier wearing red in the staff room turned to watch them emerge. One of the soldiers shouted, "Get them! It's the large rabbit and annoying baby!"

Everyone charged at Bunny and Sweetie. Luckily, Bluebush and Bink were prepared to battle. Everyone except Bunny started fighting. All he could do was plop. But then he remembered his slapper!

Next to Bunny, Sweetie took out her weapon.

"You're going to fight us with a broken slinky?" one of the soldiers asked.

"Yeah," Sweetie responded. Then she took out ten soldiers, all of them groaning on the floor.

"I didn't know that parts of this triathlon would hurt," one of them said.

"We have to pick up our game if we want to win," the other responded. Bunny was confused by what they meant, but he kept fighting with his slapper anyway. Suddenly, one of the fairy godmothers, who was counting the members in the break room, realized something.

"Aha!" she exclaimed. "None of these guards are beavers, and they said something about a triathlon." Bunny still didn't get it.

But apparently Bluebush did. "So Gewis must have tricked them into joining his army by convincing them that it was a triathlon."

Then Bunny caught on. "I get it…" he started to say. But one of the guards lunged at him and smacked him to the ground.

"Ow," he said.

"Well, well, well. You're a very realistic robot."

Bunny tried to explain what was actually happening, but he realized that it was no use.

"Prepare to meet your doom!" the soldier shouted.

But Bunny pulled out his slapper. *SLAP, SLAP, SLAP!*

The soldier started laughing. "That tickles!"

Good enough, Bunny thought. Then he moved on to slap some more.

He slapped another soldier so hard that her mask fell off, and Bunny gasped.

"You're…one of my relatives!"

And then it all made sense. Gewis had sent a soldier to place that bomb in Bunny's lair. Then, the soldier found his relatives' rabbit hole and recruited them for the triathlon.

"WAIT!" Bunny shouted. "If you're a rabbit, take your mask off!"

There was some hesitation, but soon about half the guards in the room had taken off their red masks and revealed their faces. Bunny recognized all of them, and they recognized Bunny too.

"Wait…" they said. "You're not a robot?"

"No!" Bunny exclaimed. "You're working for a villain!"

There were some puzzled looks across the room. Even the non-rabbits had stopped fighting. Sweetie, Bluebush, Bink, and the fairy godmothers watched Bunny with surprise. "Let me explain," Bunny said. Then he told his relatives about how the triathlon was fake, and they weren't fighting robots. It took some time, but eventually the rabbits caught on, and they took off their red gear, thanked Bunny, and hopped away. Bunny was surprised at how little questions were asked and a little annoyed that they didn't want to stay to help.

However, the rest of the soldiers laughed at Bunny and continued fighting. Although half the soldiers were gone, the remaining ones seemed to handle just fine.

"Bunny!" Sweetie called to him. "We don't need to fight them all. We just need to get out of this room and find Snow!"

Then he remembered something from the tunnel. "Get back in the tunnel!" he called to the fairy godmothers and his friends. So, they did, and Bluebush locked it just before the soldiers rushed in.

"Follow me," Bunny instructed them. They followed him to where the ceiling looked extra breakable.

"Good idea," the fairy godmothers noticed.

"Hurry!" Bink said, sensing that the trapdoor behind them was going to break soon. (The soldiers were banging on it with quite a lot of force.)

Sweetie pulled out the S.A.S. weapon and gave the ceiling a whack. Right away, it crumbled. They all pulled themselves out of the tunnel. About fifty yards down the hallway was the staff room, full of commotion. But no one expected them to sneak out into the hallway.

"Wait," one of the fairy godmothers said. "I have to go back into the tunnel. I'll draw them past this spot and make them think we're retreating."

"Okay," the second fairy godmother agreed. "I know the code that will get us into the jail cells."

"Great!" Bunny exclaimed. "Then we can rescue Snow and save the world!"

But there was still more to do. The fairy godmother jumped back in the tunnel while the other led Bunny and his friends to the door that led to the jail cells. She typed the code into a black keypad, but right when she did, an alarm went off. "I should have known better," she grumbled. "I guess it's my turn to distract the guards." Then the fairy godmother ran off. Once again, it was just the four of them. Sweetie yanked the door open, and they stepped into a long hallway of jail cells. Bunny spotted a really big shelf full of supplies.

"Quick!" he said. "Hide behind here!"

"That's what the guards are expecting us to do!" Bink pointed out. They all scanned the room for a good place to hide. The sound of stomping feet came closer.

Suddenly, a familiar voice said, "There's a good hiding place back here!"

"Snow!" Bunny said happily.

"Hurry!" his friend called back. The group raced to the closet Snow was talking about, passing Snow's cell. It was small and cramped and Bunny immediately felt bad for Snow. Just staying in there for a minute looked like torture! Finally, they arrived at the closet. Bink threw open the door and they waited in silence.

Bunny heard some voices talking. "Those animals that everyone fought in the staff room must have been a diversion for someone else," one of the soldiers said.

"Hold on," another responded. "I'm uploading the security footage."

Oh no! Bunny though.

"It looks like five of them. Apparently, both of the small ones ran away."

"Ha!" they both laughed. "Trying to start another diversion."

"Well, I guess we'll just stay here and make fun of this polar bear until the others reveal themselves!"

"Ha! Guess what, he tried to outrun the guards who captured him!"

Snow cleared their throat. "I'm non-binary."

"Non-binary?" one of the soldiers looked puzzled. "Whatever. Looks like you're about to be trapped here for the rest of your life."

"Looks like you're about to be ambushed," Snow said. The soldiers turned around, but they couldn't draw their weapons in time. Sweetie zapped one of them with the S.A.S. weapon while Bunny slapped the other with his slapper.

One soldier grabbed his walkie-talkie and said, "We need backup."

Bunny looked nervously at his friends. *Please say never mind*, he thought.

"Never mind," the guard spoke into the walkie-talkie.

"Why would you do that?" the other asked. Then she reached for her own walkie-talkie, but thinking quickly, Bink took both of theirs away.

"Wow," Bluebush said. "Why would he say never mind?"

"Well," Bunny told them in disbelief. "I'm not sure. I just…I don't know. I didn't want him to say never mind, so right after he said that I thought, 'please say never mind'."

"Now that sounds like magic!" Sweetie exclaimed.

Suddenly, one of the fairy godmothers from before appeared. "I realized that making a diversion didn't help, so I found this key." The fairy godmother held out a large key. Bunny took it and unlocked Snow's cell.

"Thanks for the help," they told the fairy godmother.

"No problem," she replied. "Hopefully, I'll see you back in Amaday."

Then the fairy godmother walked away, leaving Bunny, Snow, Sweetie, Bink, and Bluebush.

"Well," Snow told the group. "I think it's about time to stop Gewis."

"Yep," Bunny agreed. "It sure is."

"First we need to get out of here," Sweetie reminded them. "We're not in Amaday yet, folks."

"Is this jail break really just halfway over?" Bunny complained.

"At least you have magic," Snow said. "That was pretty cool to watch."

"And I have my weapon," Sweetie added.

"Stop calling it yours," Bunny told her. "It's actually Giraffey's." This reminded him of the S.A.S. Although he was mad at them for kicking him out, Bunny was missing them. The team decided on using the tunnel to get back to Toy City. Most of the guards had gone back to the staff room, assuming the trouble was over, so they got to the hole in the floor pretty easily. Then they jumped back into the tunnel and started running again. Far behind them, an alarm went off, but it was too late for the soldiers, because the group made it out of the tunnel and were safely back on the streets of Toy City.

Snow read a nearby clock that was on a tower. "Wow. It's only 1:00 p.m. We have nine hours to get to Amaday and stop Gewis."

"We should take the Amaday Express," Bluebush said. The five friends headed for the exit of Toy City, and Bunny realized that his goal was coming true.

He was returning to Amaday.

CHAPTER

NINETEEN

BLUEBUSH CRACKS THE CODE

"You have to be kidding me," groaned Bunny. "At least there aren't as many," Snow responded.

The group was almost at the secretive train station that would lead them back to Amaday. But first they had to get past even more soldiers.

"This is getting ridiculous," Bunny said.

"I never said that it would be easy," Bluebush replied. "After all, we are saving the world." They approached where the soldiers were stationed. Sweetie yawned. Once again, she pulled out her weapon and defeated them.

"Actually, this is just getting annoying, rather than hard," she said.

Bunny noticed something on one of the soldier's uniforms, but he shook the thought away and turned around with Snow to admire the beautiful Toy City. In the distance was the large tractor show stadium. Its circular shape looked like a pancake beside a milk carton when sitting next to the tall buildings.

Bunny looked even farther out and saw the snow peaked Rocky Mountains. He couldn't believe how far he, Snow, and Sweetie had hiked. Their adventures in Toy City were exciting. *Hopefully we will be back soon*, Bunny thought. But if they couldn't manage to free the S.A.S. and beat Gewis, he and his friends might never have the chance to return to Toy City. But Bunny convinced himself to think positive.

Up ahead, Bluebush sighed. He was at the entrance to the Amaday train. "What's wrong?" Bink asked.

"There's a code." They all gathered behind Bluebush and studied the door. It was way too thick and not bustable. Usually, fighting allies and people who wanted to visit the squad would use the train to ride to Amaday. But, of course, Gewis had blockaded Toy City and all transportation to Amaday.

"Well, I hope that we can get lucky," Bluebush said, and punched a random set of numbers into the keypad.

"Password invalid," said a creepy computer voice.

"I wouldn't mind more walking, although it would take too long," Snow said. Everyone started shouting out random suggestions for the code.

"Gewis!"

"Evil!"

"555?"

"Froggy!"

"Password!"

"1234!"

Bluebush started to type some of these in, but Snow stopped him. "I have a feeling that you only get three tries until it sets off an alarm." This seemed pretty reasonable.

"We only have two more tries," Bunny said. They all sat down to think.

"Is there some way to figure this out?" Then Bunny remembered something important.

"Those soldiers back there that Sweetie defeated," he told everyone.

"Yeeeeaaaahhhh?" Sweetie asked.

"They all had numbers on their uniforms. Five, six, four, and one."

Bluebush stood up straight and typed in this code. But it didn't work! He grumbled.

"This is an outrage," Bink said.

"Well, this is a super villain about to take over the world," Snow pointed out. "He probably wouldn't just put a top-secret code on his guards' uniforms."

"You're right," Bunny agreed. "But those numbers must mean something.

Bluebush was getting impatient. "We only have one try left," he said. Bink suggested thinking some more, but Bluebush did not like this idea. "I'm tired of thinking!" Bluebush shouted. Then, without thinking, as he was tired of it, Bluebush slammed his fist into the keypad.

"Wait!" Snow told him.

But it was too late. For a while, nothing happened. Then the keypad dinged and said in a friendly voice, "Access granted."

The heavy door slid open.

"Lucky guess," Bluebush said. He shrugged, and then walked inside. They all followed him. "Sorry that I lost my temper."

"Well, it turned out to be a good thing," Bink responded. A dim light turned on. Behind them, the door slid shut again.

"There aren't any fighting allies to run the train," Bunny explained. It occurred to him that only he and Sweetie had ridden it before. He led the way and clambered into one of the train cars, plopping down in a seat. The last time Bunny had done this was exactly two weeks ago after he had been kicked out of the squad. Snow, Sweetie, and Bink sat next to him. Each car could only hold four people, so Bluebush had to ride in another. Bunny pushed a button, pulled a lever, and they left the station! This train ride was much different than the last one. This time, instead of feeling sad, he was extremely nervous. None of them had any idea of what to expect. The thing that really lingered on his mind, though, was that he had magic. But Bunny still didn't know how to control it.

They rode in silence for ten minutes, winding through the underground train tracks, heading up mount Amaday. Behind them, in the rearview mirror, Bunny saw Bluebush's car do the same. Finally, they arrived at the Stuffed Animal Squad's base at the top of the mountain.

The five of them hopped off and huddled on a bench. "I'm so excited to meet the whole Stuffed Animal Squad," Snow said.

"Me too," Bink and Bluebush agreed in unison.

Out of nowhere, Bunny picked up on someone yelling something. He listened some more, and then picked out what they were saying.

"Quick, hide!" Bunny shouted. They all jumped behind a bush. Bunny had heard one of Gewis's soldiers say that they saw the trains arriving.

The soldiers came into view. "This wasn't here yesterday," one of them said. "Check the perimeter."

Bunny could already tell that Gewis's original beaver soldiers were much more competent than the new recruits. When the soldiers weren't looking, the five friends ran behind a wall. "Let's go for it!" Sweetie said. Then, before anyone could argue, she took off running and the others followed her. Fortunately, the soldiers who saw the train were the ones guarding the door. There was no one there to stop the friends from entering Amaday.

"Alright, we have to be sneaky," Snow said. "Does everyone remember the plans?"

Bunny reached the handle and pulled it down. Slowly, the door creaked open, and the group jumped into Amaday's entry room. Inside, it was strangely vacant. The computer desks where Bunny used to work before getting kicked out of the S.A.S. were empty of carrot bacon that he stashed there, and OHM's office didn't even have a desk.

"I just remembered something," Bunny whispered. "Gewis will be able to sense us with his magic."

Bluebush grumbled. "Just as I suspected. There's a flaw in our plans."

"No," Bunny told him. "All we have to do is find where everyone is and free them."

"Yeah, but how will we do that without getting caught?"

"That's what we have to figure out."

"Can we just go already?" Sweetie groaned. While the group discussed what to do, she turned around and observed Amaday. Much had changed since Giraffey had sent her on a mission to find Bunny. Usually, stuffed animals would be swarming the area, but no one was to be seen. Then suddenly, she broke into a fit of laughter.

"What is it?" Bunny asked.

They turned around to see what Sweetie was laughing about.

Bunny gasped with shock. "This is not funny at all."

"But..." Sweetie giggled some more. "His face is so funny!"

Gewis, who had just stepped out of Rudy's office, grumbled. "You won't be laughing any more after this. Guards, get them!"

CHAPTER
TWENTY

ONLY SWEETIE REMAINS

I f you were wondering what Sweetie was laughing at, well, it was Gewis's old and wrinkled face. It looked hilarious and cartoon-like. But of course, no one else was laughing. Because they were caught. Gewis's soldiers charged at them. (And these are his personal soldiers, who were actually trained well.)

"Run!" Bunny shouted. He was getting tired of this constant boinging. Everyone split up and started running around the base. Unfortunately, Bunny was the first to get caught. A tall and muscular beaver grabbed him and escorted him to another set of soldiers who tied him up and threw Bunny into the squad's jail. Then Bink was caught, and he went through the same process.

Pretty soon, only Sweetie was left, still full of energy and running away from the soldiers and Gewis, teasing him about his face.

"I will get you, ya little baby!" he shouted.

"I'M A TODDLER!" Sweetie yelled back.

They ran around for a bit, before Sweetie quickly changed directions, and ran out the door.

"Oh well," Gewis said. "I don't think she can do much anyway."

Then the guards closed the doors to the jail, locking Bunny and his friends inside. Snow grumbled, "I've been captured enough already." Then they realized something. They weren't alone in the jail.

"Bunny…"

"You're back!"

"H-how?"

"Darn it, I had a bet going!"

"Who is this?"

"No, who is *this*?"

These were just a few of the squad's reactions, and, despite the circumstances, Bunny was super excited to be reunited with the S.A.S.

"Welcome back!" they shouted. Bo Bo came over to untie them, and there was a big reunion. After that, Grey came over and apologized. He explained to Bunny how most of them had gone crazy because of Gewis's strong magic.

"I knew something was wrong," Bunny said. Then he introduced the S.A.S. to Snow, Bink, and Bluebush. Soon everyone realized that they had to hurry.

Rudy stepped forward. He cleared his throat. "I know that our meeting room is not available," he stated. "But I know that we can get out of here and stop my father and his scheme." The other seventeen listening nodded. "Let's start brainstorming ideas."

"Quietly!" Giraffey added. "We don't want to draw attention."

They took turns whispering ideas. But none of them seemed good enough to work. Then Giraffey asked, "Where's Sweetie?"

"She might be our last hope," Bunny explained. "She's outside, hopefully trying to free us." The talking and planning started again, but it turned into bickering. Everyone was stressed.

Finally, Rudy spoke. "Just pretend that we're fighting the bad guys, like our usual battles."

Suddenly, a familiar voice shouted, "You know we are still here!"

It was Lizhat.

Everyone turned to look at the bad guys, still there in a dark corner.

"You never escaped?" Bunny asked, surprised.

"Well, no, obviously," Lizhat grumbled. "That darn Gewis made it too hard, with all his new security."

Bunny's face lit up. "You don't like Gewis either?"

"Of course not! No one likes him, not even us, you nincompoop," Lizhat replied.

"Now we just need to figure out how to get out of here," Giraffey said. "Gewis has control over the purple pear tree, so our magic is limited."

Rudy cleared his throat again. "But we have Bunny's magic." There were gasps from all around. No one besides Rudy, Giraffey, Bunny, and his friends knew about this magic. Suddenly, stuffed animals started talking at once and asking questions. Pecan came over to congratulate Bunny on his power.

"Thanks," Bunny mumbled in return. But really, he was thinking about how badly their plan had gone wrong. Right away, Gewis had found them. There they were, trapped in jail.

Then suddenly, Sweetie's head appeared in vent towards the top of the jail room. "How's the weather down there, Giraffey?" Sweetie said. "Looks like you owe me some pineapple."

A FEW MINUTES EARLIER, SWEETIE HAD RUN OUTSIDE AND WAS hiding behind a tent, out of sight from any soldiers. After catching her breath, she thought of something. "The vent!"

The soldier inside the tent heard this and peeked their head out, but Sweetie was already long gone, heading back towards Amaday. She quickly arrived on the platform in front of Amaday, which held the squad's jet. She took the time to appreciate the view, something she would never do in front of her friends. But while Sweetie made fun of them for enjoying nature, in truth, she enjoyed it herself.

The beautiful mountains surrounded Amaday, although they were all shorter so Sweetie could see the distant skyline of Denver, miles away. The bad guys' mountain sat to the left, directly across a canyon. Other than the remains of the base, the mountain was quite beautiful. Sweetie sighed and turned her attention back to the mission at hand.

Rudy had once told her that Amaday wasn't originally meant to be a base, so there were some flaws in the design that he had to fix. Fortunately for her, though, the person he hired never got around to addressing one flaw. Bluebush and Bink had found this vent in the blueprints of Amaday, and it became their plan B. Obviously, plan A of sneaking into Amaday and freeing the squad from the jail's doors had backfired.

Sweetie found a toolkit and snatched a screwdriver before bending down and examining the vent. It was small for humans, but perfect size for most stuffed animals to fit. She used the screwdriver to take out the screws that held it to Amaday's walls, and it clattered to the ground. Sweetie grimaced at the loud noise but determined that nobody had heard. She set the screwdriver down and jumped into the vent before crawling through it, towards the jail.

After a lot of crawling, spiders, and dead ends, they reached the jail. Down below, the squad chatted nervously, and Sweetie realized that she would be the hero! She reminded Giraffey of his promise: if she found Bunny and returned to Amaday, he would give her a bunch of pineapples! Sweetie's mouth watered as she thought of her favorite food. But first, there was a slight problem. She couldn't get the vent door open.

"Use the screwdriver," Snow said from below.

Sweetie reached for the screwdriver, but Rudy stopped her. "Wait! I installed an alarm so that if the vent is ever opened it alerts Amaday."

This disappointed everyone. They thought in silence before Lizhat sighed. "Okay, we made a truce, so I guess I should follow it."

Everyone turned to him. "I know you've always wondered how we escape the jail. Well, it's through that vent right there."

"So that's how you always get out!" Bunny said.

"Yes," Lizhat explained. "And there's a secret electrical circuit that disconnects the alarm." Another bad guy showed the squad a small box installed in the wall.

"Well," Grey said. "What are we waiting for?"

Lizhat walked over to the box in the wall and pried its lid open with his fingers. On the inside was a scrambled mess of wires and buttons. Lizhat jimmied with it a bit, pulled a red wire, and there was a quick static noise. "Open the vent now!" he told Sweetie.

Sweetie saluted and banged it. The vent door popped off and clattered to the floor below.

"Hooray!" Bunny shouted.

Quickly, Alfredo put his hand over the rabbit's mouth. "Shhhhh."

"Nice job Lizhat," Bo Bo said approvingly.

"I was wrong to not trust you," Grey told him.

There could have been more praises, but they had to hurry. Gewis would be striking soon. "Anyone who can fit, follow me," Sweetie said.

One of the bad guys, who was super strong, threw stuffed animals up into the vent. For the slightly larger ones, Sweetie dangled out of the vent and pulled stuffed animals up. This process was repeated over and over until only the large stuffed animals that couldn't fit in the vent remained.

"Sometimes I really wish I was smaller," Pecan said, exasperated.

"Keep calm," Sweetie told them. "I'll find the key and free you."

She was about to close the vent when Rudy said, "Stop." Every stuffed animal turned to face him. (Except for a few in the vent, who only got a view of a rump.) "We need these stuffed animals. Finding the key and freeing them will be risky and will waste time," Rudy said. "Bunny is the only one with magic now. The sheep dolls gave me a prophecy, and he must come."

"But how?" someone asked. "He and the others can't fit in the vent!"

Rudy looked firmly into Bunny's eyes. "You know what to do."

For whatever reason, Bunny did. Something in the back of his mind told him. Focusing, he pointed his hand at the vent.

"Be calm, Bunny," Rudy said.

Some of the bad guys started laughing. (The scene probably looked ridiculous. I don't blame them.)

Bunny took a deep breath and ignored this. He thought of the Nobles, and how much he missed Miles. He thought of the S.A.S., and how he would be welcomed back into the squad if they defeated Gewis. He thought of Toy City, and all the stuffed animals on the planet, who all relied on him. But most of all, Bunny thought of Snow, who had become a great friend over the last month.

Then, out of nowhere, a blast of green light came from his paw and hit the vent passage. Slowly, the vent got wider and wider, until it expanded over two times the size as before.

"You did it!" Snow exclaimed.

"Now we can all fit," Bluebush said happily. Everyone else stood there in shock. Rudy smiled and nodded at Bunny, who, although he was very dizzy, smiled back.

CHAPTER
TWENTY-ONE

THE LARGEST BATTLE YET

Bunny set down his backpack, which he had been carrying the whole journey. Then he plopped on the nearest beaver.

When the guards posted at the doors of Amaday saw 28 stuffed animals charge out of a vent, they wet their pants and ran, thinking that facing the consequences from Gewis would be better than being beaten to pancakes.

The squad burst into Amaday and immediately started fighting, to the huge surprise of Gewis, who had been in his usual spot reclining in Rudy's office. Even though they had the element of surprise, the odds still weren't good for the squad. The S.A.S. and the bad guys had been in many battles before. But they had never teamed up; working together turned out to be a bit of a problem. There was also another problem. No one besides Rudy, Squiddy, and Giraffey were prepared to battle Gewis. His magic and his soldiers were extremely powerful.

Bunny found out that he had become a much better fighter. With his slapper and his plopping, he gave a big advantage to the S.A.S. But still, Gewis had the obvious upper hand. Bunny sat in awe on top of the beaver he plopped, watching Gewis use his magic. The villain was in front of a closet door, zapping various stuffed animals with flashes of brown. Bunny wondered what was in the closet.

Then he realized that he should start fighting. But while he was distracted by Gewis, a soldier snuck up on him and started to tie him up. "Help!" Bunny shouted as he struggled against the soldier. Fortunately, Pecan came to his rescue. She started pecking away at the soldier, who yelped, dropped his rope, and ran away in fear.

"Thanks," Bunny whispered to Pecan, who was still one of his best friends.

"Anytime," Pecan told him. Then she zoomed away to help Albert fight a soldier.

Bunny watched the scene play out. It was clear that Gewis's plan was to tie the S.A.S. and place them against the wall. A few bad guys and a few squad members were already sitting there, helpless. Bunny realized that this would be the perfect position for Gewis to zap them with the S.T.L. Bunny couldn't let this happen. Although the plan he had in mind was going to take a lot of guts, it would be worth it.

I need to find the Nobles, he thought.

"I'll start first thing tomorrow," the handyman said.

Miles was eating his lunch, but when this guy (who was supposed to fix their living room) arrived, he quickly stopped and put on his mask.

Another thing about this story that you can't forget: it takes place in the middle of a global pandemic. Although Covid-19, the virus that started this pandemic, doesn't exist for stuffed animals, it does for humans. The Nobles were careful about Covid-19, but apparently the handyman was not. He had no mask on and was coughing all over the place. Leigh, who was working and, in a meeting, gave the man a stink eye.

After fifteen minutes of examining the living room damage, the handyman walked back to his pickup truck. "I'll get to work first thing tomorrow morning," the handyman told Darren. "But first I need to know how your living room got destroyed."

Darren didn't want to tell the handyman about Bunny and the bomb. Besides, he wouldn't believe it! Instead, Darren informed him, "We watched some dogs last week. They were pretty wild."

The handyman nodded. "Sure looks like it indeed." He opened the door to his truck and hopped in the cab when a non-stuffed animal rabbit scurried across the yard.

"You know, that rabbit reminded me that just a week ago, I saw the craziest thing," he said, rolling down the window. "I had just done an odd job up in Winter Park. I was on my way back here, going down highway 40. Then I noticed a family pulled over on the side of the road. I sped away, of course. Didn't want anything to do with those green-faced city slickers."

"Wait," Darren interrupted. "If you don't like the city, then why do you work here in Denver?"

"Money," Jeff replied. "People here don't know how to fix a thing! But anyway, they said something about a doll who was alive, and when I passed their car, there was indeed an alive doll! I still don't believe it. And then, even wilder, as I went around a bend, I noticed a stuffed animal rabbit and polar bear signaling to her or something."

Miles, who had just walked outside to see why the handyman hadn't left yet, gasped.

"Anyway, you might think I'm crazy, but that ain't true. I saw those stuffed animals with my own eyes!" Then the handyman sped off. "Jeff out!"

Miles walked back into their house and up the stairs to his room. Once he got there, he sat on his bed. *Was Bunny really in Winter Park?* This didn't seem possible. But from the way that Jeff had explained it, one of the figures he saw sounded like Bunny. Then Miles got another thought. The handyman had also talked about an alive doll. *Could that be Sweetie?*

It must have been. Right around the time Darren had kicked Bunny out of their house, Sweetie had gone missing as well. That was also the case with Grey, which Miles thought was somehow connected with Bunny. But he never realized that any other stuffed animals besides Bunny were alive.

How have I never assumed that? Miles thought, feeling confused. *I guess I just accepted that Bunny was part of the family and never really considered how weird it is that he can talk.*

Now Miles felt uneasy. He knew all about Bunny's personality, but not the other very important parts. *Where did he come from? How was he made?*

The Nobles still hadn't recovered from when Darren kicked Bunny out, but Miles knew that even his dad was feeling sad and guilty. However, could they trust Bunny? He was a talking stuffed animal after all! He could just as well be an alien.

Miles went downstairs and decided to talk to Leigh about this. Then Miles walked past a closet and froze when he heard something.

"Owner?" Miles jumped. The closet door opened, and Bunny pulled him inside.

"You're back!" Miles shouted with joy.

"Yes," Bunny replied. "But is it safe for me to show up in front of Big Guy?"

"I think so. He really misses you. We all have." Bunny and his owner stepped into the hallway. Once Louisa saw him, she ran over to hug Bunny.

"I think you owe us an explanation," Leigh said, coming out of her office. Darren appeared and apologized for losing his temper and kicking Bunny out, and Bunny apologized for throwing a live bomb into their living room. Then the Nobles listened carefully as Bunny explained all the important parts of his story. Then Bunny mentioned his new friend.

"Who's this new friend of yours?" Darren asked.

Bunny looked at Leigh. "Snow."

Everyone else looked puzzled, but Leigh smiled and explained all about Snow. "I used to snuggle them all the time. Snow even went to college with me."

Then Miles asked a question, even though he already knew the answer. "There are other stuffed animals who are alive?"

Bunny sighed, "Yes. And I need your help." He talked all about the S.A.S. and answered many questions. Then, Bunny quickly told his human family about how the squad was in danger. "It's urgent. We need to leave now to save all stuffed animals and toys. Including me."

The Nobles believed Bunny. They all knew that he was not imagining things. So, a few minutes later, they had packed some weapons and things for battle. Bunny led them downstairs and into the closet that had the door to the train station. The Nobles pushed past all of the stored items in the closet, including books, pictures, and much more, and finally met up with Bunny at the wall.

Bunny knocked on the wall three times and said, "This is Bunny, an esteemed member of the Stuffed Animal Squad."

Nothing happened.

Bunny grumbled. He didn't have time for this. It was becoming nighttime and Gewis would use the S.T.L. soon. Behind him, Louisa yawned.

"Wait a minute," Miles said. "Where are you taking us?"

"Great question," Bunny replied. "But first we need to actually open the door."

"I've got it," Darren said.

He rustled through the storage until he found an old toolbox. Inside was a hammer. "This'll do." Then, with a single whack, the door was down. Bunny easily boinged through, but for the Nobles, it was a bit of a tight squeeze.

Finally, they were all in the small train station that led to Amaday. "This has been underneath our house for how long?" Louisa asked in disbelief.

"About a century," Bunny told her. "Back when this block was a park."

This train station was similar to the one back in Toy City. Three train cars sat on the track. "Can you fit in that small car for twenty minutes?" Bunny asked. Miles and Louisa definitely could, but the adults might have trouble squeezing in. But there was no time to decide. Bunny boinged into the first and Louisa sat next to him, while Miles and Leigh took their own cars behind. But there were only three, so Darren had to stay behind.

"Good luck!" he called. "I'll catch you all on the flip side."

Bunny half expected him to just walk back to the house. But Darren stayed there and would hop on the next train as soon as possible. Then Bunny, Miles, Louisa, and Leigh sped off! *So having a relationship with humans turned out to be a good thing*, Bunny thought. The Nobles were about to meet many more stuffed animals, that's for sure.

The train sped away at top speed towards Amaday, and the passengers on board started preparing for a heroic battle!

GREY SIGHED. THE S.A.S. WAS ALMOST DEFEATED.

After more than a century, Gewis had returned, with an even larger army, cut off all the leaders' access to the Purple Pear Tree, meaning that their magic couldn't be fulfilled, and captured the S.A.S. What a nice guy.

The only members of the squad still free and fighting were Giraffey, Bo, and OHM. But that was it. Grey couldn't believe that Bunny had abandoned the S.A.S. There was still a chance that he was recruiting allies, but how many more did he know? Grey couldn't blame Bunny. The S.A.S. had let him down, and that was mostly his fault. Now it was 7:00 p.m. They still had five hours, but all hope seemed lost.

Then a very familiar sound came from right outside the base's door. "Boing, a boing, a boing, a boing, a boing!" The fighting stopped, and all eyes turned towards the door to Amaday. But when it opened, everyone gasped. Even Gewis fell back in surprise.

The Nobles? Grey thought in shock.

"Who are these humans?" Gewis demanded as Miles, Louisa, and Leigh stepped into the room, followed by Bunny.

"I'm Louisa, nice to meet you," Louisa told him.

Bunny cleared his throat. "Gewis is the villain we're fighting."

Louisa looked confused for a moment before understanding. "Oh, right."

Quite suddenly, the battle started up again. Thinking quickly, Leigh, Miles, and Louisa started untying various stuffed animals. Soon, Louisa got to Grey. Keep in mind that Grey is her stuffed animal, so she untied him and gave him a hug. "I missed you!"

"Me too," the grateful leader replied. "We can have a conversation later." Then Grey got up and started fighting again, using the small bit of magic he had left.

Louisa watched him in awe. "Wow!" she exclaimed.

Nearby, Bunny saw this happen and thought, *if only I could get my magic to work again.* He thought back to when he insisted on bringing a tent when he and Snow started their journey to Winter Park. Was that magic, or was that just a coincidence? Bunny watched Gewis work his super powerful magic. The villain levitated stuffed animals and even froze them for a few seconds.

If only the purple pear tree had been better guarded, Bunny thought. But it was too late for that now. He had to keep fighting. Then everything went silent. Snow, who had just been freed by Leigh, said, "Uh…Bunny?"

"What?"

"Turn around."

Bunny whirled around and his mouth hung open.

Looming over all of the stuffed animals (and humans) was a totally different creature than ever seen before, with a grayish face, humongous feet, and a head that topped out at 7'2".

"I AM THE GREAT HOLDER, AND I WILL SMOOSH YOU ALL TO PILES OF STUFFING!

COWER IN FEAR! HA HA HA…Um Gewis, can you give the order now? My voice is getting tired."

Everyone was speechless. Except for Gewis.

"Attack!" The evil tortoise ordered Room Decor.

BUNNY FINALLY GRASPED WHAT WAS GOING ON. HE HAD NEVER stopped to think about how Gewis had returned, but now it made sense. There was an old stuffed animal legend, about a tall creature called the Great Holder. The Great Holder had a different kind of magic than the leaders, one that could hold stuffed animals in a magical item.

Bunny thought of Rudy's story about the day Gewis disappeared, back in the 1800's. He and his army had held hands and right when Giraffey struck him with the S.A.S. weapon, Ruth Demor, a soldier, bit him. And Ruth Demor sounded suspiciously similar to Room Decor…Bunny thought back to when Room Decor was leader of the bad guys. She always carried around that purse. *What if she was magically holding Gewis in it the whole time?*

But Bunny didn't have time to think any longer, because, of course, Room Decor went for him first. He took off, boinging away from Room Decor, the Great Holder.

"She put on some weight," OHM said as he ran past.

"Yeah," Bunny told him. "Good observation."

But on the bright side, now Room Decor was extremely slow, even slower than Bunny. So instead of catching him, Leigh, Miles, and Louisa, being the closest to her height, teamed up on her. Now the battle was getting really intense. Bunny thought about Darren. Was he actually going to come?

Over by Gewis, Room Decor tried to outrun the Nobles and went for Rudy, who barely dodged her. Gewis laughed and watched in pleasure as his son tried using his magic, but it was just too weak. Rudy just kept dodging Room Decor until he became exhausted. Not having magic really paid. If he was in this scenario and fighting the bad guys, he would have stopped and let another leader rescue him. But this battle was different. Rudy couldn't slow down, no matter how old he was, no matter how much his legs burned. *Would Gewis lock the S.A.S. up, or something even worse?* Then another question popped up in Rudy's head. *Why was his father so evil?*

All these questions were simply wearing him down more. Room Decor was about to whack him in the head when Leigh ran over and tackled her from behind. Miles and Louisa also came over to help, but they still couldn't stop Room Decor from standing back up. She growled and threw Leigh!

Rudy gasped. But Leigh snapped to her feet once again, mad, and charged at Room Decor. Let me say that taking on a 7' 2" giant is hard. She only managed to take down Room Decor the first time with the element of surprise. But now Room Decor was prepared, and she blocked Leigh's attack. She laughed, pleased with herself.

"Room Decor," Louisa called from behind her.

The great holder whirled around and stepped towards the kids. Unfortunately for her, she didn't notice the long rope they were holding at her feet.

What happened next was totally worth it. In slow motion, she fell right on top of Gewis.

"Turkeyed Turtles!" he shrieked.

Louisa snickered. Even evil villains said embarrassing things.

When Room Decor stood up again, Gewis had turned a deep purple in the face. Everyone, even some of his soldiers, laughed at him. Since Gewis was not used to this level of disrespect, it made him mad. Super mad. He muttered something under his breath, but Giraffey prevented anyone from hearing these bad words.

"Bleeeeeeeeeeeeeeeeep!" he said over Gewis.

After that, Gewis started shouting commands. "You soldiers are useless! Get to work for once. Come on, hup hup, hurry it up!"

Multiple beavers started scrambling around and the fight started back up again. Then Bunny looked at the clock on the wall. It was now 8:15 p.m. In a way they had plenty of time, but if they failed, the S.A.S. would no longer exist in just under four hours.

Meanwhile, Gewis noticed that one of his soldiers was not working very hard. "Hey, you! Do you know how to fight?" he asked the beaver in a babyish voice.

The soldier nodded nervously.

"Well, then start fighting!" Gewis shouted in the opposite voice as before.

"But sir," the beaver said, "You're not doing anything either!"

Suddenly, Gewis's face turned gnarly and frightening. He raised his foot and prepared to attack his own soldier. "How do you like this?"

The poor beaver braced for impact. There was a large crack. But it was not what you were probably thinking. Gewis groaned and held his back as he sat down.

"Darn father time!" he moaned. "I can't go a day without getting a sore!"

Once again, everyone laughed at him. Now Gewis was outraged. "So far, I've taken it easy on you," he announced, his face turning into a creepy grin. "ROOM DECOR, NOW!"

Room Decor ran to the closet that Gewis had been protecting earlier. She opened the door. Gewis laughed in delight, like a kid on his birthday. "This weapon isn't some lame slapper."

Bunny looked down at his mini weapon, still fit snugly in his paw.

Gewis continued, "This weapon can actually destroy things! Prepare to be defeated! Because when the clock strikes midnight, I will take over the world with the Sleep Then Listen!"

"I'll accept that as long as you lower the prices for coffee!" Lizhat called out. "I mean, even Starbucks prices are outrageous these days!"

"Yeah, sure, whatever. I'll add that to my 'ruler of the world' list of priorities," Gewis responded. "But anyway, I hope you enjoy your last few minutes of freedom, because soon, I will have control of your minds!"

There was a mysterious whirring from the S.T.L. as Room Decor rolled it out from the closet. Bunny stared at the machine in horror. It didn't look too evil at first, more like a high-tech frozen yogurt machine. But once you noticed the details, it looked much more dangerous.

First of all, it was a large metal square placed on wheels. It towered at about twice Bunny's height, painted an ugly green that matched the color of Gewis's skin. There was a keypad and screen on the backside with all sorts of buttons and a leather chair for Gewis to recline on while he controlled the machine. And then there was the laser. The front side of the machine had a long antenna with wires connected to the keypad. Just from the look of it, Bunny could tell it produced a strong laser, prefect for zapping stuffed animals with.

While he observed the machine, Gewis had been rambling on. "And by the way, I'm not one of those cheesy villains who tells everyone what their secret weapon is," Gewis matter-of-factly commented.

There was a long silence.

Finally, Gewis grew upset at the lack of fear. "Well? What are you waiting for? Gasp, run away, surrender! Just do something!" It was apparent that he was trying to bottle up his anger and failing miserably. "Alright, fine! But just you wait, the S.T.L. is the most powerful machine ever created!"

Room Decor started the fight again, slashing her weapon madly. The Stuffed Animal Squad seemed to be running out of energy. More and more got tied up and placed against the wall, staring at the antenna of the S.T.L. Room Decor managed to tie up Leigh, Miles, and Louisa.

Pretty soon, the only members of the S.A.S. remaining in the battle were Giraffey, Pecan, Rudy, Sweetie, Bunny, Snow, and one of the bad guys. Bunny knew that the fight was almost over. "Keep going," Snow told him. But even their voice was weary.

Bunny kept fighting, feeling helpless as more and more stuffed animals were captured by Gewis's army. *SLAP! SLAP! SLAP!* His arm was getting tired. Bunny watched as the soldiers surrounded Snow and tied them up. They were thrown right next to Bink and Bluebush, who grimaced.

"Ha!" Gewis exclaimed. He eyed Room Decor, who was fighting with anger like never before. "Just three more to go."

Right on cue, Darren hopped into the base. "I'm here!" he announced triumphantly.

Gewis huffed. "Of course, another bothersome human shows up."

Darren looked around curiously, "A nice place you got here."

"Well, it's not mine. But it will be soon," Gewis informed the Noble.

"So, what am I here for exactly? Isn't there like a tea party with stuffed animals or something?" Darren asked.

Bunny sighed exasperatedly. So did Gewis, who figured that Darren wouldn't be a threat.

"Yeah, there sure is a tea party!" Room Decor said in a friendly voice.

"Follow me."

Darren started to go after her before he noticed all the stuffed animals tied up on the wall. And his family! He looked at Room Decor suspiciously, then at his wife and children. "I don't think so."

The battle continued, although the good guys were obviously outnumbered. Giraffey was clearly the best fighter. He jumped around with breeze, attacking different beavers from all sorts of angles. Watching him, Bunny remembered something. *Giraffey's S.A.S. weapon!* he thought with excitement. Quickly, Bunny boinged over to his backpack. He pulled out the weapon that Sweetie had been using for their journey. He couldn't believe that everyone had forgotten about it.

Gewis looked over and frowned. "You think that you can defeat me with that?"

Bunny didn't think this. But he remembered what Snow always told him. *You have to believe.*

Giraffey stopped to watch the moment, and Room Decor used this to her advantage. She pounced on him and tied him up. Now everyone was bound except for Bunny. There was a stare down between him and Gewis.

Bunny, with all of the S.A.S. and the bad guys cheering him on, spoke to Gewis. "I think I can defeat you!"

This was a very dramatic moment. But unfortunately, Gewis ruined it by using his magic to lift the S.A.S. weapon out of Bunny's hands and move it over to him. "Well, too bad," the villain bragged. "This is mine now."

Bunny grumbled. "How did your magic get so strong?"

Gewis thought for a moment. "Do you really want to know?" Gewis laughed. Bunny got a feeling that the answer would not be good.

"It's because of you!"

Bunny gasped. How could this be true? It just didn't make sense.

"Yes. It's a lot to take in, but if you join my side, your magic will grow even stronger!"

Bunny imagined dramatic music playing in the background. But the more he thought about it, Gewis wasn't really doing a good job of convincing him. "Exactly how will this work?" Bunny asked, putting him on the spot.

"Well, Rudy, my son, gave you magic. Right?"

"I'm following," Bunny replied.

"When he made that decision, some of my magic transferred to your body. So, when you come to my side, and we combine forces, your magic will grow stronger."

Bunny still didn't get it. He gave Gewis a puzzled look.

Gewis sighed. "Maybe you shouldn't come to my side. Your intelligence isn't that high anyway."

Bunny was offended.

"When my magic gets stronger, yours does too," Gewis said slowly, trying to get Bunny to understand.

"But why don't you ask Rudy? He has more magic than me. At least when there was access to the purple pear tree."

"I know that there is no hope for my son to change sides. You see, I can control how much magic you and Rudy have. And I decided to give you more."

This was not tricking Bunny into changing sides. He looked around. No one else was left standing. He knew that he was the last hope.

"Now rabbit, you are the only obstacle left for me to overcome," Gewis chuckled. "I don't know how you didn't get tied up, but I've got you now. Unless you come to my side."

Bunny kept his rump planted to the ground and shook his head.

"I will hire top chefs and you will have a lifetime supply of carrot bacon," Gewis bribed.

Bunny's mouth watered. Carrot bacon was his favorite food in the world! But he thought about the long journey with Snow and Sweetie. If it weren't for them, he wouldn't be there and the S.A.S. would have already been defeated.

Bunny thought some more. He looked over at the S.A.S. and the Nobles. They were all his friends, even the bad guys.

Everyone had a grim look. Except for Snow. They were hopeful.

"I will not join your side," Bunny told Gewis confidently. "Friends are better than food."

The evil tortoise huffed. "I should've known. You never think with your mind. Now finally, I will take over the world! I am positive that this will not turn out to be one of those lame stories where the good guys come back and win." He turned to Room Decor. "Capture him. Who cares about waiting till midnight? It's time to fire up the S.T.L."

CHAPTER
TWENTY-TWO

THE SOUVENIRS HELP (ACCIDENTALLY)

Giraffey was tired. He had never fought this long before. Also, it seemed as if everyone else had just given up. *Well, except for Bunny*, Giraffey thought. He was impressed by the rabbit's new skills.

But now things appeared to be hopeless for the S.A.S. They even teamed up with the bad guys, yet they were still defeated quickly. Bunny boinged away from Room Decor and around Amaday.

"It's over. Gewis is going to take control," Giraffey told him.

"Don't give up hope," Snow replied.

One of the things Giraffey didn't like about Bunny's new friend is that they were *way* too cheerful. Every 15 seconds Snow would say something like, "Stay hopeful", or "Don't give up", or "Keep fighting". It was annoying.

"The day has come!" Gewis announced triumphantly. "PREPARE TO MEET YOUR DOOM!"

"We can get through this," Snow told the squad.

Giraffey rolled his eyes. He looked away from Snow and thought of a different topic. He couldn't believe that Room Decor worked for Gewis and was the Great Holder the entire time. He remembered the S.A.S.'s last battle against the bad guys, and how she just watched everyone fight. Giraffey also wondered why she never used her true form. If the bad guys had a 7'2" beast on their side, they could have dominated the S.A.S.

Giraffey snapped out of his deep thought as he noticed Bunny boinging away from the S.T.L. and towards the squad's library.

"Oh, just let him hop. Pretty soon he will run out of energy," Gewis ordered. "Now, I know I was supposed to do this at midnight but why wait?" He hopped in the chair on the S.T.L, pressed a button and the machine whirred to life.

Giraffey's eyes caught the sharp end of the antenna that would probably fire the laser. He really hoped Bunny had a plan.

Then Gewis turned the S.T.L. to face the leaders.

Oh boy, Giraffey thought.

RUDY KNEW WHY HIS FATHER WAS BEING SO EVIL. HE WAS angry.

Rudy remembered the mysterious curse that swept through Africa, back when he was a tortoise. He hadn't thought of the curse in a while but knew a lot. A few years ago, without telling anybody, Rudy had been studying this curse. He discovered something that made him realize how evil his father was. The last time he had seen Gewis was when the S.A.S first formed. Gewis, at the time, was furious with the curse for taking away his friends and family. He never found them.

Rudy sensed that they were alive somewhere, as did Gewis. It had been centuries since the curse swept through and his relatives disappeared, but he knew Gewis still had the burning desire to find them. So maybe he was taking over the world to gain power, power that he could use to recover his friends and family.

Somehow, Rudy would have to talk to his father. Convince him. *Like that will be easy,* he thought.

The beaver soldiers had arranged it so that all the leaders were sitting next to each other. Rudy desperately thought of a way out of this, but all he could think of was stalling. "What does the S.T.L. do?" Rudy asked his father calmly.

"Why would I tell you?" Gewis rudely responded.

On the side of the S.T.L. were some numbers that Rudy took note of. They were: 5,6,4, and 1.

"What do those numbers mean?" Rudy asked, which may have seemed like a silly question to most, but he understood that no question is silly. Besides, anything would do.

"Son, why would I tell you that?"

Rudy sighed. He looked around. Whatever the S.T.L. did, it probably wasn't good.

Everyone was anxious. Especially the bad guys, who were regretting allying with the squad. But Rudy was grateful for their help. If it weren't for them, everyone probably would have been zapped by now. It was a grim moment. The fact that Gewis had one was sinking in. The end of the S.A.S. was near. And then there was Sweetie, who sings annoying songs when she's nervous.

"Baby Shark, doo-doo, doo-doo, doo-doo."

"Be quiet you nincompoop!" Gewis shouted. "You're ruining the moment!"

Sweetie started crying.

"Get me a pacifier," Gewis instructed one of his soldiers.

"Yes sir!"

The soldier came back and stuck a blue pacifier in Sweetie's mouth. Sweetie calmed down a bit and started sucking on it. But the sweet silence only lasted a few seconds. Right away, she started bawling again. "This is mint flavored! I want pineapple!"

Gewis's head looked like it was about to come off. "Who buys pineapple flavored pacifiers? That's the stupidest thing I've ever heard of."

Of course, all this did was make Sweetie cry even more. She started blabbering nonsense.

But surprisingly, Gewis calmed down. It seemed as if he had an idea. An evil one. "I will use her as my test subject!" he announced.

Everyone gasped as Gewis typed something into the S.T.L.'s keypad. He moved it so that rather than facing the leaders, the antenna was aimed directly at Sweetie, who was completely oblivious to the fact that she was about to be zapped by Gewis. She kept on crying, whining about getting a pineapple flavored pacifier. Suddenly, there was a flash of blinding purple light as the antenna zapped a powerful laser towards Sweetie. Rudy closed his eyes until it was over. The blast only lasted a few seconds, but it felt like hours.

Rudy looked at Sweetie. She was curled in a ball on the ground, snoring peacefully. *Sleep,* Rudy thought.

There was another zap, although this one much less intense.

Then, Rudy thought.

Sweetie slowly got up and yawned. "Good day, sir."

Listen, Rudy thought.

"Welcome to my side," Gewis said with delight.

SNOW FELT HELPLESS AGAINST GEWIS'S POWER. HE HAD IN-sanely strong magic, and his weapon was even more powerful. Gewis was about to take over stuffed animalkind, destroy the S.A.S. and their fighting allies. He said that he would try to take over humans too. Snow wasn't sure about that. But from the way things were going, it was starting to seem more and more possible.

He's so evil, Snow thought. Even Room Decor, the magical and ancient great holder, was scared of him.

But Snow wasn't afraid of Gewis. Or the S.T.L. Instead, they started wondering what Bunny was up to. They were proud of Bunny for getting this far, but where did he go? Snow said, "don't give up" and hoped Bunny had listened.

"Gewis," Sweetie was saying. "I am happy to join your side."

"Wonderful," Gewis replied. "If that's the case, go ahead and fetch me that rabbit."

Snow sighed. It was sad to see Sweetie controlled by Gewis. Her personality had shifted completely, although it seemed she still had her memory. Somehow, the S.T.L. could make it so that Sweetie followed Gewis's orders. Hopefully it could be undone.

"Why him, sir?" Sweetie questioned.

"Because" Gewis laughed, "I'll zap him next."

"Boing, a boing, a boing, a boing, a boing!"

Bunny's rump banged against the library floor. All he needed was a break. Everything going on made him stressed. He needed to find a room where Gewis would not find him. *I just need time to relax and think of a plan,* he told himself.

"Plop!" He plopped down and pulled out the two souvenirs that he scored from the tractor show in Toy City. He started fidgeting with them behind a bookshelf, thinking about what to do. But pretty soon, he realized that it was a waste of time.

I should be helping the...

But Sweetie interrupted his thoughts. She threw open the door to the library and quickly saw him behind the bookshelf.

"Hi Sweetie!" Bunny said. "I was just coming to help the squad. How did you get free?"

She didn't answer.

"Are you okay?" Bunny asked.

She leaned out the doorway and motioned to someone.

Bunny looked at Sweetie again. Something about her didn't seem right. He hopped toward her.

"Stop right there, plump dude," said one of Gewis's soldiers, who had just stepped next to Sweetie.

Bunny frowned. First, he had just been insulted, and second, he was trapped. He couldn't believe it.

"Follow us," she ordered. The other soldier stayed behind him while Sweetie took the lead. They marched down the hallway and arrived in the room where the S.T.L. was. Sweetie ordered him to sit down on a wooden chair in front of the large machine. He followed the order and Sweetie quickly tied his arms to the back of the chair.

Gewis walked over to him.

"Well, well, well," he said evilly, with about five seconds in between each 'well'. "You put in a lot of effort trying to defeat me."

Bunny nodded, understanding that this was Gewis's final speech before taking control of his mind.

The villain grinned and continued, "But alas, you have failed."

Then a thought came to Bunny's mind. He had never stopped to consider what exactly Gewis wanted to do. "You know," Bunny told the villain. "You haven't told us what your evil plan is."

Gewis raised an eyebrow. "Of course I have. I'm going to take over the Stuffed Animal Squad, destroy them once and for all."

"Yeah," Bunny said. "But why? What are you going to do after that?"

An evil grin spread across Gewis's face. "I'm glad somebody asked. You see, rabbit, I'm going to have control over stuffed animals. And sooner or later, I'll gain control of the world. And when I have control of the world, I will have control of humans. The S.T.L. is more powerful than you think. And once I have all of the leaders' magic, any-thing is possible!"

"Wow," Bunny said. "That's an impressive plan."

"Yes, and…" Gewis sighed. "I see what you're doing. You're stalling, trying to make me perform every villain's weakness. Gloating."

Bunny didn't know where Gewis was going, but he decided to let him keep talking. "Every legendary villain gloats. The Joker, Darth Vader, Voldemort. Every time a villain gloats, the same exact thing happens: the hero uses this to their advantage and ends up saving the day. But that's not the case for me. I mean, really, I deserve a coffee mug that says: *World's #1 Villain for being able to resist gloating.*"

"But you were just gloating by saying that," Bunny pointed out.

Gewis's face turned deep purple again when he real-ized this. But once again, he turned this embarrassment into anger.

"Oh, shut up! You won't be making snappy comebacks when I take control of your mind."

Then he marched over to the S.T.L.'s keypad, pushing past a soldier who looked disappointed, almost as if wanted to work the machine and take control of an innocent rabbit's mind. Gewis slammed a button on the keypad and said, "Say hello to my new friend."

Bunny glanced at some writing on the side of the machine. In large, silver letters was the acronym: *S. T.L.*

"What's your friend's n-name?" Bunny asked, stuttering in fear just a bit, trying to distract Gewis.

"Nice try," Gewis said. "I know what you're up to."

He typed something into the keyboard and the S.T.L. was ready.

Bunny felt uneasy. Quickly, he looked at the souvenirs still in his paw. "What about these tractors?"

"Ah, just keep them. They're not living anyway."

Gewis was about to take control of his mind. Time was running out. So, using all of his ear strength, Bunny chucked both tractor souvenirs at Gewis with his ears.

"Catch!" he yelled.

Everyone watched them fly across the room towards Gewis.

Then... wham! Both tractors slammed into the center of his face. Gewis was about to say some bad words again, but before he even got the chance, he fell over on his back.

Everyone sat there in shock.

Then, without any sympathy, Room Decor walked over to the S.T.L.'s keypad. "Pick him up and give him some medical treatment," she ordered a soldier, happy to be in command. "I've got it from here."

But Gewis had underestimated Bunny's ear strength. If he could throw something across the room, surely he could untie himself. He realized that all of the battle came down to this one moment.

Oh, how I miss hanging out in my lair and eating an endless supply of carrot bacon, Bunny thought.

CHAPTER

TWENTY-THREE

A FATHER-SON SHOWDOWN

Bluebush and Bink hadn't been of any help. They got tied up right away and watched the battle helplessly. But now they could both be of major advantage because they were sitting directly behind Bunny.

"This stupid machine!" Room Decor yelled, slamming her fist into the keypad. Bunny frantically used his ears to untie and free himself, but it was slow progress. But this is where Bluebush and Bink came in.

Room Decor finally got the S.T.L. to work and started to position it so that it would hit Bunny square on.

Yikes! he thought.

Bluebush found the knot that Bunny had been working with. It was just a bit looser now, thin and unsturdy. Without another thought, Bluebush leaned in and bit right on the rope. It loosened even more, but still didn't split. It was one sturdy rope, that's for sure.

"Bunny!" Rudy called as Room Decor aimed the S.T.L. "Your magic!"

Bunny understood. He needed to use his magic. With the ropes loosened by Bluebush and Bink, he focused like he did in the jail. In slow motion, Room Decor lowered her hand, about to press the red button that would diminish the squad's only hope.

There was a bright flash of light. Everyone closed their eyes. And then it sank in. Bunny hadn't harnessed his magic in time. Room Decor had zapped him. It was over.

Snow didn't open their eyes when the light stopped. They were wrong. There was no more hope. Room Decor cackled evilly, then suddenly stopped. Snow still didn't open their eyes. Now Bunny was controlled by Gewis!

Rudy looked down, tears welling in his eyes. He put his bound arms behind his back and looked at the floor.

"Looks like we finally won," Room Decor said proudly. "I finished Gewis's job for him. I am just as powerful as him! Now I will zap you all and rule the world!"

"Too bad Bunny freed me," Rudy said.

Room Decor had been so distracted by her gloating, she hadn't bothered to look at the chair Bunny was in. "Wait, where did he—"

But she couldn't finish her thought, because at that moment Bunny whacked her from behind with the S.A.S. weapon!

By now, Rudy had untied Snow, Bo Bo, and Squiddy. These three started untying others, and pretty soon the whole squad and the bad guys were free again.

Room Decor immediately became flustered. "Soldiers!" she shouted. "Get these dirty cows! Th-these loaves of bread! They're refrigerators! Refried beans! Ahhhhhhhh! Now Gewis will never trust me again!"

The soldiers were not prepared for this sudden attack, and the S.A.S. slowly started knocking them out and getting the upper hand.

Snow started fighting beside Bunny, talking at the same time. "H-how?"

Bunny shrugged. "That flash of light wasn't the S.T.L. It was my magic. I used it to get free then boinged over to Rudy. He sensed me and put his hands behind his back, pretending to cry, while I untied him. Then while Room Decor was distracted, I snuck behind her to the place where Gewis had left the S.A.S. weapon and hit her with it."

Snow was so excited, they couldn't put their shock into words. They kept fighting, using martial arts, while Bunny swung the S.A.S. weapon like a professional.

When Gewis had been hit by Bunny's souvenir tractors, his soldiers whisked him away to Flatbeak's office, where all the medical supplies were. But now he regained consciousness and walked into the room looking like he usually did…mad.

"Room Decor!" he bellowed. "When this battle is over, you're fired!"

Meanwhile, Room Decor, who was already 7'2" and clumsy, stumbled around even more than usual.

Gewis started using his magic again, but it wasn't quite as powerful. Watching him, Bunny got an idea. *What if I use the S.T.L. to take control of him?*

Bunny knew it would be risky, but it was the best way to stop the villain. Gewis created a powerful weapon, but it could be used against him.

Bunny boinged towards the S.T.L. as quietly as he could, but someone jumped out at him. Sweetie.

"You're a traitor!" Sweetie snapped at him.

"Me?" Bunny asked in disbelief. "What do you mean?"

Sweetie rolled her eyes. "No more talking. A lot more fighting."

Bunny knew how good of a fighter Sweetie was. Although he did have the S.A.S. weapon and she was fighting with her hands, so it was a pretty even matchup. Then Rudy came to his aid.

"Try to use the S.T.L!" Bunny whispered to him.

"Can you hold off Sweetie?" Rudy asked.

"I hope so!"

Rudy went off to execute Bunny's idea. He sneaked over to the S.T.L., which was a much easier task for him. Soon he reached the large machine and looked at the keypad. There was a button next to the small keypad. *Of course, there's a password!* Rudy thought. He thought for a moment, then looked at the numbers on the side of the S.T.L.: *5641.*

Rudy typed this in, but slowly, realizing this was probably a silly guess. But to his surprise, after he typed in the numbers the screen lit up. Rudy was excited for a moment, but then he realized that something was wrong.

This is way too easy.

There was another button that fired the laser. Rudy cautiously moved his hand toward the button. Then he stopped himself.

This is a trick, he thought. He looked at his father, who was fighting Giraffey across the room.

Rudy aimed the S.T.L. towards the chair Bunny had been sitting in a few minutes ago and selected the button that would fire it. Hopefully, no one would get in the way of the blast. (But just in case, there was a *cancel* button.)

Rudy took a deep breath and fired the S.T.L. A countdown from ten was displayed on the screen. But looking at this, he noticed something that made him jump.

An antenna just like the one on the front emerged from the screen and faced Rudy. "Intruder detected. Reverse-firing activated."

It is a trick! Rudy thought. Luckily, he managed to leap out of the way. But behind him, Albert was not prepared. The purple light blasted him, and he fell down, falling asleep.

Gewis turned around, looking surprised.

"Well, son…"

Giraffey used this opportunity to whack Gewis with his weapon. (His backup, since Bunny was using the S.A.S. weapon.)

"Owww!" The villain turned around and hit Giraffey with a magical force.

Rudy turned his attention back to Albert, who was still sleeping. He walked over to the S.T.L.'s keypad again and tried to figure out if he could reverse the blast.

There was yet another button that read: *Undo (In case of accidental blast.)*

Rudy was about to press the button when Gewis slammed into him, knocking him to the floor.

"I'm giving you one last warning. Join my side, or feel the pain," Gewis said menacingly.

Rudy sighed. "I know you have good in you, father. And I know you aren't alone."

"Aren't alone?" Gewis snarled. "What are you talking about?"

"Someone gave you powers. Someone is responsible for your evil."

Gewis hated how wise his son was, but he stood up, keeping his cool. "You may be right, but your squad is no match for me. One day my boss will be revealed, and he will not be pleased with you."

"Everyone has goodness deep inside them. Even you. Eventually you will see this father, no matter how long it takes," Rudy told him calmly.

Gewis grumbled and lifted his hands, ready to use his magic. "Oh well, I guess I'll just have to get rid of you."

MEANWHILE, BUNNY WASN'T LISTENING. HE WAS STILL BAT-tling Sweetie, who backed him down into a corner with a series of advanced kicks. Bunny slashed the S.A.S. weap-on, but she ducked and jumped at him, knocking him to his rump.

"Finally!" Sweetie shouted. "Gewis will promote me, and I'll take the place of Room Decor! Ha, who needs a magical being when you have me!"

A few yards away, Snow looked over their shoulder.

I need to help Bunny! they thought. But there was also Rudy. Snow looked back and forth between the two, trying to figure out who needed help the most.

This battle is never ending! they pondered, getting frustrated. *First, there was the beginning fight, but then Gewis captured us all. Bunny freed everyone but now the battle has started again!*

Snow's head started spinning. Figuratively, of course, but if they didn't decide who to help soon either Bunny or Rudy's head was going to start spinning. Literally.

Sweetie smiled at Bunny. "You're working for the wrong side, bub. I hope you realize that before we have to force you to join us."

Then Snow jumped from out of nowhere and slammed Sweetie into a wall, making Bunny wince. Sweetie got to her feet once more but seemed too dazed to even move straight, let alone fight.

"Let's go save Rudy!" Snow said. The two friends ran towards the S.T.L., where Gewis and Rudy were having a magic duel. Gewis was clearly winning.

Gewis lifted a stick that someone had been using as a weapon and launched it at Rudy with his magic, who barely dodged it. Then Rudy responded by shooting one of his spikes. It landed in Gewis's arm, but the villain pulled it out, only wincing a bit. In retaliation, Gewis blasted a flash of his magic at his son. Rudy turned swiftly, but his back was hit.

Bunny boinged to Rudy and plopped at the leader's side with Snow. "We're going to win this battle!" he said.

"Confidence isn't a strategy," Gewis replied.

But Bunny didn't listen. He boinged straight towards the S.T.L.

Gewis just watched him, not scared at all. "Oh, but how will you find out my password?"

Bunny peeked at the numbers on the side of the machine.

"It's 5641," he informed Gewis.

"Oh no!" The villain pretended to throw a big fit over this. Then he stopped. "Ha! You think that I would just put my password on the side? Well, I think you better look again."

Rudy nodded solemnly. "He's right, Bunny."

"My invention is unstoppable!" Gewis boomed. "Surrender! You can keep on freeing yourselves, but you will never best me!"

Rudy blasted his father with a dark green light, sending him reeling.

Gewis steadied himself and glared at Rudy. "Son, you have betrayed me."

Rudy shook his head. "I think it's the other way around."

Gewis growled, "You could have ruled the world with me!"

"Ruled the world evilly, like you're trying to do now. Power always comes with a price, father."

Gewis slowly walked forward. Bunny and Snow stayed silent, watching the showdown.

"The brown mist curse ruined my life!" he told Rudy.

"Actually, I've been studying this brown mist curse," Rudy said. "I know you had the choice to get our relatives back. Yet you turned it down for power."

Gewis acted dumbfounded. "Who told you that lie?"

"Nobody," Rudy replied. "My magic told me that this was true."

"Bah!" Gewis grumbled. "Magical foretelling is over-rated!" He ran over to the S.T.L., knocking Bunny over, and punched in his password.

Before anyone could do anything, he aimed the weapon directly at Rudy and was about to press the fire button when Rudy asked, "Remember when I was little and we used to eat grass?"

Despite the circumstances, the question was so random it nearly made Bunny laugh.

Gewis paused. "Uh…"

Rudy nodded at Bunny, who used his magic to blast Gewis away from the S.T.L. Gewis screamed in a mix of fear and shock as Bunny plopped on the machine's keypad.

"Plop!" he exclaimed.

Rudy and Snow ran over to make sure Gewis didn't jump out of the way as Bunny aimed the S.T.L. at the villain. He didn't want to do it. But he reminded himself of how evil Gewis was.

"Do you really want to zap me?" Gewis asked, reading Bunny's mind. "It would be so rude of you to do it."

Bunny could be mischievous at times. He could be annoying. But he wasn't a bad person. He looked Gewis in the eye and thought of Sweetie and Albert who had been zapped already. He couldn't let this happen to anyone else.

Bunny took a deep breath and pressed the button with his ear. At the last moment, Snow and Rudy jumped out of the way. But Gewis wasn't fast enough.

ZAP!

When Bunny reopened his eyes, all was silent. Everyone turned their attention to Gewis, who was sleeping on the floor. After a long silence, Miles shouted, "We did it!"

A cheer went up through Amaday. Bunny couldn't believe it. The S.A.S. had done it. *He* had done it. Gewis was defeated, and the world was saved!

Miles, Leigh, Louisa, and Darren ran up to hug Bunny. "You saved us!" they exclaimed.

"Not to brag, but I sure did," Bunny replied.

The Nobles threw him in the air and chanted, "Bunny! Bunny! Bunny!"

It was Bunny's dream come true.

Without their boss to keep everything under control, Gewis's soldiers started running around maniacally. Only Room Decor was thinking clearly. Right when Gewis was zapped by the S.T.L., she fled for the door.

"Stop her!" Pink Nose Guy, the only one who noticed her, exclaimed.

A bad guy jumped in front of the door, but Room Decor punched him in the nose, sending him flying. She threw open the door and ran out of Amaday before anyone could stop her.

But it didn't matter too much. She was just the helper. As long as they had Gewis, they had won the battle!

The beaver soldiers were jailed, although the fresh re-cruits weren't charged, as they were tricked into thinking the whole thing was a triathlon. Many fighting allies who had been absent during the fighting came and scooped up the beavers, escorting them to the S.A.S.'s prison.

Finally, it was just the S.A.S., the bad guys, and the Nobles.

"I should have realized sooner that Room Decor wasn't on our side," Lizhat admitted.

"It's okay," Rudy told him. "I think that it's a good thing that we worked together."

"Yeah." The bad guys promised that they would team up with the squad again and left Amaday.

Then there were 22 beings– four were humans, 18 were stuffed animals. But nevertheless, they were all friends.

When Gewis had been zapped by the S.T.L., his mind was no longer what commanded Sweetie and Albert. In-stead, it was Bunny's. So, he told Albert and Sweetie to go back to being themselves.

"Man," Sweetie told the group. "I can't believe I was working for Gewis. It's like I knew it was wrong but couldn't help my–"

"What may I do for you, sir?" someone asked.

Bunny turned around to find Gewis staring at him ex-pectantly. Bunny got scared for a second, thinking that they hadn't really defeated Gewis, before realizing that now *he* was in command of the former villain. While everyone was distracted, the S.T.L. had blasted that second, less intense laser that made Gewis wake up again.

Bunny looked at Grey and Rudy. "What should I say?"

"Tell him to listen to me," Grey said.

"Gewis," Bunny told the tortoise, "Listen to him."

It was crazy how much the villain's personality had changed. First, he was cold, devious, and evil, now he was respectful, nice, and quiet.

"Alright," Grey began. "Your name is Greeny the Tortoise. You are a retired fighting ally who doesn't want to move away from Amaday. You may sleep and live here for now, until we build a small house for you down the mountain. You may never leave Amaday, never help another stuffed animal unless I say so. We will put tight security around your house so no one finds you, but don't let these requirements stop you from living a quiet and peaceful life. Now go and wait in the library."

Gewis understood the orders immediately, and he shuffled off to the library. Bunny wondered if he, like Sweetie, knew his past and what he really wanted to do. But it didn't matter. The villain would no longer be evil, no longer try to take over the world.

Then, although Rudy didn't want to ruin the good mood, he instructed everybody to start cleaning up Amaday. The battle had made the base a pigsty. Weapons were scattered about, random red gear lay on the floor, and ropes were everywhere.

Bunny dug through the piles, looking for his slapper. Then Snow came over, holding the weapon in their hands.

"Thanks," Bunny said.

Snow smiled. "No problem. You did it. You saved us!"

Once the base was cleaned up and in better shape, Bunny looked at the clock at the wall. It was 12:00 a.m. on the dot. If Gewis hadn't decided to execute his plans a little earlier, he wondered where he would be right about now. But more importantly, it was extremely late. He yawned.

"I guess we'll see you in the morning," Squiddy said.

"Sure thing," Leigh replied.

"And thanks for helping us defeat Gewis," Bo Bo added.

The Nobles nodded and looked at Bunny. "Good thing the rabbit thought of it."

They opened the door and walked outside with Bunny, Snow, and Grey. Bunny started talking about the adventure he went on, but he got tired and couldn't make it to the train.

"Carry me," he told Miles.

His owner sighed. "It's back to the good old times."

CHAPTER

TWENTY-FOUR

THE AWARDS CEREMONY

B unny yawned.

"Good morning," Miles told him.

Bunny sat up and looked around. He followed Miles out of the bedroom. Louisa was waiting right outside the door with Grey.

"Good morning," she said.

"Where's Snow?" Bunny asked.

"Right over here," said a recognizable voice. Snow appeared from Louisa's doorway with a big smile on their face.

"Good morning."

"You too."

Miles, Louisa, Bunny, Grey, and Snow walked downstairs together and played a card game until Leigh and

Darren came downstairs and joined. And then they heard the basement closet door open.

"What was that?" Bunny asked.

"Oh," Snow said, "Those must be the guests."

Bluebush and Bink were the first to walk upstairs, and many stuffed animals followed. Once every member of the squad was there (including the fighting allies and bad guys), Snow announced, "Let the real party begin!"

The Nobles' house suddenly got much louder, with conversations recounting the details of the night before. Piggy helped Leigh make some casserole, and the smell wafted from the oven to the living room. Pretty soon, Rudy told everyone to gather around in the living room. He signaled for Grey to come up onto the chair with him.

Once the audience settled down, the two leaders cleared their throats. "In case you have not heard," Grey began, "Gewis, just yesterday, attempted to take…"

"We know, Grey," Bunny interrupted.

"Oh. Right."

He continued, "Anyway, Rudy and I decided to hand out some awards. So, the first of six medals goes to…. drumroll please…."

Nothing happened.

"I *said*, drumroll please."

The sound of thunder filled the Nobles' living room as Rudy held up a ribbon.

"This award goes to…me!" Grey exclaimed.

Rudy glared at him.

"Oh, sorry. I mean, Bink!" Grey announced.

Bink blushed as he stood up and walked to the chair. He let Rudy hand him the award. Everyone cheered. As Bink sat down, he high-fived Bluebush, who ended up getting the next award. After Bluebush sat down, Grey called up Sweetie, followed by Snow.

"Nice job!" Bunny told Snow, ready to receive the last award. (It wasn't much of a secret that he was getting it.)

This time, Rudy spoke. "Our last award is for someone who improved a lot with his bravery and kindness. He helped me and the whole squad win the battle against Gewis. I know it's a tad early, but I am going to give out the Stuffed Animal of the Year, S.A.Y., award, despite the law that states it cannot be given to a member of the S.A.S."

Grey tried to make the moment dramatic and suspenseful, but everyone knew who the award was for.

"Bunny, come on up," Rudy said.

A cheer went up and Bunny boinged forward, filled with joy. "Boing, a boing, a boing, a boing!" Rudy placed the gold ribbon gently in his paw, and Bunny turned to face the audience.

"Everyone contributed to helping us win the battle against my father. Who, in case you're wondering, is under control after being zapped by the S.T.L. Hopefully, we can get some security and build a nice hut for him to live in."

There were some murmurs about this, but for the most part, everyone seemed fine with it.

Rudy continued, "Even if Grey, Giraffey, Bo Bo, Squiddy, and I are considered the leaders, the whole squad is just as important. So, everyone should be proud, and the

Stuffed Animal Squad will continue to lead all stuffed animals fairly."

When Rudy finished his speech, Pink Nose Guy started chanting, "Peace! Peace! Peace! Peace! Peace!"

Then OHM joined, "Peace! Peace! Piece-a-pie! Piece-a-pie!"

"Speaking of food, the casserole is ready!" Piggy and Leigh called from the kitchen.

In under a minute, everyone in the living room had moved to the dining table. It was pretty crowded, and thankfully, Squiddy brought up the subject.

"Um, there's a slight problem," he said.

Piggy, who was about to serve the casserole, looked around. "What? That there's not enough room?"

"Uh, yeah."

It took a while to sort it out, but soon a small fold-up table was set, and a few stuffed animals sat on the floor. The casserole was delicious. Everyone gobbled it up. Afterward, Bunny talked and received congratulations from almost everyone in the house.

Finally, he boinged away from the main floor and had some alone time to think. *The last few weeks were full of excitement*, Bunny thought. He recalled getting kicked out of the S.A.S., and then the Nobles' house shortly afterward.

Luckily, he met Snow. Snow introduced him to skiing in Winter Park, and they went on the journey to Toy City with Sweetie. There, they met Bluebush and Bink, went to the tractor show, and freed Snow from Gewis's jail after they were captured.

Bunny, Snow, Sweetie, Bink, and Bluebush came back to help the S.A.S. Yes, the battle was the hardest part, but they had made it through, defeating Gewis in the end.

Now Bunny stood there, enjoying the moment of silence and peace. He knew that the S.A.S. would probably experience more battles (because that's just how it goes), but not for a while. They were at peace with the bad guys, who were rebuilding their base that the squad had blown up previously.

Bunny decided to boing back to the main floor and take part in the celebration.

"Congratulations on the medal!" Giraffey called out to Bunny the minute he appeared.

"Thanks," Bunny replied. He found Snow standing by the entrance of his lair.

"It's been a while since I've gone to my lair," he said.

"Your lair?" someone asked. Bunny turned around to find Miles with a puzzled expression.

"Uh…" Bunny knew that he needed to tell his owner the truth. "Well, I have a giant lair filled with carrot bacon down there."

He expected Miles to be surprised, but his owner didn't show any reaction. "Yeah, I should have known."

There had been many surprises in the last 24 hours for the Nobles, and this one didn't really compare. Bunny said thanks again and boinged over to Rudy.

"I hope you realize how wise you are," Rudy told him. "In fact, since I've taught you about wisdom, maybe you could teach me a thing or two about humor."

Bunny smiled. "Sure thing."

Bo Bo came over and whispered to Rudy, "It's time."

Rudy nodded and hopped back on the Nobles' living room chair. "It's time for a speech!" he announced.

"Again?" Bunny asked the leaders.

"Yes," Squiddy said. "Everyone gather round! This'll be quick."

This turned out to be a bluff, and Bunny had almost fallen asleep by the time the leaders got to the good part.

Giraffey was speaking. "Well, I know this speech was kinda boring…" (He gave a thumbs down sign.) "But now, I will share the big news."

The S.A.S. and bad guys got excited.

"I could make this another long speech, but the point is that, well…"

Silence.

"We're expanding Amaday!"

Just like when Bunny got his award, a cheer went through the crowd. Then the leaders took turns explaining about how they would not only expand the base, but also find more Fighting Allies.

When this speech was done, the leaders jumped off the makeshift stage and got many compliments. Pretty soon, the party was over. Everyone left, filled with joy, and announced that they would be at Amaday the next day.

Finally, the Nobles' house quieted down, and left standing there was Bunny, Snow, Sweetie, Miles, Louisa, Darren, and Leigh. "Wow," Leigh told everyone. "We did it. Defeating Gewis *and* hosting 30 stuffed animals for a party."

Bunny and Snow hugged in celebration. Sweetie, always one for dramatics, fainted when she saw this.

"I'm going to Amaday with Snow and Sweetie," Bunny told the Nobles. "We'll try to be back by dinner time."

"Have fun," Darren said.

Bunny hugged his owner and followed his friends into the basement. They went inside the closet, through the secret door, and rode the Amaday train together.

"Today was a great day," Snow said.

"Yeah," Bunny agreed. "But it's not over yet."

Sweetie nodded. "I have a feeling that the squad has a party ready for us."

"There's been a lot of partying lately, but I'm always down for boinging to the next one!" Bunny remarked.

They all laughed.

THIS BOOK IS ALMOST OVER.

Bunny, Snow, Sweetie, and the whole S.A.S. (I hope you were able to keep track of them all), had a break from battles for a while.

The Stuffed Animal Squad still leads all stuffed animals (and toys) in the world peacefully. But despite this, little did anyone know, many more big adventures were waiting…

BUNNY, SNOW, AND SWEETIE GOT OFF OF THE AMADAY TRAIN and knocked on the door to the Stuffed Animal Squad's base.

"Maui, maui, maui," Bunny said (the code to get in), and OHM opened the door.

Bunny was so glad to feel welcomed in Amaday again, and ready to continue having fun with the squad. Giraffey came up to them. He looked at Snow.

"I'm happy to announce that, if you want, the leaders have all agreed that you should become a fighting ally!"

Snow blushed. "I would love to be a fighting ally! Thanks, Giraffey."

"No problem," Giraffey replied. "You really deserve it, just like Bink and Bluebush."

"Are they going to be Fighting Allies too?" Snow asked.
"You betcha!"

Sweetie ran off to pull a prank on someone, but Bunny and Snow kept walking until they ran into Rudy.

"Hello Bunny," he said. "Do you want to have dinner with me and the leaders?"

Bunny looked at Snow, but his friend pointed over to where some stuffed animals gathered in a circle, chanting, "Plop! Plop! Plop!"

"Thanks," Bunny told Rudy. "But I have a plopping contest to attend."

And, with Rudy smiling and Snow laughing, Bunny boinged away.

"Boing, a boing, a boing, a boing, a boing!"

The End

BIOGRAPHIES OF THE S.A.S

RUDY - THE ORIGINAL AND WISEST MEMBER OF THE S.A.S. was born in southwestern South Africa as a Tortoise. His parents, Mwana and Binti, took care of him for seven years until the Brown Mist Curse swept through, separating Rudy from his parents. He never saw his mother again, but after a long journey as a stuffed animal dinosaur with magic, he tracked down his father, who was creating tons of stuffed animals.

After discovering that his father had turned evil, Rudy met Rodger, Squiddy, and Giraffey. Together, the four of them fought in the Father-Son war. One day, Rodger went on a dangerous mission that saved hundreds of stuffed animals and helped win the Father-Son war. This mission became known as the Freedom Trail, but after being jailed, Rodger mysteriously disappeared. Rudy searched for him day and night, but he never reappeared.

A few years later, Rudy, Squiddy, and Giraffey founded the Stuffed Animal Squad. Although he claims everyone in the squad is equal, Rudy is oftentimes considered the most powerful. He is very kind, wise, and loves peace—and smoothies. His major accomplishments include founding the S.A.S., signing the Stuffed Animal Document of Independence, and defending all stuffed animals.

SQUIDDY - THE SECOND MEMBER OF THE S.A.S. IS VERY QUIet. But he can catch you off guard with his fighting skills and magic. He is in charge of Stuffed Animal Security and has passed tons of laws on Stuffed Animal safety.

Squiddy was born in the waters of Vancouver as a market squid, and, after about 5 months, was caught by a fisherman. Miraculously, he made it to Denali alive, where he escaped the fisherman's boat and was found by Gewis and turned into a stuffed animal. Shortly after, he befriended Rodger, where the two of them ran away from Gewis's evil troops only to be stopped in the cold. Luckily, Rudy saved them and the three became friends.

Squiddy is also great with computers. He loves to code, teach fellow squad members, and make up for his quietness by standing up for all stuffed animals. He also loves to eat brunch foods such as pancakes, waffles, and fruit salad.

Squiddy's major accomplishments include signing the Stuffed Animal Document of Independence, creating the Fighting Allies (which he left for Giraffey to be in charge of) and leading S.A.D.S., the Stuffed Animal Department of Safety.

GIRAFFEY - THE THIRD MEMBER OF THE SQUAD IS ALMOST THE opposite of Squiddy: he is noisy. Stuffed animals have mixed opinions about this leader. Some extremely dislike his sense of humor and outgoing personality, while others think he balances the seriousness of the other leaders. But either way, all agree that Giraffey is a great fighter. He is a menace in battle, using the silver weapon that Rodger gave him as a gift.

Giraffey was born in northeastern Chad as a real Giraffe before being captured by Gewis's troops, brought to Denali, and turned into a stuffed animal. At the beginning of the Father-Son war, he started fighting for Gewis. But after realizing that his boss was evil, Giraffey started pranking his own troop, resulting in him being thrown defenseless into the wild. Fortunately, Rodger found him before it was too late and trained him to fight for their side.

Giraffey loves to fight, eat leaf bars, talk and joke, and play sports. Some of his major accomplishments include signing the Stuffed Animal Document of Independence, leading the Fighting Allies, and training several famous stuffed animals, many of which include S.A.S. members.

GREY - THE FOURTH MEMBER OF THE S.A.S. HAS THE STRONGEST magic of all the leaders. He was born as a puppy in 1881, outside of Chattanooga, Tennessee. At the age of two, Grey followed his uncle and visited Denali with his friend Bo Bo, where the two became some of the last stuffed animals Gewis ever created.

After the Father-Son war ended, Grey traveled back home to Tennessee and lived quietly with his family for 5 years, until some members of Gewis's army escaped the

Stuffed Animal Jail, which, coincidentally, was in Chattanooga.

The S.A.S. was notified too late, and Rudy rushed to Tennessee, only to find that Grey had taken care of the 15 soldiers single-handedly. (He was panting happily when Rudy found him.)

Rudy declared that Grey should join the squad (Squiddy and Giraffey were hesitant at first, but eventually agreed), and brought him back to Gewis's castle, their base in Denali, and gave him a purple pear from the purple pear tree that supplied him with magic.

Grey loves to eat peanut butter and bananas, have fun, and talk with fellow squad members. Some of his major accomplishments include signing the Stuffed Animal Document of Independence, passing various laws to improve stuffed animal education, and using his magic to defend his kind.

BO BO - THE FIFTH MEMBER OF THE SQUAD AND LAST OF THE leaders is also a dog. She is one of the favorites because of her laid-back personality. Bo Bo hardly ever gets mad, but when she does it's not pretty.

Bo Bo was also born in 1881 outside of Chattanooga and has been friends with Grey her entire life. After traveling to Denali and being turned into a stuffed animal with Grey, she went a different way and moved outside of Denver, Colorado, on her own until the S.A.S.'s base (Gewis's old castle) burned down in a forest fire and Grey contacted her for the first time in a decade, asking if the squad could build a new base by her home. After some hesitation, Bo

Bo agreed, and the four members of the S.A.S. built their base and told Bo Bo that they were looking for a fifth member. Although it took two years of convincing, she became the last leader.

Bo Bo created Fairy Godmothers, the mini stuffed animals that create larger stuffed animals. She loves to hang out with Grey, attend fashion shows, and watch movies with her friends. Some of Bo Bo's accomplishments include leading the Fairy Godmothers, creating stuffed animal currency, and founding Amaday.

TUSKEY - ALTHOUGH THE SIXTH MEMBER OF THE S.A.S. IS not a leader, Tuskey the elephant is very smart and powerful. He has created almost all of the squad's weapons and is always coming up with more. On top of that, he has invented useful machines for stuffed animals all around the world.

Tuskey was the first stuffed animal made by fairy godmothers, created by the 'German Steiff' that was founded by Margarete Steiff. Bo Bo transformed Steiff, who was a fairy godmother, to look like a human so no humans would get suspicious.

Tuskey was made in 1897 in Germany but didn't come to life until he was shipped to Amaday. There, the five leaders inspected the fairy godmother's work and Bo Bo declared that he should join the S.A.S. The other four did not agree, however, so Bo Bo convinced them by saying that Tuskey wouldn't eat purple pears, therefore not having magic.

Tuskey loves inventing and being creative, helping others, and eating oranges. (Although he doesn't have a huge preference for what he eats.) Some of his major accomplishments include founding S.A.T.S.–the Stuffed Animal Transportation System, and inventing thousands of things.

ALBERT - UNFORTUNATELY, THE SEVENTH MEMBER OF THE squad and his accomplishments are often forgotten. The reason for this is probably because he hasn't done much in the last few decades, so only the oldest stuffed animals remember when he was powerful. However, he is still very lovable.

Albert was created by fairy godmothers as a dog and lived all over New York City until moving outside of Amaday. Grey, who had just founded Toy City, asked Albert to be its first mayor. Albert gladly accepted, and after his third term was offered a spot on the squad.

Some of Albert's major accomplishments include supporting the stuffed animal entertainment and business industries, starting many charities for stuffed animals, and overseeing the growth of Toy City. Albert is known for being super funny and clumsy, but also super loveable, and his favorite food is pears.

FLATBEAK - THE EIGHTH MEMBER OF THE S.A.S., A PENGUIN, was made in Japan and lived there for a short period of time before moving just outside of Amaday and founding the first stuffed animal university. His intelligence and extraordinary medical skills caught the attention of Giraffey, who decided to train him. However, Tuskey strongly objected and asked that Flatbeak would be sent on a quest to prove his talent. The leaders agreed, but made Tuskey go along with him. As it turned out, Tuskey liked Flatbeak a lot, and became great friends with him after the quest, learning not to judge so quickly.

Flatbeak loves to snack on chocolate cake (although, being a doctor, he only has this treat occasionally), help others, and teach. Some of his major accomplishments include founding the first stuffed animal university, helping many with his medical skills, and his ability to float!

PINK NOSE GUY AND ALFREDO - THE NINTH AND TENTH members of the S.A.S. are very close. Pink Nose Guy, a small rabbit, is one of the loudest and most popular members of the squad, despite the fact that she's a spy. Alfredo, a small moose, is quieter, however, and is the one who plans their spy missions.

Pink Nose Guy was made in 1987 in London by 'Jellycat', a group of fairy godmothers who pretend to be a company in order to sell stuffed animals. She was brought to a nearby toy store and awakened there. However, after a few weeks, she and her friend Alfredo got bored and escaped. Soon, they were taken in by a stuffed animal street gang, where they infiltrated countless toy stores throughout London.

Soon, the problem got so severe that the 'Jellycat' fairy godmothers called Bo Bo in to stop Pink Nose Guy and Alfredo. After a long hunt, Bo Bo tracked the gang down and used her magic to defeat them. But during the fight, she saw their talents and brought them to Amaday where Giraffey trained them.

Pink Nose Guy loves to talk, compete in gymnastics, eat all sorts of food, and help Tuskey with his inventions. Alfredo loves to read, watch American Ninja Warrior, eat peppermint, and help Tuskey with his inventions as well. Some of their major accomplishments include spying and busting many villains.

OHM - THE ELEVENTH MEMBER OF THE SQUAD IS KNOWN for being loud, hilarious, and annoying but also a useful member of the S.A.S.

Orange Hairy Monster (or, for short, OHM) was made in Mexico City and taught by fellow stuffed animals how to fight at a very young age. While on vacation, Albert met OHM and brought him back to Amaday. Giraffey was currently training Pink Nose Guy and Alfredo, so OHM was taught a little bit from all the leaders, giving the monster a wide range of fighting, lawmaking, and general skills. Since his main talent is fighting, Squiddy asked for him to help with security. OHM became the person who opened the door, which might not sound important, but it saved the squad from a lot of trouble.

He loves to eat garbage, talk, cause mischief, and fight. Some of his accomplishments include being the squad member who's gone on the most missions and standing up for stuffed animals outside of the United States.

BUNNY - THE TWELFTH MEMBER OF THE SQUAD, DESPITE THE fact that he is extremely lovable, did not get a lot of credit until recently. He was made in London by 'Jellycat' in 1987, but shipped to a store in Denver, Colorado, where he was awakened and freed by some other stuffed animal rabbits who introduced themselves as his relatives. (The reason why he still thinks he's related to everyone.) After 24 years, though, he was found and caught by a toy-store owner and put up for sale, where he was bought the next week by Leigh, who was pregnant with his future owner, Miles.

The secret entrance to the Amaday train used to be in a park. But around 2010, they destroyed the park to build some houses, including the Noble's future home. But the S.A.S. refused to rebuild the Amaday train, so whenever someone wanted to ride it, they had to sneak through the Nobles' house.

One day, Louisa found Grey in the basement and declared him her stuffed animal. Grey didn't have the heart to run away from her, so she became his owner. Since Miles had Bunny, Grey met the rabbit soon and decided he could be the one to escort stuffed animals through the Nobles' house so no one else would get caught.

After about two weeks on the job, the leaders got to know Bunny more and saw past the silliness. A few days later, he was brought to Amaday to be trained by Giraffey, who, at times, lost his patience. But he eventually became the 12th member of the squad, and, for six years, was completely unrecognized. But, as you might know, he saved the Stuffed Animal Squad from Gewis and his army, getting as much attention as the leaders.

Bunny loves to eat carrot bacon, hang out with his friends, and plop. His one major accomplishment (so far) is defeating Gewis and his army and receiving the S.A.Y., Stuffed Animal of the Year award, defying the law that states a member of the S.A.S. can't win it.

PIGGY - THE THIRTEENTH MEMBER OF THE SQUAD IS SUPER kind, gentle, funny, and everything you would want in a politician. Made in Argentina as a pig, Piggy lived with an owner for just a year before being donated to a company that shipped her all the way to Boulder, Colorado. On a truck that was driving to Boulder, some mean stuffed animals pushed her off, leaving her stranded in the wilderness. After a super long journey, she made her way to Toy City, where she found shelter.

During her years in Toy City, Piggy became a famous chef and public speaker, while secretly training in karate so she wouldn't be bullied again like she was on the truck. Eventually, she became so famous that Rudy wanted to see her for himself. The leader was immediately impressed by Piggy's talent and resilience and brought her to Bo Bo for training.

Piggy is the official caretaker and cook of Amaday, and she loves to talk with Bo Bo, bake unique recipes, and practice yoga and gymnastics. Some of her accomplishments include making the first homeless shelter for stuffed animals, training a few stuffed animals who became great heroes, and winning multiple awards for cooking and karate.

PECAN - THE FOURTEENTH AND FINAL MEMBER OF THE SQUAD, and emu, was made in Sydney, Australia. Soon she was shipped to Alice Springs as a souvenir. She was purchased by someone who took her to Paris, France, where she lived for a few years. One day, some anti–S.A.S. villains led an attack near the Eiffel Tower, but Pecan saved the day along with some of her friends. Afterwards, she was asked by Giraffey to become a fighting ally and Pecan agreed, going through training and becoming the fighting ally with the best reputation.

Pretty soon, her talent was so good that Rudy declared her a member of the S.A.S. But this decision led to some of the longtime squad members to start complaining about how many members the squad had. So, the leaders decided that Pecan would be the last member, reaching the squad's limit of 14 stuffed animals.

Pecan is the jail guard, and she is pretty good at fighting and is extremely fast. She is also kind and witty. She enjoys eating pecans (nobody is sure if her name came from her favorite food or if her favorite food came from her name), chatting with friends, and competing in races. Some of her major accomplishments include starting the stuffed animal justice system and improving the relationship between stuffed animals and toys.

ACKNOWLEDGMENTS

WRITING A BOOK, ESPECIALLY WHILE I WAS GOING TO SCHOOL, was not easy. I want to thank all the people who helped me along the way. Without them, this book would not exist.

First of all, thank you to my parents and my sister for encouraging me.

I want to acknowledge my teachers from McKinley-Thatcher Elementary School who helped me grow into the writer I am today. Shoutout to my 3rd grade teacher, Ms. Evans, who inspired my first novel, *Where Is Ms. Evans?*, and my 4th and 5th grade teachers, Mrs. Keller and Ms. Stenftennagel who supported me while I was writing this book.

I thank my friends and classmates for cheering me on. For those of you who like tortoises, I hope you aren't too offended that I chose Gewis to be the villain in my story.

Thank you to the Community Resources, Inc. Academic Mentors program for introducing me to Jason Henderson, author of the Young Captain Nemo and Alex Van

Helsing series. Thanks to Jason for giving me tips and helping me make this story the best it can be.

Finally, thank you to all of my stuffed animals for providing countless ideas!

ABOUT THE AUTHOR

MILES NOBLE IS A MIDDLE-SCHOOL STUDENT AND LIVES WITH his family and Bunny in Colorado. His first book, *Where Is Ms. Evans?*, is a story about his 3rd grade teacher who goes to great lengths to get to an art competition. He started writing his second novel, *Bunny and the Stuffed Animal Squad*, when he was nine years old.

Miles likes to play sports, ski, hang out with family and friends, and go to school (because he doesn't want to break the law). In his free time, he loves to write. Miles has many ideas for future books to share with his readers!

Made in United States
Troutdale, OR
11/11/2023

14503925R00192